TWO
CENTURIES OF EVIL

The house in Amityville, Long Island—most infamous of all haunted houses, scene of repeated unspeakable horrors—what lies behind its strange, evil aura? In this blood-chilling novel, internationally known parapsychologist Hans Holzer follows the bloody trail of a fabulous gem and its powerful curse through violent acts of piracy, betrayal and murder, from eighteenth-century England to the shores of the New World, and an Indian burial ground presided over by a vengeful spirit. In a shattering climax, a full-blooded American Indian pits his skill and the power of ancient ritual against the Powers of Darkness in a final desperate effort to remove the hideous curse once and for all . . .

THE SECRET OF AMITYVILLE

HANS HOLZER

LEISURE BOOKS   **æ**   NEW YORK CITY

A LEISURE BOOK

Published by

Dorchester Publishing Co., Inc.
6 East 39th Street
New York, NY 10016

Copyright © 1985 by Hans Holzer

Printed in the United States of America

A WORD TO THE WISE

Rarely has a house caused such a commotion, aroused such fervent interest, such controversy and, yes, fear, as has the house on Ocean Avenue in the little town of Amityville, Long Island.

Those of my readers who are familiar with my two earlier works dealing with this infamous dwelling are of course aware of its sinister history. One of these days the house may be no more, swallowed up in a final burst of that destructive energy that has accumulated on that site for all these long years.

But how many know what lies behind the terrible happenings in Amityville? Its origins stretch back far beyond our time and far away from the shores of the New World. We may trace the horror forward to its inevitable resolution; and at last we may discover why so much terror has been associated with that house.

Read on, then, and learn what there is to be gleaned of the Secret of Amityville, for this is all there is to say.

The Author

Prologue

"Why is there an empty lot here when there are all those houses on the land round about?" Franklin Adams asked his companion, Reggie Brewen, as they strolled together down Ocean Avenue.

Reggie worked at the Amityville library on Saturdays when school was not in session and the library needed some extra help. Franklin Adams, who was several years older than Reggie, had just opened his own law offices down the road. Born in New Jersey, he had only recently come to Amityville, and he knew little about the town. He was keen to take advantage of Reggie's own fascination with local lore and history to find out more about the past of the town where he now made his home.

"That's the place where That House used to stand," Reggie replied, almost too quietly, "only it burned down, of course . . . you know . . . when the last guy in it got killed."

Now Franklin Adams understood, for one of his own relatives had once lived in that house, years ago, when the horror of the DeFeo murders was still fresh in everyone's minds.

"But isn't somebody going to build on it again? After all, it is a valuable piece of land, on an attractive residential street in the best part of town."

Reggie shook his head. "Nobody in their right mind would touch it," he replied, "and I can't say that I blame them. I would not touch it either."

Franklin Adams' practical approach to life rebelled against such a superstitious notion. After all, there are lots of houses where murders have taken place, and accidents have happened, even fatal ones, and yet other people move in and live there happily ever after. Clearly, he thought, someone must be profiting from keeping this valuable piece of land off the market. It was gaping at them like a toothless mouth, somehow menacing, reaching all the way back to the water as if ready to swallow up anyone who might dare to venture on to it.

Reggie laughed at this notion when Franklin voiced it. Then he explained that the land was in the care of the town of Amityville now, having been taken over in lieu of taxes when the last owner had abandoned it . . . and Amityville.

"Well, now," Franklin said impatiently, "I'm not going to stand here and let a dirty piece of acreage make a fool of me. Come on!" With that, he lightly scaled the rotting barbed wire fence that now only symbolically protected the land from trespassers. He stood inside the enclosure, waiting for the younger man to follow him, but Reggie shook his head.

"No thanks, Mr. Adams," he said, "but I'd rather not. And if I were you, I'd come back out right away."

"Rubbish!" a defiant Franklin replied. "I'm not about to give in to a silly superstition. I'm sure lots of curious people have walked all over this place just to say they've been here. Come on!"

But Reggie remained firm. "If you want to go in there, I suppose I can't stop you. But I've got to get back to do some homework. I'm sorry." He started to turn as Franklin walked out onto the most notorious piece of land in all of Long Island.

He found the ground uneven and at times slippery, but otherwise devoid of any unusual features, and not even remotely chilling. Here and there there were bits of debris, perhaps final remnants of the big fire of some years ago. When he reached the center of the lot, he turned and saw Reggie still standing at the barbed wire fence. Reggie, perhaps more out of curiosity than concern, had changed his mind about going home right away.

"See? Nothing to worry about!" Adams shouted back at him, waving his arm. Reggie acknowledged the greeting. He began to feel silly about his own reluctance to join Franklin out on the lot. While he began to wonder if perhaps he ought just to jump the fence and go to where the man stood, he noticed that the weather had begun to change. There seemed to be some moisture in the air now, and as he watched Franklin poke his foot at some piece of debris in the center of the land, a patch of fog drifted down from nowhere and rapidly engulfed his friend.

A moment later the wind had blown the fog away again, and the view was as clear as before. But where was Franklin? At first Reggie thought the lawyer must have gone on down to the edge of the land where it met the ocean. But the land is flat and you cannot possibly miss seeing a man on it, unless he is lying on the ground.

Reggie was suddenly filled with nameless fear. A part of him wanted to jump over the fence and look for Franklin, but another part, warned by an inner voice, wanted to turn and run.

And then he heard a faint voice coming from the center of the land, crying for help. It was the unmistakable voice of Franklin Adams, the bravura gone, and stark fear in its tone.

"Reggie! Help me . . . get me out of this

hole . . ." Then the voice trailed off and a terrible silence fell all around.

Reggie no longer had control over his actions. He turned and ran down Ocean Avenue, as fast as his feet could carry him.

Franklin Adams was never seen again, neither in Amityville nor anywhere else, and his offices were eventually closed down. Nobody came to look for his body, least of all in the center of that accursed piece of land, because no one knew of his visit there. Reggie had decided to keep quiet. Who would believe him, anyway?

PART ONE

How it all began

Chapter One

The Pig and Whistle was owned by a certain Mrs. Margaret Donleavey, whose ancestors had no doubt come from Ireland. The inn stood on the south bank of the River Thames at a point where you could actually see Whitehall in the distance. Its neighborhood was far from elegant: as a matter of fact, it was probably one of the most disreputable of the south bank. Lately, because of the unrest which affected the whole of England, the area had become even less safe for the unwary.

But the Pig and Whistle was a pleasant, well-established inn, kept reasonably clean by its mistress; thus far at least it had been free from any official criticism. This was of course due in part to the fact that Mrs. Donleavey acted rather generously with the law, whenever its minions came around. Even so, she didn't hold much with fights or violence on the premises, and her reputation was formidable enough to keep the peace.

The year was 1717, the month January, and a downright raw day it was. At this time of day, four o'clock in the afternoon, it was already getting dark, but the flickering candles and a warm fire in the huge fireplace at the far end of the room gave the inn much needed warmth and an almost home-like atmosphere. The inn was reasonably full at this hour; of people from the neighborhood, a stranger here and there, all taking refuge from the freezing winds outside.

At one of the corner tables, near windows giving onto the river, sat two men. One of them was redheaded and on the short side. The other was tall and stately; he had long, dark brown hair, and an aristocratic bearing. Between them there was a jug of wine and two glasses. The conversation seemed to have ground to a halt at this moment.

The taller of the two men was in his late twenties. His clothes marked him out as a gentleman—and a wealthy one at that. His eyes were blue, and his brown hair almost black, though the reflection of the flames made it appear lighter than it was. This was John, Lord Howell, a scion of one of the oldest and most illustrious families of England.

Lately, some of the family had not done too

well financially, partly due to the recent political strife during which some Howells had taken the wrong road. They had thus been deprived of the fruits of victory when the new Protestant government had come into power. Then, too, some Howells harbored Roman Catholic sympathies, and that did not help family prestige in England at this juncture of events.

Lord Howell's own father, Richard, had openly backed the candidacy of James III, the Catholic pretender and son of the late King James II. After the arrival of William III, of Orange, such sentiments were not looked upon with favor, and the political consequences had proved long-lived. Lord Howell was well off, for his estates in Wessex yielded sufficiently high revenues for him to live comfortably wherever he chose. On the other hand, there was no position of importance open to him, try as he might. The present government distrusted a man with so many Jacobite and Catholic relatives.

Lord Howell's companion was clearly of a much lower social order. The earring he wore suggested that he had been to sea, and his tanned face reinforced that observation. In fact, Tom Masterson was a professional sailor and had been all over the world, despite his young age, which was then a mere twenty-four years. What had drawn Masterson together with the aristocratic Howell was nothing more than a chance meeting the night before at another tavern. Both had been at loose ends that evening, and a conversation had sprung up between them at the bar. They had decided to dine together the following night, and so here they were at the Pig and Whistle.

Masterson set down his glass on the wine-stained surface of the table. "Tell me, m'Lord," he said softly, "have you ever heard of the Queen Anne Opal?"

"No," Lord Howell said, shaking his head, emphatically, "What exactly is it?"

The red-headed sailor threw his head back, holding his tongue for a moment, to make a greater, more dramatic impression. Then he smiled, his mouth opening wide from ear to ear, as if he were about to disclose one of the most profound truths of the age. "The Queen Anne Opal, m'Lord," he finally said, "is a very special jewel. Three years ago, when my ship cast anchor off Bombay harbor, I asked permission from my captain to go inland for a while, to explore this strange country. He wouldn't let me go, but I had a hankering to go anyway, and one dark night, I jumped overboard and swam ashore, unmindful of the dangers that lurk in the harbor."

"So you deserted your ship, eh?" Lord Howell said, evidently none too pleased with what he had heard so far.

But the sailor ignored Lord Howell's command. "After weeks and weeks of travelling, I managed to reach the north of India. I had heard of the fabulous treasures of Tibet, and

I intended to see for myself."

"Tibet?" Lord Howell exclaimed. "A sailor in Tibet?"

Tom nodded. "Aye, aye, sir," he said. "In the end I made it all the way up to what they call the roof of the world."

"Amazing," Lord Howell admitted. "Was it worth your efforts?"

"Indeed it was, sir," the sailor replied. "I entered the forbidden land of Tibet, dressed like a native, and after great difficulties I reached the monastery of Saskya. It is located way up north of the holy city of Lhasa, m'Lord, and I wager that not too many Englishmen have ever set foot there."

"Not to mention sailors," Lord Howell added.

"I made friends with one of the Lamas, and somehow we understood each other even though I did not understand their language. But after a few weeks of staying with him, I began to grasp it, and he, I suppose, learned a few words of English. That is when I heard for the first time about the opal."

"You referred to it earlier as the Queen Anne Opal, I believe," Lord Howell said. "Why is that?"

"What I was told about this enormously beautiful blue opal, probably the largest of its kind on earth, has to do with the coronation of her late majesty, our good Queen Anne. It appears that many years ago the Grand Lama of Saskya had received a gift and an expression of friendship from the

Queen's father, the late King James II. Somehow word got back to Tibet that one of his daughters was to be crowned Queen of England."

"That was fifteen years ago."

"Yes, exactly, sir. But when I spoke to my friend, he told me that this fabulous stone had appeared at the monastery shortly before the Queen's coming to the throne, and the Grand Lama wished to name it in honor of our late Queen. You see, sir, his intention was to send it to London for the coronation, to be presented to the Queen as a token of his respect. Unfortunately, the Grand Lama died before this could be effected, and thus the Queen Anne Opal is still at the monastery, or at least it was when I was there three years ago."

Lord Howell had listened to this silently, and didn't answer immediately. When he spoke, he seemed rather preoccupied. "Why are you telling me all this?"

"I felt perhaps you might be interested to hear about this strange piece of jewelry, seeing that you told me last night how fascinated you are with strange and mysterious objects."

"Oh, but this is merely a large and valuable opal, is it not? There doesn't seem to be anything so mysterious about it."

"Oh, but there is," the sailor replied, saving his juiciest bit for the last. "You see, sir, the opal isn't just an ordinary piece of jewelry.

The original owners had put a terrible curse on it."

Lord Howell became more interested. "Did you find out what this curse was? And who pronounced it?"

"Yes, indeed I did, sir," the sailor replied. "I took great pains to ask questions as much as I was able to with my limited knowledge of the language. It appears that this same blue opal had originally been embedded in the head of a statue of a protective demon, what the Tibetans like to call the Third Eye."

"The Third Eye?" Lord Howell frowned. "I have never heard of that."

"Nevertheless, sir," the sailor replied, "there is this belief that some extraordinary people, those who have been chosen for tasks —such as prophecy and spiritual guidance —have a third eye in the middle of their foreheads with which to see better and know things that other mortals cannot. This demon—and you know, sir, there are lots of strange demons all over Tibet—this demon, sir, appeared to have a particularly powerful Third Eye. Naturally, it wasn't the human eye, it was this blue opal, you see, and it gave the statue a certain degree of fame."

"Then why the curse?" Lord Howell demanded to know. He was getting slightly impatient.

"I'm coming to that, m'Lord," the sailor replied, sensing Lord Howell's feelings. "This figure of a demon stood in a monastery called

Rva Sgreng, in another part of the country. I soon enough learned that in Tibet individual monasteries are often competitive with one another, and sometimes even go to war against each other. The monastery of Rva Sgreng was famous for its demon and the blue opal, and the faithful came to it all the time to derive certain benefits from touching it."

"Oh, like the Catholics and the statues of their saints," Lord Howell commented.

Tom nodded. "Precisely. Now the way I heard it, in the year twelve thirty-nine, a certain officer by the name of Hunai, in the services of Godan, the son of the Mongol overlord of Tibet, came to the monastery of Rva Sgreng to loot it. At that time, my friend the Lama told me, Tibet was part of the Mongol Empire, but had been granted a certain degree of autonomy by the Mongol overlords. In fact, the leading Lama had been given the title of King, or Ti Shih in their language. This happened under the reign of the terrible Genghis Khan. Now Godan, the grandson of the Khan, was anxious to maintain good relations with these strange people and learn from them about their mysterious ways, including the ways of magic."

"Magic?" Lord Howell asked.

The sailor nodded. "Magic plays a big role in Tibetan life. But to get back to the story about this opal, sir, if you do not mind, it appears that this officer, Hunai, took the opal from the forehead of the statue, and ran away with it. When the Abbot of the monastery discovered his great loss, he pronounced a terrible curse not only on Hunai, but on anyone who possessed the opal, until it was returned to its rightful place as the Third Eye in the statue of Rva Sgreng. That is, I believe, how the curse started."

Lord Howell thought this over for a moment. Clearly, the story intrigued him. Anything out of the ordinary had always held great fascination for him, bored as he was with life in London society. "And where is the opal now?"

"That's just it, m'Lord," Tom replied. "Nobody really knows. As you recall, sir, it had been named in honor of our good Queen Anne upon her coronation, but of course it remained in the possession of the Grand Lama of Saskya. Now how it got to Saskya I never found out, but there was no love lost between Saskya and the rival monastery of Rva Sgreng. They knew very well that the opal was in the possession of the Grand Lama, but the Grand Lama of Saskya, far from being willing to give it up, or back, simply proclaimed that it had been found one day in front of the main altar in his private *Stupa*, and that he had accepted it as coming to him by divine guidance. Thus, the Grand Lama of Saskya retained the opal, and after it had been dedicated in honor of Queen Anne, it nevertheless remained at the monastery."

"Then that's where it is, isn't it?" Lord Howell commented. "Why do you say no one knows?"

"Because, sir, some time ago I received a letter from my friend, the Lama at Saskya. He and I write to each other from time to time, his English getting better and better as a result. In this letter to me he told me that two men had appeared at the monastery, claiming to have come with secret messages for the Abbot. They were left alone with the aged Abbot, but when the Abbot failed to emerge the next morning, other Lamas went into his study to discover him quite dead, and the opal missing. All my friend knows is that the two seemed to be Englishmen. Presumably they had returned to England with the precious jewel."

"Then it may be here in England," Lord Howell exclaimed, not disguising his mounting interest. Tom nodded gravely.

"Very likely. You see, sir, the theft occurred three years ago, according to my friend."

Lord Howell suddenly jerked upright in his seat, almost upsetting the glasses before him.

"What is it? What is it, sir? Have I offended you?" the sailor said quickly. His fear was instinctive: a poor sailor could not afford to antagonize an influential peer of the realm.

Lord Howell sank back in his chair. "No, no, it's nothing like that. Just that, well, I've realized a connection."

"A connection?" Tom asked, puzzled in his turn.

Lord Howell nodded. "Last Christmas, I

recall, when I was at Court, I heard a strange tale about two Englishmen who had been to the Far East and had come back with a strange jewel. It was said that this jewel had supernatural powers, and that it had been at one time part of a statue of an idol."

"Did you hear whether it was an opal?"

"The bluest of blue opals, I was told."

"Well, then," Tom exclaimed, "it must be the same."

"Very likely."

"But what happened to it?"

"That's just it," Lord Howell replied. His face grew thoughtful. "As I understand it, and mind you this is just a story I was told by two men at Court, all this happened about three years ago in the last year of our good Queen Anne."

"That would be correct," Tom exclaimed. "That is exactly when the theft is said to have occurred, according to my friend the Lama."

"Well, then," Lord Howell continued, "the mysterious gentlemen presented the jewel to Queen Anne. Shortly afterwards, the Queen died. All attempts to make James III, her brother, the heir to the throne failed, and the crown went to the House of Hanover. There was a lot of confusion, of course. I wonder, where is the opal now?"

Tom smiled. "I believe sir, you are in a better position to make enquiries about that than I."

"Quite so," Lord Howell said. His face became thoughtful. He drummed his fingers on the table, staring in silence at the bleak grey river beyond the window.

When the two men drained their glasses for the last time, the gathering dusk had made the river invisible. Lord Howell left a coin on the table to settle their score. He and Tom shook hands. Neither believed he would be likely to meet the other again—their stations in life were too different.

They set off in opposite directions. Tom's mind was occupied with the possibility of returning to India on the very next ship, to look for other treasures, for he knew that the opal had not been the only valuable jewel at the monastery. Lord Howell, on the other hand, was toying with the idea of trying to lift the veil from the mystery of the accursed opal, if only out of curiosity.

The next day Lord Howell hurried to Court. His wealth, wit and connections always made him welcome there, though the doubts concerning his political and religious loyalties prevented him from attaining a position of real influence.

His first call was on Lord Buckminster, an old friend who was the Deputy of the Royal Chancellor of the Exchequer. Surely, something as valuable as this opal would have to be known to the treasury! But Lord Buckminster shook his head. He knew nothing about it. Of course, it was just possible, he opined, that among the many, many gifts which kept streaming in from the colonies, there might be such an opal as Lord Howell was enquiring about. But to search for it was entirely futile, and even to know where to begin was impossible.

Lord Howell shrugged and made his departure. He was not disconsolate—there were plenty of other people he could ask. But by the end of the third day he had been forced to accept that the opal was a remarkably well-kept secret, if indeed it existed at all.

He began to have second thoughts about Tom's veracity; knowing that sailors would sometimes spin tall tales, he started to wonder whether perhaps Tom had invented the story as a result of a pleasant evening over a bottle of wine.

He was about to dismiss the entire incident when he ran into an old friend in a coffee house near Covent Garden. Robert Dingleberry, despite his funny name, was a very serious fellow. A don at Oxford, Dingleberry had an enormous knowledge of history and politics, and was just the kind of man who might have some sort of information about the mysterious opal. At any rate, Lord Howell decided to take a chance and brought up the matter in conversation soon after they had left the coffee house.

"Yes, yes," Dingleberry replied, as they were walking arm in arm down the Strand. "I've heard that story somewhere before. Of course, you realize it's just a legend, but I've heard it talked about. Some beautiful blue opal from India that is supposed to cause all the troubles. Well, if you ask me, there aren't any troubles. After all, we should be very pleased with the great change that has taken place in England, now that we are finally rid of Popish intrigues. James III indeed! It is a good thing that the Elector of Hanover is at the reins of the country." Dingleberry was a committed Protestant, and the idea of a return to a Roman Catholic monarchy was totally abhorrent to him.

"But what about the opal? Where would it be now?" Lord Howell pressed. As far as he was concerned at present, he couldn't care less who sat on the throne of England; just now his interest was focused on the mysterious opal and on nothing else.

"Oh, well," Dingleberry said, as if it were the most obvious thing in the world, "I suppose they have it somewhere at the Tower."

"The Tower of London?"

"Of course. It is the obvious place, isn't it?"

"Is it?" Lord Howell replied, not sure what to say. But at least he had his first real lead.

Chapter Two

At first the idea seemed ridiculous. Lord Howell tried to ignore it, but it returned to his thoughts time and again. The great blue jewel even glowed in his dreams. It was as if the stone had somehow enchanted him from afar. Finally he allowed himself to examine the idea in the cold light of reason.

He wanted Queen Anne's opal more than he had ever wanted anything in his life. If it was in the Tower, he was going to steal it.

It was not that he needed the money. Rather, he craved adventure, for he was becoming increasingly bored with his life. Unable to enter politics in a serious way because of his past political affiliations, he thought himself condemned to a life of luxury without purpose. This would never do for the adventurous John Howell. Consequently the idea of undertaking so extraordinary and dangerous a venture as stealing the opal from the recesses of the Tower appealed to both his sense of adventure and his need for personal achievement. The idea was also attractive for another reason. The opal was technically in the possession of the German Elector who sat on the throne of England. Howell was a Jocobite at heart: as far as he was concerned, King George was a usurper. Lord Howell might be tolerated at Court, but the King had effectively blocked all his hopes of advancement. That fact alone would make it a pleasure to steal the opal.

Not for a moment did he consider the consequences of failure. Howell valued his life very highly, but at the same time he could not have cared less if he were to die tomorrow, provided the cause was just. In the circumstances, he decided to seek out the sailor again. Together with Tom, he would attempt the impossible: to whisk the opal out of the Tower in such a way that no one would notice its absence until they were safely out of reach. Fortunately, it was not difficult for one in his position to gain access to the fortress itself, provided he could offer a reasonable explanation for his visit.

His first requirement, however, was to find Tom; a colleague would be essential for the scheme he had in mind. He tried the Pig and Whistle without high hopes, for he knew that Tom had been considering a voyage to India.

But he struck lucky: he found Tom propping up the bar. The sailor was very nearly penniless; he was happy to postpone his journey in return for the handful of gleaming guineas which Howell tossed onto the bar.

Within a week of formulating his plans, Lord Howell arrived at the outer gates of the Tower, dressed in his richest, most fashionable clothes. He sauntered gaily into the gatekeeper's lodge, and requested an interview with the governor of the Tower.

"Are you expected, m'Lord?" the gatekeeper asked unemotionally. Evidently he was not impressed by his vistor's rank—nor by his appearance.

"Nay," Lord Howell replied, unruffled, "but pray present this note to His Lordship." With that, he handed the gatekeeper a letter of introduction which had been provided by a mutual friend at Court.

A few moments later, the gatekeeper returned with a somewhat friendlier expression on his face. "His Lordship will see you now. Follow me." Leaving his mount outside, Lord Howell followed the gatekeeper into the recesses of the Tower. The air inside was heavy, the atmosphere one of doom. Lord Howell had been inside the Tower before, and although that was several years ago he had never forgotten how depressing the place had seemed.

Shortly they arrived at the entrance to the governor's apartments. The gatekeeper withdrew, and Howell was ushered into the governor's study by a footman.

"What can we do for you, Lord Howell?" the governor asked, offering his hand in greeting.

"A mere whim, if you please," Lord Howell replied lightly. "If you will do me the great favor of showing me through the treasury, I would be much obliged to you, sir."

"The treasury?" the governor asked. "What is the purpose of such a visit, may I ask?"

"Very simple, sir," Lord Howell said. "I am an avid collector of precious jewels, and I would like to know just how insignificant my own collection is in comparison with what you have in this fortress."

"Very well, I see nothing wrong with that," the governor replied, and rang the bell. After a moment, a guard appeared. "Will you tell the Keeper of the Keys that Lord Howell is permitted to be shown through the treasury," the governor said, and nodded to Lord Howell.

Howell followed the guard along the winding corridors of the fortress until they arrived at a heavy iron gate. The gate formed the border between that part of the fortress where prisoners were kept and matters of government were taken care of, and that part which served as a treasure house.

The guard rang a bell by pulling a handle to the right side of the iron gate. After what seemed an eternity, heavy, shuffling footsteps could be heard approaching the other side of the gate. An elderly man appeared; his face was deeply furrowed, and he wore the peculiar uniform of the Keeper of the Keys. His name was Geoffrey London. Much had been made of the fact that his name was the same as that of the city. He was a well-respected man who had served the Crown all his life. By now he was nearing retirement age; his eyes watered and his back was stooped, for the many years spent in the dark recesses of the fortress had left their mark on him. The guard explained their mission, and the Keeper of the Keys nodded.

"Wait here a moment, m'Lord," he said, and returned to where he had come from.

Now what? Lord Howell thought. How long is this going to take? But he did not have to wait too long. A moment later, steps resounded once again from inside, but they seemed much lighter than the ones he had heard before. Then there appeared at the gate a young woman, fragile and slim, with long, flowing, blonde hair. In her right hand she held a large key.

"I am Merryn London," she said when she reached the gate. "My father has asked me to take you around the treasury. He begs to be excused for he does not feel well to-day."

With that she opened the gate from within, and let Lord Howell inside. The guard saluted, and went back to his post.

Intrigued by the lovely appearance of the young woman, Lord Howell did not know what to think. Gaining access to the treasury had been much easier than he had anticipated. But whenever he tried to strike up a conversation with his guide, she seemed oddly silent, though perhaps she was only shy. Under the circumstances he thought it best to concentrate his attention on the task at hand, looking with feigned collector's interest at the fabulous treasures now before his eyes.

Eventually they came to a glass box, within which an enormous blue stone rested. Lord Howell's heart beat faster: could this be the fabulous opal he was seeking? With a casualness that belied his excitement, he pointed at the blue stone in the glass box and asked what it was.

"Oh that," Merryn said. "It comes from Tibet, I believe. Someone wanted to give it to Queen Anne for her coronation, but it came too late."

Lord Howell could scarcely suppress his feelings of jubilation. He had located the precious jewel. Quickly he thanked Merryn for the tour she had given him, bent down to kiss her hand, rather to her surprise, and then made his departure. But when they arrived back at the iron gate something within him made him halt once more.

For the first time he took a good look at the girl. She was perhaps twenty-four or twenty-five years old. Her figure was elegant and her face was very beautiful, with those blue eyes and that cascade of blonde hair. With a start,

Lord Howell realized the color of her eyes was almost identical to that of the opal.

"Merryn," he began.

"I am Lady Merryn," she corrected him with a smile and took the edge off the remark. "My father has been made Earl of Whitechapel."

"I beg your pardon," Lord Howell replied. He should have known he was dealing with a gentlewoman. He began again. "Lady Merryn, may I express my gratitude to you for this remarkable tour by inviting you to dine with me some evening?"

Clearly the invitation came as a total surprise. Her face displayed a kind of pleasant shock, and for a moment she seemed flustered. "You're very kind, m'Lord," she finally managed to say, "but I don't know—"

"That is, of course, if you are not married or betrothed?" Lord Howell continued.

"I am neither, m'Lord."

"Then I see no difficulty."

For a moment she hesitated. "Perhaps," she said carefully, "perhaps if you will speak to my father?"

"By all means," Lord Howell said. He walked through the archway into the court-yard. "I shall speak to Lord Whitechapel anon."

Without looking back again he made his departure. He left behind a very puzzled young woman, who stood fixed to the spot for a long time after Lord Howell had disappeared from her sight.

Howell himself was puzzled, as he strode across the courtyard to the gatekeeper's lodge. Why was that young, attractive woman neither married nor engaged to be married? And why did she need to have her father's permission to dine with him? But then other thoughts entered his mind, thoughts of high adventure, and perhaps also of the dangers that certainly lay ahead.

When Lord Howell awoke the next morning he realized that the encounter with Lady Merryn was a perfect gift from fate to help him accomplish his ends. Consequently he immediately dispatched a short note to Lord Whitechapel, requesting the pleasure of his daughter's company at dinner.

The request was soon granted, and, before the week was out, he sat opposite Lady Merryn in the dining room of his town house, admiring her fragile beauty even more. Her shyness was not something she displayed to impress him, he realized now, but an affliction from her childhood that she had never been able to overcome.

The conversation revolved around historical treasures and kings and queens of England, and nothing romantic passed between them. Much as he wanted to take her in his arms, for he felt rising within himself a great desire for the woman, he behaved like an old-fashioned gentleman. He sensed that it would be better to bide his time. Eventually, hee took her back to her father's apartments at the Tower.

By now he had learned two things about Lady Merryn: that she had been engaged twice to men of rank but had declined to fulfill the engagements for reasons of her own, very much to the distress of her father; and that she had a mind all her own which would not permit her to marry a man unless she felt deeply in love with him. This not having been the case in the past, she was still unwed.

Lord Howell also discovered that she was a widely read woman, extraordinarily so for someone in her position. Her learning could have put to shame that of many men he knew who had attended university. Merryn, it seemed, was fond of books and spent most of her time reading.

The following week, he called on her again, this time without first asking her father's permission. Once more they dined together, and the conversation became somewhat livelier, involving some of the legends attached to the great treasures guarded at the Tower. Lord Howell skillfully brought the conversation around to the opal, and enquired whether Lady Merryn had ever heard of a curse being attached to it. To his utter surprise, she knew of it and assured him that the story was based on fact.

"I wouldn't touch that jewel for anything in the world," she said with a shudder.

That evening, when he brought Lady Merryn back to her apartments, he asked her to take him once again to view the opal. He made it sound like a casual whim of the moment. Somewhat surprised by his sudden request, she nevertheless assented. She fetched the huge iron key. Together they descended into the treasury.

"Remarkable, remarkable," Lord Howell murmured as he viewed the object of his desire again. And he meant it.

The treasure house was dank, and Merryn shivered as she gazed at the opal. Lord Howell noticed, and courteously insisted that he should escort her back to her apartments.

At the iron gate they paused to relock it. Lord Howell chivalrously took the key from her. There was a screech of ancient metal as he turned the tumblers in the rusting lock. Under cover of darkness, it was an easy matter to press the notches of the key into the pad of wax concealed in his left hand. He returned the key to Merryn with a bow. She noticed nothing amiss.

The following evening he met Tom again at their usual rendezvous, the Pig and Whistle.

"That's easy, m'Lord," Tom assured him when he saw the wax impression, "I'll have me friend have it ready for you by tomorrow night. He's a skilled locksmith—and always happy to make a little money on the side."

"Splendid," Lord Howell said. He congratulated himself on his foresight in hiring Tom: the sailor had many acquaintances in London's underworld. "Then perhaps we can proceed this coming Saturday?"

"Right you are, sir," Tom said. A slow smile spread across his face.

Shortly afterwards, Tom excused himself to attend to the business at hand. Lord Howell decided to linger on a bit and finish his glass of wine. As he sat there in the tavern, contemplating what lay ahead and the possible dangers that might be lurking in the depths of the Tower, his eye fell on a table at the far end of the inn. It was occupied by a small, dark-haired woman in her fifties or early sixties. For some reason his gaze was attracted by her and he asked himself whether he might not have encountered the woman somewhere before. Eventually, his curiosity got the better of him and he got up from his table and sauntered over to hers.

"Begging your pardon, madam," he said with a polite bow, "but it appears to me that we know each other from somewhere."

"Not likely," the woman replied, and looked him straight in the face.

No, Howell thought to himself, I've never met this woman before, and yet why is it that I *seem* to know her?

It was as if she had read his mind. "Care to sit down and share a glass of wine with me?" she said, pointing to the chair opposite hers.

"You are most kind, madam." Lord Howell sat down and looked across at her. "Who are you?"

"I am Maureen Grayner," the woman replied. "They call me the seeress of London."

Of course, Howell thought, the seeress of London! He had heard of this extraordinary woman whom the church could not touch because many of the leading clergy were her clients. A pious woman, she had always ascribed her powers to God and no one in London had ever dared accuse her of anything in the nature of witchcraft. She lived in a modest cottage at the outskirts of town. Maureen had the reputation of not wanting much from anyone, spurning wealth and invitations to reside at the mansions of the great. As yet, so the story went, the king had not commanded her presence, but it was rumored that some of the royal family had visited her in secret.

"So you are the seeress of London," Lord Howell said. "I'm honored to share this wine with you."

"Give me your hand," Maureen commanded, and he obeyed immediately. As she touched the lines of his right hand, a serious expression crept over her face. Her dark, sparkling eyes widened considerably as she looked at him with an expression of utmost urgency.

"Lord Howell," she began, and he wondered how she knew his name without him having offered it. "Lord Howell, you must be very careful. I see the greatest of dangers surrounding you. Do not tempt God."

Immediately he withdrew his hand. "What

exactly to you mean? What sort of dangers do I face?"

Maureen made an evasive gesture with her right hand. "I can't give you any more details than that. But I see great danger to you and your loved ones, if you are not very careful. I sense some sort of high adventure, and while I do feel that you will succeed, m'Lord, I also feel no good will come from it. Whatever it is you are planning, I urge you not to do it. But if you will not listen to me, and you do go ahead, remember that I warned you. From it will come great tragedy for you, from it will come a total change in your life that you had never anticipated. Beware."

While Lord Howell stared at her, not sure what to say next, Maureen rose abruptly, waved at him and quickly left the inn.

Chapter Three

Everything was in their favor on Saturday night: the moon was full, allowing them to see just enough without the need for artificial light; and because it was a Saturday night, very few of the Tower guards were about.

Howell and Tom slipped past the gatekeeper's lodge like a pair of ghosts. The gatekeeper himself was slumbering heavily in front of a roaring fire, with a steaming tankard of mulled wine at his elbow. Howell had tipped the man well on his last visit— and his investment had evidently paid off.

While Howell himself waited in the shadows, Tom engaged the two guards at the entrance to the treasury in conversation. Deftly he brought the talk around to the injustice of all, that they had to stand guard on a Saturday night while all of their colleagues were out celebrating with their girls. He then offered them a drink from a flask which he had brought with him.

Both sentries had a couple of long swallows of the fiery spirit, draining the flask. The senior soldier, a corporal, merely belched his gratitude; his younger colleague handed the flask back to Tom with a few words of thanks. But the words tangled in his throat as he tried to speak. A few seconds later, both sentries slumped to the ground, heavily drugged.

Howell, who had secretly observed all this, now joined his associate in the corridor. With the key he had made they were able to unlock the heavy gate. Moments later they stood in the damp cellar that housed the treasury. Enough moonlight filtered in through the high windows close to the ceiling to allow them to find the position of the opal. Without so much as a moment's hesitation, Howell broke the glass and took the opal into his hands. For a moment he stood there transfixed, gazing at his prize.

But Tom was getting nervous. He insisted they leave at once before they were caught. The guards were still unconscious; they met no one on their way out; and the gatekeeper slept on in front of his fire. Out in the street, they mounted their horses and rode off as quickly as possible.

When the loss of the precious opal was discovered, the corporal of the guard was accused of having stolen it. Even though subjected to torture, the man would not and could not confess to anything more serious than having had a drink with a stranger and remembering nothing more afterwards. Soon the matter of the opal moved to the background of public interest, there being far more important and more controversial issues of the day in politics. As the prosecuting magistrate could not find another suspect to pin the theft on, the matter was put *ad acta*.

Now that he had acquired the opal he had determined to add to his possessions, Lord Howell tried very hard to pay attention to a matter of another kind: his courtship of Merryn London, which by now had taken on serious overtones. Before long he was proposing marriage to the lady and, to his utter surprise and joy, she accepted him at once. The wedding which followed was a quiet one at his country house near Chester; it was almost as if he wanted to hurry it, and get on with their lives.

Lord Howell's marriage to Merryn London fared well, as marriages go. The gentle lady gave him a daughter a year after they were married, whom they baptized Mary. Life for Lord and Lady Howell was no different than life for many country gentry of means, but eventually Howell's restless nature came to the surface again. Still unable to play any major part in the affairs of state, he began to write, a book of poetry at first; but that soon bored him. Eventually he wrote a book dealing with the adventures of a famous seventeenth century pirate, partially fantasy and partially based on public knowledge. This pleased him and took his mind off the essential placidity of his day-to-day life. But not for long.

England was now being ruled with a firm hand by the very Protestant King George I, who had lately come over from the continent. So German was George I that he hardly spoke English, and surrounded himself mainly with those whom he knew well back home in Brunswick. Nevertheless, because he was a Protestant and the nearest Protestant heir of the old royal family, most of the British accepted him as their rightful king.

But not all. Many Scots, particularly in the Highlands, vehemently refused to acknowledge the foreigner, and continued to consider the Stuart heir, James III, their rightful king. But even in England itself, there were many who opposed the Hanoverian rule, some openly, some secretly. The Jacobites who opposed it openly did not dare say much about it, for that would have jeopardized their positions, if not their lives. Those who opposed George I secretly, however, were bound to take action sooner or later, waiting only for the right moment to unseat the "German king."

One of those who wanted to depose the king was a young lawyer by the name of Frederick Sykes. Sykes came from an impeccable family, had had all advantages at Oxford, and was now in the forefront of those who wanted to organize a plot against King George. During a country weekend, Sykes managed to meet John Howell. One word led to another, and by the time the visit was over, Lord Howell himself had added his name to those who would unseat the King. He knew of course that discovery was tantamount to imprisonment and, should the venture go further than merely plotting, would bring his certain death at the gallows. However, his loyalties had always been strongly pro-Stuart, and he felt that joining the potential rebels was a just and fair use of his energies and abilities; and he was willing to risk it. Sykes merely provided an opportunity for which Howell had long been waiting.

During the succeeding weeks he and Frederick Sykes met several times at the latter's London apartment near Whitehall, and also at Lord Howell's own house. Merryn knew nothing of the purpose of Sykes' visits, and she did not think it was her business to question her husband concerning his doings. Then, too, she was preoccupied with their daughter, Mary, and seldom interferred with her husband's daily activities. That there was great love between them, she knew, and that was enough for her. Little did she know that her husband had misused her trust before their marriage and stolen the opal she had innocently shown him. There was a side to Lord Howell she was yet to discover.

One month after Howell's initial meeting with Frederick Sykes, the young lawyer brought two other men to Lord Howell's house. They had developed a scheme to murder the King while he was on holiday at Bath. It seemed plausible enough, and likely to succeed, because most of those who would be involved in the plot were known to the King and would have ready access to the royal presence. Much as he disliked bloodshed, Lord Howell agreed to take part in it, in fact to be the one who would draw the attention of the King away from those who would carry out the murder. There were now enough men involved in the plot for them to be able to secure the King's lodgings and disarm his guards, so that the conspirators could make good their escape if necessary. By then they hoped the country would rise against what they called the foreign usurper, and be with them in their just cause. Calmly, the plotters went their separate ways that night and Lord Howell went to bed secure in the knowledge that he was about to contribute to history and the greater glory of Britain.

He was rudely awakened in the small hours of the night by knockings at his door. He hurried down the stairs to find out who wanted to break into his sleep. On his way down, he glanced out a small window which overlooked the street. To his shock he saw six fully armed soldiers of the royal guard clustered around his door; their officer was hammering on it with the hilt of his sword.

Fortunately, the door was not the kind that could easily be broken down. Howell at once realized that something had gone amiss. Quickly dressing, he managed to say a few words of farewell to his wife, and then ran out of the back door.

By the time the soldiers outside had managed to break down the front door and question a terrified Lady Howell, her husband was well on his way out of London.

The following day the official gazette carried news of the discovery of the plot, prominently mentioning Lord Howell's name among those who stood accused of trying to overthrow the monarchy. Most of the culprits had been caught except for Frederick Sykes and Lord Howell. Knowing that the authorities would expect him to make for France, Lord Howell rode hell-for-leather to Scotland, where he thought himself safe from what he called the Hanoverian minions. Rightly so, for the lairds of the Highlands were in no mood to turn over a man who stood loyal to the Stuarts against the Hanoverians. It was clear to him, however, that he would have to hide, perhaps for a very long time, if he were to survive, and the Highland lairds promised him all the help he would need.

The following week he managed to write a few lines to Lady Howell, explaining as much as he could and assuring her of his undying love and ultimate return. But the messenger was caught and destroyed the note before it could be delivered to Lady Howell. Not that she needed any note from her husband, for he had told her of his intended destination before he left; as the gazette had not mentioned his capture, it was safe to assume he had arrived.

Later that year, Howell managed to send off another letter to her, and this time she received it. In it he assured her that he would one day return and perhaps seek a royal pardon. In the meantime, he explained, he had to stay hidden, until the hue and cry died down.

But it soon became apparent that such a time would not arrive in the present King's lifetime. George I was not a forgiving man, and he did everything in his powers to apprehend those still at large among the plotters. Frederick Sykes was caught in an unguarded moment while visiting his fiancee, and promptly hanged. Only John Howell remained at large.

As time went by, Lord Howell became restless. The Highlands were dull, remote and impoverished, he missed his wife and daughter, and he felt he was becoming a burden to his hosts.

Eventually he reached the point where he felt that nothing could stop him from seeing

Merryn. A considerable length of time had now gone by since the plot was discovered, and he thought he might risk going to London secretly, so long as he was careful. His Scottish friends urged him to reconsider his decision, but Howell was adamant. Fate intervened in his favor at that point: King George I died.

His greatest enemy was out of the way, and the authorities would be more concerned with the uncertainties of the succession than with a fugitive Jacobite. Lord Howell disguised his appearance and set off on the long road south. It was 1717—almost exactly two years since he had left London.

Some days later he reached the capital. Though travel-stained and weary, he went directly to his town-house. He was shocked to find that Lady Howell and his daughter Mary were gone, and the house itself was in a state of disarray, as if it had not been kept well for a long time. Only one person was still living in the house—the former butler, who was now acting as a caretaker. His name was Philip Babb, and Howell had known him all his life.

From this loyal servant Lord Howell discovered the bitter truth: Lady Howell had gone off about a year before to Ireland, in the company of an Irish chieftain by the name of O'Halloran; their daughter, Mary, was being cared for by an elderly relative, an aunt of Lady Howell's who lived not far from the Tower of London.

Lord Howell immediately left his former home to seek out the house of the relative. When he arrived at her modest quarters, a tearful woman shook her head. The little girl, never very strong, had passed away the month before. Stunned by this news, Howell retraced his steps to his house.

He spent only an hour there, still reeling under the double shock he had received. He brushed aside his old servant's anxious questions and locked himself in the room which had been his study. There was only one consolation: no one had discovered the wall-safe concealed behind the oak panelling.

Working swiftly, Howell transferred the gold and letters of credit it contained into a small bag. Lastly he tossed in the small box which held the blue opal. He now realized that Maureen, the seeress of London, had indeed foretold truthfully what was to become of him!

But was it his fate to be so cruelly treated, or was it the accursed opal that had robbed him of his honor, most of his wealth, his wife and his child?

Lord Howell stayed in London. He found a room in a seedy lodging house south of the Thames. There was little chance that he would be noticed. Sufficient time had elapsed now, he reasoned, and perhaps no one was really looking for him. He couldn't be sure, of course, because in those perilous times political sentiments ran high and lasted for many years. He had taken certain precautions; for one thing he had allowed his hair to lengthen and had grown a fierce moustache; even those who knew him well might not have recognized him now. He changed his clothing from the impeccably elegant attire of a well-to-do aristocrat to that of a somewhat flashy adventurer; he looked more like a returning sea captain than a distinguished member of one of England's oldest families.

Despair haunted him, but he kept it at bay by making plans for the future. One person would be vital to their success—Tom Masterson. Howell hired his landlord to scour London for the sailor.

The landlord ran Tom to earth in the port area, and arranged for him to meet Howell at six o'clock one evening at their old rendezvous, the Pig and Whistle. The inn was noisy and filled with people having a drink at this time, and Lord Howell was scarcely noticed as he made his way toward one of the rear tables. There, already waiting him, sat Tom Masterson, with a mug of beer in front of him.

"Welcome, sir," Tom said, rising to his feet. The two men shook hands. As soon as Lord Howell had seated himself opposite the sailor, he began to explain the reason for this encounter.

Tom was visibly shaken by the bad news of his friend's misfortune, and he wondered what Lord Howell was going to do next with his life.

"That's just it," Howell replied. "I have decided to go to sea."

Masterson choked on his beer. "You, sir, go to sea?" he said, unable to disguise his surprise.

"Don't be too surprised, my lad." Howell smiled. "I've been on many a ship, and I know what makes them sail. I love the sea, and I want to try my luck on it. England now makes me feel—well—it makes me feel unwanted and unhappy."

"I can well understand that, sir," Tom Masterson said, "but how exactly do you plan to accomplish this? And how can I be of help to you?"

"I have the means to purchase a medium-sized ship," Lord Howell said, "and I need your counsel both in purchasing her and in getting her ready to go to sea."

Tom Masterson blinked. Somehow he could not quite imagine the aristocrat going out to sea as a sailor, and he said so.

"Well, not exactly as an ordinary sailor, my lad," Howell commented drily. "I shall be the captain."

"Buying a ship costs a great deal of money, sir," Tom Masterson said thoughtfully. "Have you sold the opal?"

Immediately Lord Howell put his hand on Tom's arm, indicating to him to be quiet. "Please," he said, "do be careful. No, the opal rests safely with me in a place no one can find except myself."

"Then how, sir?" Tom's question remained unfinished. He himself had had a generous payment, based on a percentage of the opal's worth, paid out to him previously by Lord Howell: and he felt that Howell must have spent most of his own fortune just for that. But perhaps he was wrong. Somehow Lord Howell seemed to read his thoughts.

"Yes," he said with a smile, "I still have some money left. Not to worry."

Now the conversation turned to more practical matters: what sort of ship they would be looking for, where to find her and how to equip her. Lord Howell wanted her to be solidly built and fast; he wasn't looking so much for a merchantman as a ship that somehow represented "his castle"—he shared the age-old dream of all Englishmen to be the lords of their own castles. Tom understood perfectly well; he promised Lord Howell that he would start making enquiries immediately and report back in three days' time.

When they met again at the Pig and Whistle, Tom's face glowed with excitement. He had managed to locate a well-built ship, not too large, not too small, but capable of sailing even the roughest seas, whose captain had just recently retired. While the owner was looking for a new captain he had entertained bids to sell her and it was precisely at that moment that Tom Masterson had appeared on the scene. He had informed the owner that a friend of his was anxious to purchase a ship and that he might want to buy the one now lying in harbor waiting for a new captain. The ship was named the *Aurora*, and Tom thought she offered all the features Lord Howell was looking for.

"Splendid, splendid, my lad," Howell replied, and jumped up. "Where is she? Where is she?"

"At Margate sir," Tom said. "We can go down there tomorrow if you wish."

By the time they arrived at Margate it was afternoon. When Lord Howell saw the proud ship *Aurora* he was immediately taken by her. "Splendid, splendid," he kept exclaiming. "This is exactly what I had in mind." Within the same evening, a deal was struck for the ship and Lord Howell arranged to have funds transferred to the owner.

"How long do you think it would take to have her ready to sail?" he asked Tom, appointing him his First Mate.

"Perhaps a week, perhaps two, I don't know, sir," Tom replied. "It depends on the quality of men you want to take aboard. What sort of men are you looking for?"

"Good sailors and, above all, men who are not afraid of anything, men without prejudices or fears."

"That shouldn't be difficult, sir," Tom replied cheerfully and shook hands with Lord Howell. They were to meet again a week hence at the Pig and Whistle. As if by an afterthought, Lord Howell stopped Tom from running off.

"Wait," he said, thoughtfully, and looked around to make sure no one was listening. "There's just one more thing. I want you to purchase some guns—I mean ships' guns."

"Guns? You mean cannon?" Tom replied, his eyes widening.

Howell nodded. "Precisely. I want her to be as strong and able to defend herself as if she were in His Majesty's navy."

He pointed at the portholes. There was ample room to mount half a dozen cannon on each side of the ship.

A week later the two men met again in London at the Pig and Whistle. Very business-like, Tom had brought with him all the necessary documents, including the official authorization which gave the *Aurora* the right to sail from Margate, and the ship's papers, which Lord Howell was to sign both as owner and captain. There had been some problem with the Admiralty concerning Lord Howell's ability to serve as captain. But somehow Howell had managed to persuade the official in charge that the sea patent he offered in evidence of his professional ability was to be accepted. Naturally, he paid for whatever extra expenses might have been involved and, true to the times, the official could not have very well refused. The little Admiralty Clerk found that a couple of golden guineas were a very persuasive argument. It didn't really matter very much that the patent was issued in the name of Lord

Howell's father, rather than in his own.

Finally, the great day arrived. It was April 30th and the *Aurora* was about to sail for a destination which was unknown even to her crew. There were rumors, of course: many of the sailors thought that the first voyage would be overseas towards the West Indies, and that they would return with a valuable cargo of West Indian goods.

But none of them was worried about where they were going. True to Lord Howell's command, Tom had selected as crew members men who qualified on two grounds: they had to be experienced seamen, but also men who had for one reason or other expressed a desire to leave England. Among the crew were several men who had served time in prison for minor offenses, though no murderers to be sure; there were others who were unable to secure adequate employment and wanted to emigrate to the New World but would settle for a two-year journey aboard the *Aurora* first. Thus it was not the usual British crew that sailed the *Aurora* out of Margate harbor that sunny morning of April 30th, but rather a motly cross-section of men bent on high adventure.

Much as he wanted to look for Merryn, Lord Howell knew only too well that he would be stretching his luck too far if he ventured to stay within the British Isles at this point. Going to Ireland would subject him to double danger: firstly, as a wanted rebel, and secondly as a suspicious Englishman, whose business in western Ireland would surely come under the close scrutiny of some of the soldiers swarming all over that part of the emerald isle in this time of unrest. Then, too, he felt deeply guilty about having deserted Merryn and he did not really blame her for going off with another man, under the circumstances. How was he to face her now? He needed more time to sort things out for himself.

The winds were favorable and eventually the men found themselves in the middle of the Atlantic ocean, bound for the West Indies. They were now at a place where turning back was as difficult as going forward, should there be no wind. In fact, just then the winds abated and for two days the *Aurora* did not move at all. It was in this intervening period that Lord Howell chose to assemble the crew of the upper deck to tell them more about his plans, and this voyage in particular. When he appeared before them, standing above them slightly to the left on the quarter-deck, he made a splendid impression in his uniform. His clothes reminded Tom of the uniforms worn a hundred years before this time, uniforms worn by buccaneers and pirates.

"I have brought you together for this journey, men," Howell began, "because I wanted to have a crew of men whose purpose was similar to mine. So I ask you, do you want to make your fortune?" He looked expectantly from one face to the other. There was a moment of hesitation, then smiles broke out on the faces of the men below him and an eager chorus of "Yes, yes!" rang out.

"Very well then," Howell said, "let me tell you what my plans are. The *Aurora* is not an ordinary merchantman."

Ah, Tom Masterson thought, here it comes. I always knew there was something he hasn't told me.

"No, the *Aurora* is a very special ship," Howell continued. "And I'm a very special captain. We are buccaneers."

A hush fell over the crew when the meaning of those words sank in. "Buccaneers?" Tom asked and looked straight at Lord Howell. "You mean pirates?"

"Precisely." Lord Howell sounded so unemotional that he might have been discussing the weather. "I have decided to become a free man of the sea, taking legitimately, of course, what my patent allows me to." With that he pulled a document from his breast pocket. "This is a patent for freebootery, issued to me by the Spanish Ambassador. It allows me to capture certain ships, except Spanish ships, and to remove all valuables."

Tom Masterson could not believe his ears. Lord Howell turned pirate? As inconceivable as the thought seemed to him at first, after a while he was not so sure that the impossible could not happen. Why not? he finally said to himself. Anything is possible in this uncertain century, at a time when men fight for their very existence, not knowing what lies ahead—a time when the old values are no more and nothing has come upon the scene to replace them. Yes, Tom Masterson assured himself silently, a time when a German prince can ascend the throne of Britain, such a time can also give birth to a pirate named Lord Howell.

As if he read his thoughts, Howell beckoned Tom forward. "Only you know who I really am," he said in a voice so low that none of the other sailors could hear. "But now you must forget that you ever heard the name of Lord Howell."

"Aye, aye, sir." Tom's face was puzzled. "But—"

Howell waved him to silence. He raised his voice again.

"From this day onward, men, you will know me as Don Pedro."

He then discussed what he had in mind: whatever prizes the *Aurora* was able to take would be fairly divided among the crew, with a larger share going to the captain and first mate. The men liked the idea; two or three of them were hesitant at first about turning pirate, but they all finally agreed that it was worth a try.

And so the *Aurora* sailed on, as the wind rose again, into an uncertain future, full of the spirit of high adventure, with a captain who had decided to turn his back on the native land that had done him so much wrong.

Chapter Four

But the piracy game wasn't as fruitful as
Lord Howell had hoped it would be; true,
they managed to pillage their fair share of
merchantmen and live a relatively decent life
from the proceeds, but soon the men were
grumbling that the *Aurora* was by no means a
particularly successful freebooter, and that
others were doing far better.

"It is as if some kind of a curse is upon us,
m'Lord," Tom Masterson observed one night
as he shared the meal with Lord Howell—
now Don Pedro—in the captain's cabin.

"Please refer to me as Don Pedro," Howell
warned. The men did not know his real name
and he wanted to keep it that way. Tom
understood. He remembered also how the
infamous opal had brought his captain

nothing but misfortune. He secretly wondered whether perhaps the jewel was at the root of their lack of success in this game. When he mentioned the idea, 'Don Pedro' shook his head.

"I've been wondering about the opal myself, Tom," he said, "and perhaps we ought to do something about it now." He rose from the table and stepped up to a large map on which their future course had been marked. "In about six or seven days, depending on the wind, we should be getting close to the American shore, about here," he said, and pointed to a spot on the map. "Let us make landfall there and see what we find in the way of a good hiding place for the jewel."

"Perhaps we should also remove some of the other gold and jewelry," Tom suggested. "The men are getting restless these days and temptation is always near."

"Quite so," Don Pedro nodded. "Especially as we have just divided the results of last year's spoils with them. There is no money due to the crew now for another year."

"The map reads Long Island," Tom said, pointing at a yellow-colored bit of beach on the map. "Is this where you intend making landfall, sir?"

"Yes, somewhere along that sandy stretch. I have been told there are many coves where a vessel our size can easily lie at anchor and not be detected from inland. We will need a little time to do our business, and it had best be done without interference from anyone on land."

"The men know to fight on land as well as on sea," Tom replied.

"Perhaps, but the very nature of this business requires us to be prudent, Tom." Don Pedro doused the candles. "No more of this to anyone, you understand, until we are close to the coast."

Tom nodded, and left his captain, seated by the cabin's rear window, staring out into the darkening night sky as the sea pounded the *Aurora* with relentless monotony.

Don Pedro sighed. There was a trace of relief in the sound. It seemed to him that his decision had removed a great weight from his soul; there might well be better times ahead. He shivered. He must be growing superstitious, like all sailors. How could the great blue opal affect the destiny of the *Aurora?*

Nevertheless, he mused, he would be glad when it was off the ship—and hidden out of harm's way in the New World.

It was a cold, clear morning just over a week later when an excited lookout came running down to the captain's cabin with the good news that he had sighted land. Quickly getting dressed, Don Pedro rushed on deck. No doubt about it, as his telescope quickly told him, there was a thin, dark line on the far horizon that could only mean one thing: land ahead.

Just then the wind suddenly changed, and the *Aurora* was being pushed farther south than Don Pedro had intended. But there was no arguing with nature; he resigned himself to letting it take its course, for he knew that in due time, the winds would shift again and carry them to their intended goal. This was the *Aurora's* first transatlantic voyage, though some of her crew had been to Panama and Mexico.

Don Pedro decided to pray for a shift in the wind, so he could make landfall at the earliest possible time. He found his praying a bit awkward, seeing that he was now in the piracy business, but then he figured that God had favored stranger causes than his; and perhaps there was some redeeming element in his past that would sway the Deity to favor him and his course!

Whether it was the power of his prayer or merely nature taking its course, the winds shifted again a week later and once more the *Aurora* set course directly for the American coast. This time, the favorable winds stayed with them to the last, and not more than five days had elapsed when the coast rose up before their eyes, close enough to prepare the anchor for landing. The crew rejoiced at the prospect of being on land again, and having fresh water and food—though the total lack of booty en route had somewhat dismayed them. On reflection, Don Pedro thought that this was just as well as it would have delayed their arrival even more. But could it not also be the consequences of having the accursed opal aboard that had kept rich merchantmen away from their course? For a well-equipped pirate ship, the *Aurora* was doing poorly indeed.

Had it not been for a fortuitous encounter with three French ships six months before, bound for the Indies with pay for Colonial troops there and sundry goods, Don Pedro doubted his crew would still be with him: they would have looked for more lucrative employment elsewhere. He hoped that things would change as soon as the opal had been removed from the ship and his possession.

The stretch of coast where the *Aurora* made landfall was deserted. They could see smoke rising from Indian settlements in the distance and, as the morning matured, the sun disclosed a sandy, white beach which looked pristine and inviting. Of course, Don Pedro knew that there were English settlements strewn along the coast of Long Island; it had been his intent to avoid them all along so as to do his business with as little risk of being disturbed as possible.

When the longboat had been lowered, he, Tom, and half a dozen men jumped into it and made for shore. In his breast pocket, Don Pedro carried the accursed stone; a heavy chest containing much of the gold and jewelry taken from the Frenchmen—mainly the share reserved to himself, Tom, and the officers of the *Aurora*—was also aboard, ready to be secreted along with the opal. A suitable place had of course to be found, and as soon as the party set foot on land, the task to find such a hiding place began.

The sun was now getting stronger; it promised to be a warm day. The seaman's chest filled with treasure weighed heavily on the shoulders of the four men carrying it, and now and then they set it down on the sand, to recover their strength. Tom looked at Don Pedro with a searching glance, as if to say, how much farther do we have to go?

"Halt," Don Pedro said, perhaps intuiting Tom's thoughts telepathically. "This is where I want to do it."

They had reached a small clearing not far from where they had made landfall. It was shaded by a clump of trees bending with the wind. Almost like a meandering river, the clearing extended to the coast; to the east the rolling dunes led to uplands in the distance. It was as if they had stepped on virgin soil, so silent was the landscape. If it had not been for the rising smoke of Indian settlements in the distance, they might have thought they had landed on some undiscovered island.

The men put the chest down with a sigh of relief, and its weight half-buried it in the soft sand. But they were not to have any long respite.

"Let us dig over there," Don Pedro commanded, and pointed at the trees. "Just below that one tree standing apart from the others."

Quickly, the sailors took out shovels, and

dug where their captain had indicated. The soil was less soft where the trees stood, and though they worked hard, it was clear it would take more than a few minutes to dig deeply enough to secure the chest from possible scavengers.

At last, the hole was deep enough for a man to stand in and not be seen from above: Don Pedro was satisfied that the treasure would be safe at that depth. He ordered the men to line the walls of the hole with wooden planks they had brought with them from the *Aurora.*

"How will we remember the spot?" Tom asked. Part of the immense treasure within the chest was his, and he wanted to be sure he could find it again.

"Not to worry," replied Don Pedro as he drew a piece of paper from his pocket and began to sketch the area. "I will always remember."

"And I will never forget," replied Tom, and smiled. But there was a false note in his voice that Don Pedro failed to notice.

The men had by now finished supporting the walls with wood. They lowered the heavy chest into the hole.

"Do you want us to cover it now?" asked the burly seaman known as Rowdy Tony, whose real name had long been forgotten.

"Not just yet, Tony," replied Don Pedro, "but in a moment."

With that, he swiftly stepped up to the hole, peering down into it. There sat the seaman's chest, safely ensconced in the wood-lined hole. Pedro drew a small pouch from his breast pocket and carefully placed it down on top of the chest, making sure it would not slip off. Then he jumped up onto the sand again, brushing loose earth from his clothes.

"Now cover it, men," he commanded. The sailors quickly shovelled the loose earth and sand on to the chest, filling in the hole in a matter of minutes. As they were busy finishing the work they had come for, they failed to notice that a pair of eyes was watching their every move.

But something made Tom look in the direction of the farthest tree.

"Look," he cried out, "we're not alone."

As Tom spoke, the owner of the eyes stepped out from behind a tree. A tall, proud-faced Indian, attired in clothes indicating his rank of Chief, fearlessly stepped forward and confronted the landing party. There was a moment of embarrassment, as Don Pedro realized his quandary.

"How long have you been standing there, friend?" he enquired, not yet knowing what to do about the unexpected and certainly unacceptable intruder.

The Indian did not move. Agonizing moments went by as they waited for his answer. Perhaps he did not understand English?

As if he had read their random thoughts, the Indian replied, "I have watched you land, yes . . . and I have seen you come to this place.

What is it you have brought here, white man?"

"That's none of your business," an angry Tom shouted, ready to attack the Indian. But Don Pedro's hand restrained him.

"It is my business, white man," the Indian said, somewhat haughtily. "You are on ancient tribal soil."

"Nonsense." Tom's temper was on the verge of exploding. "This is part of His British Majesty's land."

"Are you of the King's men, then?" the Indian asked. A furtive smile appeared on his thin lips, indicating his disdain.

While this conversation was taking place, two of the men had quietly moved around the clump of trees and come up behind the Indian. With a sudden move, he noticed them and prepared to defend himself with his hunting knife. But it was too late: the two burly sailors had him firmly in their grip.

"Don't hurt him," commanded Don Pedro, "but bring him to me."

With the Indian a reluctant prisoner, the two sailors led him down the dune to Don Pedro.

"Who are you?" the captain asked. He motioned to the men to release their grip on the Indian, which they reluctantly did. The Indian did not move.

"I am Chief Rolling Thunder . . . this is our tribal land."

"Which tribe?"

"I am of the Shinnecock."

"We are a peaceful people. We do not want your land."

"You have come to place . . . something . . . into our sacred soil. This is our land."

"We will not stay. Have no fear."

Tom had been watching the exchange with mounting discomfort. Now he bent close to Don Pedro and whispered in his right ear, "We can't leave him . . . he has seen everything."

Don Pedro realized the dilemma had to be resolved quickly. The sailors stood around, their eyes focused on him with increasing hostility. After all, they all had a share in the treasure they had just buried.

As Don Pedro was groping for a solution, Tom suddenly lunged forward, his seaman's knife high in his fist. He seized the Indian in a deadly hold, in such a way that the man could not free himself unless his strength was greater than his attacker's; and Tom's strength was clearly superior.

"We can't let him live, Captain," Tom said matter-of-factly, as he prepared to slit the Indian's throat. The Indian's face was serene as he prepared himself for death.

But something in Don Pedro's mind snapped at this instant. With all his weight, he threw himself against Tom, forcing him to release the Indian. Tom sprawled on the ground, his eyes filled with anger. Don Pedro stood waiting, prepared to defend himself against his own men. The Indian did not move. Why wasn't he taking advantage of the situation to run away? Don Pedro wondered.

Even Tom took this in, and as he got up, he seemed a calmer man.

"I am still the captain," Don Pedro said, casually touching the pistol in his belt. "And you will please refrain from taking any action without my command to do so."

The Indian now extended his hand to Don Pedro. "You have saved my life, white man, and I owe it to you."

"I do not kill a man in cold blood, Rolling Thunder," Don Pedro replied. "But it is a pity you saw us hide the chest here."

"You must not concern yourself about it," the Indian said. "It will not be touched so long as the Shinnecock walk this land. We will guard it for you."

"You will, really?" Tom said, coming closer with an expression of astonishment in his brutal face. "Then I am truly sorry I tried to kill you."

But Rolling Thunder did not reply. Instead, he once again extended his arm to Don Pedro, then took a small knife from his belt and quickly cut into his skin, drawing blood immediately.

Don Pedro understood at once. Extending his own arm, and baring it, he let the Chief cut his skin as well. Each man sucked the blood of the other, while the crew watched in disbelief.

"We're blood brothers now," the Chief said. "We are as one."

He waved at Don Pedro, and then turned away. Without so much as another glance, Rolling Thunder walked past the clump of trees and disappeared toward the Indian settlement in the distance.

For a moment, nobody spoke. There was a brooding silence in the air, chilling it even though the sun now stood nearly at the zenith.

"Let us go back to the *Aurora*," Don Pedro said, and the men obeyed. Only Tom seemed ill at ease. For a moment, he hesitated.

"Coming, Tom?" Don Pedro asked, waiting for his mate to make a move.

"I don't think it is wise to let the Indian go, sir," Tom said, as he slowly joined Don Pedro in walking down the dune toward the boat. "How do we know he won't come back tonight and take our treasure?"

"No, Tom, he won't. I know enough about Indian taboos to be quite sure our treasure could not be safer."

"You're the captain," Tom replied, but there was a tone of subdued anger in his voice.

Don Pedro noticed it, of course, but thought it would quickly pass. Still, he did not want his mate—and old companion—to feel unhappy. Putting his arm around the reluctant man's shoulder, he said, "It's going to be all right, Tom, believe me. But we'll come back with the fall tides just to make sure everything is as it should be—all right?"

"Very well, sir," Tom replied. "I hope you're right."

Nothing further was said about the matter, and soon they were back aboard the *Aurora*. The afternoon tide was favorable, and within the hour she set sail, heading due south toward the rich trade lanes where a lonely French merchantman might offer new treasure.

Chapter Five

Ten years had gone by since he had left England and become Don Pedro. Lord Howell, secure in his new identity, felt it would be safe to venture back for a brief visit. Of course, the *Aurora* was by now too well known as a pirate ship for him to risk taking her into English harbors, but Ireland was different. He knew that they would be perfectly welcome on the west coast of the Emerald Isle, where English dominion had never been absolute to begin with. They made for Newport, hoping to reach land within two weeks, if the winds continued to be as favorable as they were when they set sail.

It turned out that they were, and the *Aurora* made excellent time. By now the men had more or less forgotten about the Indian

Chief, and even Tom seemed his old, friendly self again. Don Pedro had drawn an exact map of the area where they had deposited the chest with the treasure, and given a copy of it to Tom for safe-keeping. Perhaps this gesture, more than anything Don Pedro could say, calmed Tom's suspicions and the old bond between them seemed fully restored.

At Newport, they were welcomed by a small landing party of traders from town. Of course, the *Aurora* had by now changed the black skull and crossbones for the Spanish flag which Don Pedro felt he had at least a moral right to display. The tradesmen who came to seek their goods knew of course what the *Aurora's* real purpose was, but they never said anything about it. The people of Newport had long since learned that it was best to be tactful with the crew of ships like the *Aurora:* it was safer—and far more profitable.

But trade was not the only reason Don Pedro had decided to head for port in Ireland. As soon as the formalities of the business at hand had been attended to, he turned command of the ship over to Tom, and purchased a horse. He would be gone for several days, but he was quite sure that his mate could handle matters in his absence.

There was some personal business he had to look after, Don Pedro told Tom, without going into details; but Tom knew perfectly well what the business was, though he did not let on. His captain's personal life was an area he wanted to stay away from, but in his heart he hoped that Don Pedro would find pleasant news of his wife, Merryn.

Despite the years of separation, Lord Howell had never ceased to love her, and now he hoped he would find her, at the very least, happy with the man with whom she had gone to live in this isle.

The ride down the coast was difficult and slow, due to the absence of good roads; but Don Pedro drew on his past horsemanship to manage it as well as he could. Leaving rocky County Mayo behind him, he entered the boundaries of Galway, heading straight for Galway city where he had been told that Merryn had gone to live. Here in Galway, the rebellious spirit was particularly strong, and he took great pains not to be recognized as an English aristocrat, lest he be murdered by these people. Pretending to be a Spanish sea captain, and laying on a slight accent, he managed to get by, and by nightfall of the second day he had reached the city limits.

The city was teeming with people; there were strangers amongst the crowds, easily recognizable by their attire. This did not surprise Don Pedro. He knew that Galway city was a place where people and sailors from all countries would congregate to exchange wares and other goods, such as information and even thoughts of rebellion against the British Crown. He knew, of course, that the government in London was well aware of such activities but could do little about them short of sending in an expeditionary force to the eternally rebellious Ireland; that would be a costly and long-drawn-out affair which the government was not likely to engage in, unless driven to it by open revolt. At the moment, however, there was no sign of any such activity. The Irish seemed peaceful enough, at least on the surface.

As he entered the city, Don Pedro looked for a likely inn to bed down for the night, for he was extremely tired and had no intention of continuing his search for Merryn until the following day. As if fate was guiding him, his eyes fell upon a sign extending into a street, reading, "Ye Old Four Leaf Clover Inn." Truly, he thought that would be the best place to spend the night, for he could use all the luck available, both the luck of the Irish and his own, to find Merryn in this teeming city.

As luck would have it, the inn had a spare room. Don Pedro consumed a hearty meal, served in the rough Irish manner and followed by a tankard of beer, or rather stout, as it was hereabouts called. Within an hour of his arrival, he fell into a heavy sleep from which he did not awake until well into the following morning.

As the sun stole into the window of his room on the second floor of the inn, he was confused as to where he was; realizing that he had arrived in Galway city, he dressed quickly and demanded his breakfast. He then

summoned the inkeeper and asked for
directions to St. Patrick's Lane, the street
where he had last known Merryn to live.
Shortly afterwards, he paid his bill and
called for his horse. He made his way slowly
and carefully through the throng. St.
Patrick's Lane, he had been told, was situated
at the very outskirts of the city, and the ride
gave him plenty of time to worry about what
he would find when he reached his destination.

His heart was beating faster as he
approached St. Patrick's Lane. How would it
be, confronting his beloved Merryn after all
those years? Would she still recognize him?
Would he recognize her? Immediately he dismissed this as a silly notion, for he knew that
he would recognize her a thousand years
hence. But then he began to wonder: was he
wise in coming here? Should he not have left
well enough alone? He rejected the idea at
once, knowing full well that his love was
forever. By the time his thoughts had been
sorted out, he arrived at St. Patrick's Lane, a
short, narrow street lined on both sides with
rather small, traditional houses, which
seemed to have stood there for a long time.
He looked for Number 22, the house that had
been indicated to him as the abode of his
beloved Merryn. When he dismounted, his
heart began to beat even faster: what if the
man she was living with should object to his
coming here? What if there was a fight? The
last thing in the world Don Pedro wanted was

to hurt Merryn again in any way whatsoever. But he had come a long way to seek her out, he finally reasoned, and now he had to find out how matters stood.

There was an old-fashioned brass doorbell mounted on the wooden door, which he rang. He heard the bell jangling inside the house, far away, it seemed. For a moment nothing happened. Then he heard shuffling feet coming down a flight of stairs toward the entrance door. A moment later the door was opened, and a slim blonde woman peered out at him. Immediately he recognized Merryn. She had hardly changed at all. If anything, she was more lovely than ever. She looked at him for a moment, wondering who this stranger was. Then she recognized him in turn and the door was flung wide open.

"John! John, is it really you?" she cried out. She threw her arms around him, pulling him towards her, as if he had never left. He responded in kind, allowing her to draw him inside the house. Quickly she closed the door and turned around to face him. "You've come back. How wonderful," she said. "We must close the door in this city, you know. There are many who would want to listen if you are not careful." She then motioned him to follow her up the stairs.

The second story contained a large living room with windows giving on to the city in the distance. There was a bedroom off to one side and what appeared to be a large kitchen to the other. Merryn led him to a couch in front of the window and there they sat down and looked at each for a moment in silence.

"I hope you don't mind my coming here," he began uncertainly, "but I would have come before if it had been possible."

"Of course not," she replied, "I am happy to see you. I have never forgotten you."

Still, he thought, there is something not quite right. He looked around as if searching for another person.

She immediately understood. "Oh I see." She laughed mischieviously. "You are looking for my husband, perhaps, or my lover?"

"Yes, as a matter of fact I am," he replied seriously, looking at her with a deep frown, as if expecting the worse.

"Rest your mind at ease," she said, "for you will not find either."

"But what about the Irishman? Did you not go away with him?"

"Oh yes, I did," Merryn replied. "He was a wonderful man. We lived together for over a year and then he went out to sea and never came back."

"I am sorry," Don Pedro said immediately. "Did you love him very much?"

"Not as much as you." Merryn looked straight at him. "Remember, it was you who left *me*. Had you stayed with me, I would not be here now."

"Yes, yes," he replied, bending his head. "I am the guilty one and I freely admit it. As you know, the cause of the Stuarts has always been strong in my heart, and the events that drove me from London, despite my great love for you, made it impossible to see you."

It was clear to him now that Merryn still loved him, and he rejoiced in his heart. He could not blame her for trying to build a new life with another man. After all, it was he, her husband, who had deserted her, seemingly forever. Now, he thanked God that they had a chance to start over.

There was so much to talk about, so much to catch up with. Over dinner they talked about each other's lives, each other's problems, and each other's hopes for the future. When Merryn learned of his new "profession," she was not as horrified as he had feared she might be. After all, many of the population of western Ireland were pursuing similar aims. But she was concerned for his safety and realized that, being a seafaring pirate, he was not likely to settle down on land. The crux of their conversation was simply this: would he now be willing to give up his ship and settle down with her, either in Ireland or back in England perhaps, if that were possible, or did he want to return to his ship and continue his restless ways? It was then that Don Pedro realized that he had reached a turning point in his life. He told Merryn he could stay with her another two days and that he must then return to the *Aurora*. During this time, a decision had to be made, that he knew.

On the third day, their last day together, John faced his Merryn, ready to discuss his future and hers. "I must go back to my ship and my men," he said, "I cannot abandon them. But I will go out once again and try to retrieve as much of my treasure as I can, distribute it among my men, and then turn the ship over to Tom, my mate. When I have done so, I shall return to you and never leave again."

"But you are leaving now," Merryn replied, unable to hide her disappointment. "How do we know when the winds of fortune will bring you back to me again? We are living in perilous times, and one never knows what fate has in store."

"I swear," he replied, becoming extremely emotional as he did so, "that I will return to you in a year and a day, never to leave again."

When she saw that she could not sway him to stay with her now, she gave him a tearful farewell. Don Pedro, with turmoil in his heart, mounted his horse again and rode from Galway city. He resisted the temptation to turn around and take a last look at Merryn, standing in her doorway, her long, blonde hair fluttering in the wind, tears streaming down her face. Had he done so and seen her, he might never have returned to the *Aurora*.

When he arrived at Newport at the end of the following day, it was already late evening. Rather than make his way to the *Aurora*, he decided to stay in town for the rest of the night. Also, he needed some time to himself before facing his men again. So he bedded down in the best inn in Newport, which was called the Thistle.

But sleep eluded him. He tossed and turned, his mind going over his life and his future and his plans again and again.

Eventually he acknowledged defeat. Although it was late at night, he went downstairs again, where a few people were still in the inn, taking a late drink. As he walked by them, he noticed a strange-looking gypsy woman, seated by herself in the corner at one of the tables, with a crystal ball in front of her. Something stronger than himself made him saunter over to her and greet her. As if she had expected him, she bade him to sit down at her table.

"You want to know, don't you?" she said with a heavy brogue. "Well now, cross my palm with silver, and I shall tell you."

Almost mechanically he reached down into his pocket and handed her a shilling. She first bit into it to make sure it was good metal, then rapidly made it disappear among the folds of her ample skirt, smiled at him and began.

"You are a seafaring man, that much I can see," she said, not impressing him very much. Anyone could see that he was a sailor. "You are about to go out to sea again, and you are going a long way off. You are leaving a blonde lady behind. She loves you very much, but you will never see her again."

"Not so," Don Pedro protested vehemently, perhaps too vehemently.

"Are you listening?" the gypsy woman

replied, looking sternly in his direction. "Now then," she continued, looking in her crystal ball at the same time, "I see you going a long way. You are going to be very lucky at sea, and someday you're going to build a great house. It's going to be far away from here, but you are going to live in it a long time."

"A great house? Far from here? Impossible."

"Don't argue with me, sir," the gypsy woman replied unpleasantly, "just listen."

He nodded and fell silent.

"You are going to be a rich man, that's for sure. But you are going to be unhappy nonetheless."

"Why will I be unhappy?" Don Pedro demanded to know.

"Because there is a curse on you," the gypsy woman said. "It's an unlucky stone that casts its curse on you."

"But I've buried it," Don Pedro said, defending himself.

"Nevertheless," the gypsy woman said and shook her head, "the curse is upon you. Them as have touched it, they cannot escape. Mark my words, sir, 'tis a bad kind of lot. You're going to be rich, but you're not going to be happy."

"But what about—the woman? What about her?"

"Ah, the woman, the blonde woman you mean," the gypsy said. "It's as I told you, sir. You're not going to lay eyes on her again."

"But how, but why? Tell me, tell me!" Don Pedro was almost shouting, and people started to turn in his direction. The gypsy woman put her hand on his arm to calm him.

" 'Tis fate, son," she said, almost like a mother. "You cannot do a thing about it."

And with that she rose swiftly and walked away from him, leaving a very perturbed and stunned Don Pedro behind. Quickly ordering a stiff drink, he downed it and stumbled to his quarters, hoping that sleep would eliminate the bad taste of the gypsy woman's predictions.

The following morning, bright and early, he rose, feeling much better and only faintly remembering the gypsy woman's predictions. As he entered into the activities of the day, he grew less inclined to believe the woman, drawing upon his own background as a British aristocrat, where curses and gypsy women played a very small part. He returned to the *Aurora*, where he was given a hero's welcome. Tom hugged him and accompanied him back to the Captain's cabin, where a meal had already been prepared for him. That very night, the *Aurora* set sail and headed out west, toward the American coast.

Chapter Six

During the ensuing weeks Don Pedro was much too busy with his sea voyage to think about Merryn, except for an occasional furtive longing to be with her again. Now and again, the mysterious gypsy woman would come back to his mind; but, as time went on, he tended to dismiss her warning as mere superstition, ascribing her dire prediction to the prevailing tendency among the people of western Ireland to see only the worst in their future. Then, too, Don Pedro's background did not allow him to put too much stock in predictions and other psychic phenomena. More to please Tom and the crew than because he himself believed in it, Don Pedro had gone along with the idea that the opal was indeed the cause of their troubles. There were times when he wondered about it, to be sure, but on the whole, Don Pedro was not inclined to take predictions, curses and other occult phenomena too seriously.

The *Aurora* was doing splendidly now. A tail wind made her race across the waves at a speed she had never attained before. If it kept up, Don Pedro reckoned they would be on the other side of the Atlantic within the next six or seven days. This time they were heading for the West Indies, a rich prize of Spain, France, and Great Britain, with the idea of intercepting a Frenchman or perhaps a Portuguese. Of course they would not interfere with British shipping in any way. That was part of his compact with Tom and the crew, that British shipping was exempt from their attempts at piracy.

The days went on, and Don Pedro's memory of Ireland faded more and more into the background. When they arrived at Port Royal, they were flying the British flag, even though Jamaica was then in Spanish hands. But he could not risk being interrogated by the governor about his Spanish connection, knowing full well that it was only nominal. Since Spain and England were technically at peace, there was no risk involved in flying the flag of his true nationality. Besides, he had no intention of staying in Port Royal very long; it was their first port of call to get food and fresh water. From there they intended to sail out toward the Lesser Antilles, in search of prey.

They spent three days in Port Royal, over-hauling the ship and taking on new provisions of water. By the time they sailed out again, Don Pedro had again taken on the personality of his adopted name: Lord Howell seemed far away, Merryn even farther, and the immediacy of adventure was at hand and occupied all his energies.

On the third day out of Port Royal the look-out saw a Frenchman approaching them. Don Pedro ordered his men to their battle stations. But what ensued was hardly a fight; the Frenchman did not offer any resistance. When the pirates boarded her, it was like taking candy from a child: the passengers and sailors handed over their possessions willingly and it was not necessary for Tom and the crew to employ any violence. Don Pedro was relieved; he had given standing orders that there was to be no violence unless they found themselves under attack. Returning heavily laden to their own ship, the crew was of course in a festive mood. The *Aurora* then set sail toward the Central American coast, because Don Pedro had decided that it was time to turn some of the booty into hard cash and this could only be done in a place like Panama, where he had certain connections with the governor.

Four days later they lay at anchor at Panama, once again flying the British flag. Don Pedro immediately paid a visit to his friend the governor, to inform him of his intention to sell or trade their cargo and to request him to clear the way through the red tape; Don Pedro wanted to avoid awkward questions about the provenance of the *Aurora's* cargo. Since the governor had traded with Don Pedro before, this was only a matter of courtesy; both men knew very well that a percentage of the profits would land in the gubernatorial pockets. Returning from the governor's palace to the *Aurora*, Don Pedro felt that his life was taking an upturn. Whatever dire predictions the gypsy woman had made, none of them had any reality in this environment at this time.

The following morning the crew of the *Aurora* began to transfer their rich booty to the shops lining the quays at Panama City, and the trading started in earnest. As promised, Don Pedro delivered one tenth of the profits to the governor in person and was invited to stay for a sumptuous banquet in his honor. Only Tom was asked to accompany him, as the governor did not feel the crew members of the *Aurora* were quite up to the standard of his guests. The crew had no objection: they were much too busy celebrating in their own fashion, in a port known for the hospitality of its citizens, especially its women, to be interested in so sophisticated an entertainment as the governor's dinner.

This time the governor had truly outdone himself: whether it was because his percentage was unusually large, or whether it was because he was in a festive mood himself, he laid on more than just a dinner. When the brandy was being served he clapped his hands and a group of dancing girls appeared in the room, giving the party a truly outstanding performance.

"How do you like my girls?" the governor asked and smiled at his guest of honor.

"I like them all right," Don Pedro replied, keeping a steady gaze on the lead dancer, a beautiful brunette woman who had just performed the most torrid dance Don Pedro had ever witnessed. His Anglo-Saxon blood began to boil, very much against his will, for he was still deeply in love with Merryn.

The governor leaned over to Don Pedro and whispered. "You like the lead dancer, don't you? I can arrange it for you."

Before Don Pedro could shake his head, the governor had waved to the dancer, who nodded briefly but continued with her dance. A few minutes later the presentation ended and the dancers took their bows. Once again the governor clapped his hands: the lights were lowered and the dancers joined the guests, all of them men, with unmistakable intentions. Suddenly Don Pedro found the attractive lead dancer clinging to him, shedding her clothes and helping him out of his. Looking around, he noticed that all the other men were doing the same. Despite a slight feeling of remorse, he nevertheless gave into the sensuality of the moment.

Don Pedro woke late the following day. The sun already stood high in the sky, and he realized that he had slept all morning. He was still in one of the rooms at the governor's palace. Dressing quickly, he took leave of his host, thanking him for his hospitality and wishing him great good fortune, in the polite Spanish manner. Then he hurried to the shore where the *Aurora* was at anchor. He found his men mostly asleep on deck or in the bunks, still heavy with alcohol, and unable to move. All right, Don Pedro thought, let us celebrate for another day: it will put them in a better mood when we must leave again.

The following day he rallied the men around him and told them it was time to get out to sea again. There were murmurs of discontent when he announced this, for the men had begun to like the easy life ashore. But he reminded them that greater prizes lay in wait outside the harbor, and that even greater joys would be theirs if they were successful in capturing other ships, more booty. Ultimately, his appeal to their greed convinced the men that it was time to go back "to work," and within a day the ship was ready to sail again.

Looking back toward the splendid port of Panama, which was receding rapidly behind them, Don Pedro turned to Tom. "I fear there is serious business ahead for us now," he said, "but also much joy."

Tom hadn't seen his captain in such a somber mood for a long time.

"What sort of serious business, sir?" he enquired. "Do you see trouble for us?"

"I don't know," Don Pedro replied, "but I have a hunch we will encounter some difficulties somewhere."

Tom laughed. "Don't tell me you've become a fortune-teller now," he said lightly.

The careless words hit Don Pedro with a heavy blow. A fortune-teller, he thought, like the gypsy woman in Galway city. He did not reply. Instead, he slowly turned and went down to the cabin, leaving a puzzled first mate behind.

As luck would have it the winds were with them this time and it took no more than two days to reach the islands. As they were approaching the West Indies, they noticed in the far distance the sails of what appeared to be a large merchantman. Don Pedro ordered the ship to be cleared for action. As yet, he had no idea who the foreign merchantman was; but, as they drew nearer, it became clear to him by the shape of the sails that they were facing a Frenchman. The captain's shrewd guess proved to be accurate.

Since the *Aurora* could outsail almost any other ship, due to her sleek construction and the additional sails she carried, it wasn't very long before they could clearly see the Frenchman up ahead. Once the *Aurora* was in range, Don Pedro ordered a volley to be fired across her bow, signifying that she should turn around.

The merchantman, however, paid it no heed. Its captain was clearly unaware of the *Aurora*'s ability to outsail her. The Frenchman sped into the wind, all her sails flying.

This time Don Pedro ordered one of the cannon men to hit the merchantman lightly in the area of the bow. Now the merchantman knew that the *Aurora* meant business and the battle was over before it had properly begun. Within a few moments the *Aurora* lay alongside the other ship.

As the pirates' boarding party, led by Tom, swarmed over the merchantman, Don Pedro stood watching on the *Aurora*'s quarter-deck. His face was melancholy. In a way, he hated this business, having never been a pirate by nature or by conviction. On the other hand, His Majesty's Government was not exactly on excellent terms with the French government, so in a sense he did not feel too guilty about robbing the Frenchman.

The plundering was going ahead with professional skill and dispatch. Contrary to the alleged cruelties of most pirates, Don Pedro's men were instructed never to kill anyone, to leave the women alone, and to go about their business in a thorough but professional manner. Their aim was booty, not cruelty, and the men of the *Aurora* were told not to fight unless someone attacked them first. Naturally, as was likely to happen, the pirates occasionally met with resistance, and men were killed during such encounters. But Don Pedro kept a tight rein on his men and, despite their sometimes violent character, by and large his law was obeyed.

As it turned out, the Frenchman, a ship out

of Marseilles named *Les Beaux Champs*, carried a number of useful goods, useful, that is, for the *Aurora*. There were manufactured goods from the French colonies in the Antilles, small arms and plenty of ammunition, and, most interesting of all, payrolls for the garrisons. All of this was immediately transferred to the *Aurora*.

Within a matter of hours the *Aurora* set sail and left the Frenchman to pursue her course. It was not Don Pedro's habit to scuttle the ships he boarded, feeling quite rightly that he might have the opportunity to empty such ships of their cargo on another occasion. As the sun set that day, the *Aurora* was a lot heavier from the treasure she had taken aboard. Piracy, after all, was just like any other business: sometimes the inventory was light, sometimes full.

As Don Pedro and Tom went over the booty from the Frenchman, it became clear to them that some of the goods they had confiscated would have to be traded for hard cash at their next port of call. The *Aurora* accordingly continued on toward the West Indies, as she had originally planned to do. After a couple of days, she made a landfall once again at Panama City.

The familiar bargaining took place; once again the governor played host to Don Pedro, and once again a sumptuous dinner was presented to Don Pedro and his first mate after the conclusion of the business. This time, however, there were fewer guests. At the end of the meal, when everyone was smoking the peculiar tobacco grown in this country, rolled into long, thin cigars, the reason for the relative privacy of the arrangements became clear. Instead of a group of dancers, as had been the case during their last encounter, the governor this time presented to them only two women, who joined the men at the table. They were not dancers, either, but two very beautiful young women whose sole interest seemed to be Don Pedro and Tom. With a gesture from the governor, a gesture which was immediately understood by the ladies as well as by Don Pedro and Tom, the dinner ended and the guests were led to private chambers by the ever-present black servants.

The governor, with a sardonic smile on his face, wished them a good night.

As Don Pedro followed the lady who had so freely presented herself to him and who was apparently quite willing to be his for the night, he had strong misgivings. For the first time he felt that he could not freely undertake such a liaison, even though most men would have had not the slightest qualms under such conditions. As soon as he had entered the room which the woman had led him to, he tried to tell her so. But the already had her arms around him and was beginning to undress him. More unwilling than willing, and with mounting apprehension, Don Pedro allowed her to proceed and within minutes they were in bed together.

Don Pedro had always prided himself on his manhood and his way of proving it to the ladies, and he had never given a second thought to his ability to satisfy them. Here, however, for the first time he failed to do so and he realized, after all, that he was not a free man anymore.

The *Aurora* left Panama City again a few days later, and went about her business, lying in wait for potential victims among French or Portuguese merchantmen. Time passed rapidly, or perhaps it only seemed that way, for Don Pedro had suddenly become very introspective. Tom noticed that the conversations which the two men had often had in the captain's cabin after dinner were now getting more and more drawn out, and more and more one-sided, as far as Tom was concerned. He questioned Don Pedro about this change of mood and got very little in reply.

But soon Tom had little time to consider the matter further. Business was booming: a couple of wealthy merchantmen came across the *Aurora*'s bows. After their capture came the work of disposing of their booty in ports along the coast.

For reasons of his own, Don Pedro insisted that they should not return to Panama City this time. The *Aurora* visited other ports, where the governors were less accommodating—and Don Pedro's memories less vivid.

The months went by and soon it was Christmas and then New Year's Day. Don Pedro remembered his promise to return to Ireland "a year and a day" after he had seen Merryn last. He turned the bow of the *Aurora* toward Europe, explaining this change in direction away from the lucrative West Indian route be saying that the ship needed to be refurbished in western European ports. As the crew had been amply rewarded thus far, no one complained.

The winds were against them this time and it took them a full month to reach Ireland during one of the stormiest voyages the *Aurora* had ever had. As soon as the ship had made port at Newport, Don Pedro arranged for the ship chandlers to come aboard and make the necessary repairs. Then he turned the command over to Tom and once again took off to seek Merryn.

As he travelled by the now well-known road south, he had the strangest feeling. Perhaps the horse sensed his master's mood, for it seemed to run faster than ever. At first Don Pedro assumed it was his eagerness to see his beloved one again, but as he approached the city of Galway, his apprehension grew by leaps and bounds. Something terrible might have happened to her, he thought, or perhaps something terrible might happen to him. Immediately he rejected such a notion; after all, he, the successful pirate, was not about to give into fears for his own safety; and, as for Merryn, she was living in a safe city, surrounded by decent people. There was no reason to assume that anything unusual might have happened to her in the meantime. Last time she had been well and eager to see him, and he knew nothing to suggest that this might not be the case now. Having thus rationalized his fears, he continued his journey, but the deep-seated apprehension would not leave him.

In time he arrived at the outskirts of Galway city. There seemed something oddly different about the suburban areas he was riding through now, as he noticed people in a state of agitation when he passed them. He paid no attention to it, however, and continued his journey directly to the house where Merryn lived.

Within the hour he arrived at the house that he remembered so well from his last visit. But this time shutters covered the windows and the brass door-bell had grown dull with lack of polishing. He secured the horse and ran up the steps, pounding the door with his fists as his own heart pounded as loudly. There was no reply from inside. Once again, even more forcefully this time, he hit the door.

After a moment, a door opened in the house next to Merryn's. Slowly the head of an elderly woman appeared in the narrow opening, peering out as if to make sure that what was happening outside on the street was of no danger to the person inside.

Don Pedro noticed the movement and immediately called out to the woman. "I say there, Madam," he said, turning toward her, "can you tell me where the lady in this house has gone to? There seems to be no one inside."

The neighbor woman ventured outside now. She turned out to be a stooping woman of small stature, gray-haired, with a wrinkled face and a charming smile: her dancing eyes belied her age. However, there was an expression of fear running across her face, and her voice was kept low, so low in fact that Don Pedro had difficulty understanding her at first.

"What is it, woman, what is it?" he said impatiently.

She stepped closer to him, again peering around to see whether they were being watched by anyone. Having reassured herself that no one was listening to their conversation, she finally opened up.

"Yes," she said and nodded. "The lady is gone indeed. 'Tis a terrible thing that has happened to us here, sir, a terrible thing."

Frantic now, Don Pedro took the woman by the shoulders, as if to shake an answer out of her faster. "What is it, what is it?" he said.

"Now wait a moment, sir," she replied, shaking herself loose from his grip. "I will tell you. Do not become upset. The lady is gone."

"Gone? Why? Where to?"

The old woman shook her head. "I don't know, sir. All I know is that she is gone. It happened three months ago, and I know you were here to see her before. I remember your face, for I was looking out me window when you came last time. It happened three months ago."

"What happened? What happened three months ago?" Don Pedro said, unnecessarily loud. Immediately the old lady put her fingers to her lips, warning him not to raise his voice.

"Don't you know?" she said, lowering her own voice still further. " 'Tis the English who have come. 'Twas the King's men who came and broke into her house. That's what happened."

"Tell me all about it." Don Pedro commanded, forcing himself to be calmer.

"Well, sir," she began, "I happened to notice a commotion outside that evening, and next thing, a group of English soldiers arrived. They were pounding on the door, just as you were a moment ago. Only when they came, the lady opened wide and let them in. I reckon she wasn't expecting them. I heard a lot of goings on inside the house, voices and some commotion, but I honestly do not know what was said. All I know is that awhile afterwards the soldiers left again, and the lady, she was with them."

Don Pedro covered his face with his hands, trying hard not to let his emotions overcome him. "But why? Who?"

"I don't know, sir," the old woman said, trying to sound as soothing as possible. "I suppose they wanted to ask her some questions."

"About what? About me?"

The old woman shook her head. "No," she said, "I do not think so. 'Tis about this other man, I reckon, the Irishman, the lady used to know some time ago. I reckon they were looking for him. But of course I don't know. I just assumed that was what went on."

"Where did they take her? Where is she now?"

The woman shook her head and Don Pedro realized that he had gotten all the information there was to be had. He thanked her, tried once again in vain to enter the house, but finding the door shut and the shutters impenetrable, soon gave up. While he was doing this the old lady stood there watching him.

"Who closed the house down? Did Merryn come back to do it?"

The old woman shook her head. "No, sir," she said. "Two or three days after the lady had gone with the soldiers, a couple of soldiers came back and did it and that is the last time anyone has been to this house, as far as I know."

Don Pedro thanked her and left.

He decided to make some enquiries in town. Perhaps someone had seen Merryn or knew where she had been taken. Of course, that was not an easy task, for he could not be sure that his true identity wasn't known. As it happened, no one challenged him, and he was able to piece together what had transpired at the house three months before his return. It seemed that a party of English soldiers had arrived in town rather suddenly, looking for the Irishman who had once been Merryn's friend. He was wanted by the Crown, for rebellious activities, not an unusual situation in those days in Western Ireland, which had never been fully subjugated by the English. Don Pedro learned at the inn he was staying at for the night that the party of English soldiers had left soon after they had arrested Merryn, and gone east; where to, no one knew.

What was he to do? He realized that without any leads to go on, there was little he could do. Going to the authorities and asking about her would only implicate himself and might eventually lead to the revelation that he was making his living as a pirate. While he could not be sure that the Crown would object to his activities in that respect, they might also try to implicate him with Merryn and her former friend. None of this suited Don Pedro. Worst of all, he knew that the authorities still considered him as a wanted man—as Lord Howell, rather than as Don Pedro. If Merryn let slip that she had once been Lady Howell, his position would be all the graver. Sadly, then, he decided there was too much danger in any kind of enquiry, and nothing else for him to do but return to the ship.

The following morning he returned to Newport, hoping that in time there would be some news of his beloved Merryn. He had left word of his visit with the neighbor woman, and he recalled that Merryn knew the name of the ship's chandlers which the *Aurora* used in Newport, and that he and his crew would from time to time come back to refurbish their ship. Thus, if Merryn were to return, or want to contact him, she could do so. That was the best he could hope for at that moment, and it saddened him that there was nothing more he could do.

Chapter Seven

During the following weeks and months, Don
Pedro and his crew kept very busy. They lay
in wait for merchantmen, usually French,
sometimes Italian; they boarded them in a
professional manner, relieved them of their
goods and did so without bloodshed.

Don Pedro, of course, was pleased that
little violence was necessary. As time went
by, his distaste for bloodshed grew even
stronger. Where resistance made killing inevitable, Don Pedro went to the extraordinary length of asking the captains of the captured ships to accept a payment for the
widows or children of the men who had been
killed during their taking over of the ship.
Nothing like this had ever happened in piracy
on the high seas, and soon word got around

the sea lanes that Don Pedro was a very special kind of pirate. Although this helped Don Pedro to come to terms with his peculiar profession, it did not improve his standing with his crew, many of whom had little sympathy for moral scruples of any kind.

About a year after this last landfall at Newport, when they were approaching the Caribbean area again in the hope of rich prizes, this problem came to a head. The crew asked Tom to raise the matter with their captain. Tom went to Don Pedro's cabin and argued their case forcibly. He wanted the crew to have the freedom to defend themselves and to do what they thought necessary in the circumstances. Don Pedro listened quietly as Tom explained the incongruity of orders dealing with violence, when in fact they were in what most civilized countries considered an illegal business. But Don Pedro remained firm.

"The crew wonders who you really are, my captain," Tom finally said. "Of course they will not hear it from me, of that you may be sure."

"I should hope so, Tom," Don Pedro replied, with perhaps more sternness in his voice than he had intended. Only Tom knew his real identity, and Lord John Howell did not exist for the rest of the crew.

"What shall I tell them about your identity, though?" Tom continued. This matter was on his mind as well. "After all, they can see that you are not a Spaniard. Don Pedro couldn't

possibly be your real name. I've got to tell
them something. They keep asking. I think it
would help your relationship with them if
they knew a little more about you."

Don Pedro thought it over. "Quite so," he
said. "I think you should tell them that
my real name is Philip Babb, that I am an
Englishman, and that I have decided to go
to sea in this manner because of injustices
done to me back in the mother country."

"Philip Babb?" Tom said. "Who is Philip
Babb?"

"It's a perfectly fine name," Don Pedro
replied with a twinkle in his eye. "It happens
to be the name of my butler when I was still
Lord Howell."

Tom enjoyed the joke. "Aye aye, sir," he
said. "Philip Babb it is."

Relations between Don Pedro and his crew
improved slightly after this. But the men
noticed that their captain gradually became a
bit harder, a bit more taciturn, less likely to
crack a joke with them, than he had been
before they had been to Newport. It was common knowledge aboard ship that the
captain's sweetheart had disappeared; and
while no one dared to bring up the subject,
they all knew and sympathized with him.

As if in fear of returning to Ireland and
finding something he did not want to know,
Don Pedro avoided going back to Newport
for several years, preferring to do his repairs
elsewhere. The *Aurora* plied her trade back
and forth between Europe and the American

coast, here and there catching a rich merchantman, taking the booty to be sold in Panama City or sometimes in one of the lush places in the Carribbean itself, such as Port Royal. Don Pedro felt that in himself a change was taking place. Somehow, the excitement of adventure at sea had gone out of his life, and he saw himself plying his trade as a pirate captain more or less mechanically, not caring very much whether he were successful, or not.

Some evenings, when he was alone in the captain's cabin, siping a glass of fine Spanish wine, he pondered his fate; had the curse of the Tibetan jewel taken his daughter and his beloved Merryn away from him? Was it possible that the accursed opal, though buried safely in the sands of America, could reach out and hurt him? He began to wonder whether he should not get rid of the jewel altogether, rather than merely having it buried and thus kept safely for his return. The more he thought about it, the more he became convinced that that was so. In the end he decided that on his next visit to the American shore he would try to reopen the hiding place and remove the stone; he would either destroy it, or take it back to where it had originally come from, though he realized that a journey to faraway Tibet was more of an adventure that he could possibly manage.

The thought of dealing with the opal became more and more an obsession with him and many a night he could not find rest because of it. If the opal was indeed responsible for his loss of Merryn, there was no gainsaying what else the accursed stone might do to him in the future. He did not relate his fears to Tom because he knew that Tom was not of that bent, and did not really believe in curses. But he knew that there was a destiny in all this, in the way the stone had reached his possession. Perhaps a kindly destiny was trying to tell him that the time had come to rid himself of the opal.

Several weeks later, the *Aurora* was approaching the shore of New England, the Massachusetts Bay Colony, as it was called. The crew was particularly restless during those days, because they knew that very little in the way of prizes lay that far north, an area frequented mainly by whalers; the southern seas of the Caribbean, on the other hand, promised far more in the way of rich merchantmen. But it so happened that the captain had decided to sail farther north, perhaps unconsciously wanting to approach that part of America where the opal lay buried. Of course, the crew did not know this, and perhaps Don Pedro himself was not aware of it; but the course had been set. The *Aurora* drew rapidly nearer the American coastline, the winds being extremely favorable at that time of year. Within a matter of three or four days they would undoubtedly make landfall along the coast of Connecticut or Massachusetts.

Unbeknownst to the *Aurora*, another ship

was approaching the same general area. This was a good-sized merchantman, called the *Wolf*, out of Londonderry, Ireland. The ship's captain, William Wilson, had just become the father of a little girl who had actually been born at sea. In addition to various goods, Captain Wilson had aboard the *Wolf* a large number of Scottish and Irish emigrants who had put all their hopes in a new life in the New World, because of repression, religious difficulties and other reasons in the Old World. Some of these emigrants had a great deal of wealth with them; others were poor but managed to take along whatever possessions they had anyway. All this gave the *Wolf* the appearance of being heavily loaded, as she lay rather deeply in the water. Anyone seeing her thus might assume that she was indeed filled with precious cargo.

As the *Wolf* approached the coast of New England, and found herself within sight of the rolling hills of the Northern Massachusetts coast, her passengers thronged the rails, pointing out to each other the approaching American coast, the land of their future where all their hopes resided. So occupied were they with the joy of looking out towards the approaching landfall that they failed to notice another ship bearing down on them from the sea. The ship was none other than the *Aurora* which had noticed the *Wolf*, sailing at so much slower a speed owing to the fact that she was so heavily laden. The *Wolf*'s lines were French, and Don Pedro had decided to attack her. As yet, he did not know what the ship was or what she carried. When the *Aurora* cut across the *Wolf*'s bow, thus bringing her around, he realized that he had for the first time in his career as a pirate given the order to attack a ship from his own country.

Don Pedro found himself in a quandary when he realized this, but it was too late. Already the orders to board had been given; the merchantman offered no resistance; and the men were eager for booty. As Tom rushed by Don Pedro on his way to go with his men, Don Pedro held him back for a moment.

"Go easy Tom," he admonished his mate. "No killings please. These are Englishmen."

"No matter, sir," Tom replied curtly. "They're ours now." Without reassuring his captain that he would follow the request, Tom brushed past him and joined the men, who were already scrambling over the *Wolf*'s side.

Under the circumstances, Don Pedro decided to join them, partly because it was his duty as the captain to do so, and partly because he wanted to prevent anything taking place that he would later regret.

The attack by pirates within sight of the American coast had, of course, caused tremendous panic among the passengers. Women were screaming, babies were crying, and men were walking around in a daze, clinging to their meager possessions. But to no avail. Calmly and professionally, as they had done many times before, the men from the *Aurora* collected whatever valuables they could from the passengers and the crew. All Don Pedro could do was to reassure them that no harm would come to them if they did not resist. The emigrants, of course, followed his request without fail, begging him only to understand that all they had for the new life was being taken from them. Much as he may have wanted to, Don Pedro could not listen to their requests to retain some of their belongings, because he knew only too well that if he did so, his own crew would rebel against him. Too many weeks had passed without a single ship coming into sight, and they were eager for booty.

While the men from the *Aurora* were beginning to take their spoils from the *Wolf*, ferrying it over to the *Aurora*, Don Pedro went down below into the captain's cabin, a privilege reserved to the captain under the unwritten law of piracy. Normally it was the captain's cabin where the most valuable possessions were kept, such as gold or jewelry. Even though Don Pedro realized that the *Wolf* carried emigrants and that their most valuable cargo was people, he felt that there would have to be some valuables in the captain's cabin, and he fully intended to secure them.

An unexpected sight met his eyes when he entered the cabin. There, instead of gold and valuables, he found an attractive lady with a little girl, scarcely more than two weeks old.

The woman was in her middle or late twenties, and vaguely reminiscent of some of the women he had known back in England. Frightened by the appearance of Don Pedro, she readily told him that she and her husband Jack Wilson, the *Wolf*'s captain, had hoped to start a new life in Londonderry, New Hampshire, the namesake of the town they had come from in Ireland.

"So you are Mrs. Wilson," Don Pedro said. "And this is your little girl?"

"Yes," the woman replied, still trembling.

"What is her name?" Don Pedro asked, looking at the little girl, who wasn't at all afraid of him. In fact, she stared at Don Pedro with searching blue eyes, as if she knew who he was!

"She's not afraid of me, is she?" Don Pedro asked, and looked directly at Mrs. Wilson.

"So it seems, sir," the woman replied, somewhat more relaxed now.

"You didn't tell me her name," Don Pedro repeated.

"Oh sir," Mrs. Wilson replied, "she hasn't been baptized yet."

"I see," Don Pedro said. "What name have you picked for her?"

"I don't rightly know, sir," she replied. "We haven't given it much thought yet."

A sudden thought struck Don Pedro. The little girl looked at him and seemed to be smiling now, as if she was enjoying the entire scene.

"I'll tell you what," Don Pedro said, never

taking his eyes off the little girl's face. "I'll tell you what: if you will name her Mary, I will do something for you in return."

"Mary?" Mrs. Wilson said. "Is that someone you know?"

"As a matter of fact," the captain replied, "it is a name very dear to me indeed." He didn't want to tell the woman that he was thinking of his Merryn, and of his little daughter Mary who had died long ago.

"Of course, sir," Mrs. Wilson said, "if it will please you."

"Yes, it will please me very much," Don Pedro replied. "And in return I will tell you what I will do for you and the people on this ship. I will spare everyone, no one will come to any harm, and all your possessions shall be returned forthwith."

Mrs. Wilson could not believe her ears. She jumped up and flung her arms around Don Pedro's broad shoulders. Somewhat embarrassed, he gently loosened her grip, sat her down again, touched the little girl lightly and then went out of the cabin up on deck.

When Don Pedro told his men what kind of bargain he had struck, he was faced with icy silence. But a look at the captain's eyes convinced Tom at that time, at least, Don Pedro meant business. Considering that what they had taken from the emigrants wasn't really all that much, Tom thought it wasn't worth making a stand for it. There would be other times.

"Give these people back whatever you have

taken from them," Don Pedro ordered, and after a moment's hesitation and much grumbling, the crew obeyed.

Within the hour all the goods taken from the emigrants had been returned to the *Wolf*. When this was done, the last crewmen of the *Aurora* left the *Wolf* and returned to their own ship, not without expressions of anger. But go they did, and a sigh of relief went up from the emigrants, who had watched the proceedings in utter amazement.

While this was being supervised by Tom, Don Pedro had returned to the *Aurora*. Now he returned once again to the *Wolf*, bringing with him a satchel. Quickly descending into the captain's cabin, he presented it to Mrs. Wilson. Amazed, she opened it and found in it a bolt of precious silk.

"For Mary's wedding gown," Don Pedro said simply and withdrew.

Moments later the *Aurora* was on her way. When it was apparent they were free to pursue their original course, the *Wolf* also set sail for the nearby coast.

"Mary it is indeed," the proud captain said, as he looked at his little girl. "It's a right nice name, too," he added, still amazed at what had transpired.

"You know that pirate captain," Mrs. Wilson said. "There was something peculiar about him. To begin with, he wasn't Spanish. I am sure he was an Englishman."

"Oh, that is for sure," Captain Wilson replied. "But you see, pirates take these names to disguise their real identity."

"I think it is more than that," Mrs. Wilson said. "It isn't just that he is an ordinary Englishman. He struck me as being one of the nobility, or someone very, very important."

"You're just prejudiced because of what he did," the captain said, and kissed her gently.

The following morning, the *Wolf* made landfall at the port of Salem, Massachusetts. The captain spent most of the day disembarking the passengers and unloading the goods the ship carried. Once the formalities had been completed, Captain Wilson, his wife and little Mary set out to spend the night in a comfortable inn in Salem. They planned to stay only a day or two and then continue onto their home at Londonderry, which lay a day's journey to the north. The *Wolf* had been his ship for many years, but this was to be his last trip as her captain. On her home journey, the *Wolf* would be commanded by his former first mate, now Captain Johnson, while Wilson and family were to settle down in the American Londonderry, to lead the life of colonists, perhaps even as pioneers. They felt that living in America would give them more peace and certainly better opportunity than the old country; and little Mary would grow up in surroundings free from the prejudices and pressures of the other Londonderry, which they had left behind.

When they arrived at the town of Londonderry, which was then part of the Massachusetts Bay Colony, they found the house they had purchased beforehand waiting for them. It was everything they had hoped for, built of wood and neatly painted in white. Since Don Pedro had given them back all their belongings, including their money, the Wilsons started life in America with the proper support.

Captain Wilson knew nothing about farming, but Mrs. Wilson did, since she came from a long line of farmers. They hired a man to help them run the little farm, a native North American named Pennington. Their needs were not terribly large, the house was paid for, and the farm should support them within the year. All in all, it was a very good feeling that filled their hearts when they began to settle down in Londonderry. Many a night, Mrs. Wilson thought of Don Pedro, and her strange pact with the pirate captain.

Time went on and the Wilsons did very well in their new home in the New World. Mary, the baby who had unwittingly saved her parents and the entire ship from the pirates, grew into a beautiful young woman, slender in form at age eighteen, very much the apple of her parents' eye. Her charm did not escape the eligible young men of the countryside either, and shortly after her eighteenth birthday, in a gown made from the silk Don Pedro had given her, she married a man by the name of Wallace. Robert Wallace was a good husband who provided well for his wife and four children she bore him.

But as often happened in those days, when medicine had not yet found the remedies, after the birth of their fourth son, Mr. Wallace became ill and shortly afterwards passed away. This left Mary Wallace a widow with four boys and a house to manage.

Somehow the years went by for Don Pedro and he wasn't even aware of the passage of time; his mind was preoccupied with the business at hand, meaning to make a fair living from piracy on the high seas. In his heart he knew that his wife was dead, and with Merryn gone, life did not matter very much to Don Pedro anymore. He developed a morose character which even Tom and the crewmen could not fail to notice. More and more, he kept to himself and spent long hours in the captain's cabin; when they were on land, he isolated himself from the others, shunning the company of women; he refused to discuss his private life, even with Tom. All this grief over the disappearance of his beloved one seemed to age Don Pedro rather suddenly. Nothing Tom could say in the way of cheer or a bright word for the future would help; Don Pedro answered merely that his life had been rendered useless by fate and that he did not know how long he could carry on as he did. Such pronouncements began to worry Tom, who was frankly concerned more with his own future than that of the *Aurora* and Don Pedro's moods. He began to wonder what would happen if the captain became unable to fulfil his duties and more and more Tom's mind began to drift in the direction of perhaps taking over the enterprise at an opportune moment.

Don Pedro had abandoned his intention of digging up the opal after the abortive capture of the *Wolf*. Fate, he felt, had loaded the dice against him. In his despair, he believed that digging up the cursed stone would only increase his ill-fortune. The nearer he came to the opal, the worse his life would become.

Many years after their visit to Newport, Don Pedro decided that the time had come for him to think of his own future and perhaps retire from the sea. He had studiously avoided making a landfall again on Long Island, where the seaman's chest had been buried in the sand. That was for an even more remote future to worry about. Meanwhile, Don Pedro had kept up a loose correspondence with the Wilsons in New Hampshire and learned from them what had become of Mary and the tragedy that had befallen her with the death of her husband. On the next landfall in the New World, Don Pedro decided to build himself a house not far from where the Wilsons still lived. He excused himself from Tom and the crew for a week, explaining that he needed the fresh air of New England to bring his ailing mind into better shape.

Meanwhile Tom and the crew were having a good time on land, celebrating and spending some of their recent booty. No one interfered with them, for in those days piracy was a way of life which everyone knew existed, and few did anything about.

In time, Don Pedro acquired a piece of land, near what is now the town of Henniker in New Hampshire. Using the name of Philip Babb, he had no difficulty getting a land grant from the local officials. He did not use his real name, let alone his title, for the British government's memory was a long one, and news of his arrival in the colonies might eventually filter back to the authorities in London. Within a matter of days he was the master of six thousand acres of fertile land and forest in and around the little town of Henniker, which was then only a village. The place was some distance from the sea, which was exactly what Don Pedro wanted. Once he had turned his back on the sea, he wanted to be safely ensconced inland to continue what was left of his life. Here, he told himself, he would build his final home.

When he returned to the *Aurora*, he made his plans known to the men. He told them that after his retirement he would transfer the captaincy of the *Aurora* to Tom. All he wanted for himself, Don Pedro explained, was their help in building himself a house. Once that was done, he would turn his share of the *Aurora* and her future profits over to Tom and the crew. This, of course, pleased them and they were eager to help Don Pedro build his dream house, the sooner to inherit the *Aurora* and all that she stood for.

Within a matter of days nearly all the ship's crew, including her carpenters, had gone to the piece of land acquired by Don Pedro and had started building his stately mansion. They soon realized that it could not be done as quickly as they had hoped and that perhaps they would have to spend a considerable amount of time on land in order to complete the job. But so eager were the men that they did not mind this interruption of their normal activities away from sea. They spent the next three months in Henniker, building Don Pedro his house.

It was a strange sight, indeed, seeing the burly seamen in their colorful outfits working on land, raising the house Don Pedro was to call his home. The village people wondered who these strange men were, but the menacing looks of the workers suggested to the villagers that no one should ask too many questions. Besides, Don Pedro had been very generous with them and his presence amongst them promised to be beneficial.

As soon as the house was finished, Tom and the crew returned to the *Aurora*, while Don Pedro furnished his home as lavishly as was possible in eighteenth century New England.

Soon after he had settled in, he received a letter from Mr. and Mrs. Wilson. They wrote to say that their daughter, Mary Wallace, had fallen on hard times since her husband's death. They were too proud to ask for help, but Don Pedro had no intention of allowing Mary—the namesake of his lost wife and daughter—to live in want. He went at once to Mary's modest home and suggested that she and her children should come and live with him. In this way, Mary Wallace became Don Pedro's permanent housekeeper.

To be sure, she was never more than that. There was no romance between them, for Don Pedro's one and only love had disappeared forever.

Don Pedro settled into a quiet domestic life in his new house, walking the countryside, fishing here and there in the little brooks surrounding it, and reading a great deal from the books he had managed to bring with him. Now and then he would engage Mary Wallace in conversations about life and philosophy, but on the whole he kept to himself. The house was then, as it is now, isolated, and few callers found their way to it. Occasionally a friend of Mary Wallace's would drop by or the Wilsons would come for a visit, but Don Pedro had not made any close friends in the village and continued to keep to himself as much as possible.

Living the quiet life now, Don Pedro needed little money, and he had brought with him enough funds to ensure that he would have no need ever to look for money again. As for the buried treasure, Don Pedro had become firmly convinced that there really was a curse attached to the opal, and even the thought of removing it filled him with fear.

He wished he had put it elsewhere, for the chest also contained much treasure, some of it belonged to Tom Masterson and the boys from the ship, who might not feel the same way about letting things rest.

At times, he wondered whether in fact the treasure was still in place. Perhaps Tom had come back for it secretly? Tom and the other sailors had been so convinced the jewel was bringing them bad luck that it seemed unlikely that greed would overcome their superstition, but the fortune that lay buried would be a great temptation.

It seemed as if Don Pedro would live out the rest of his natural life gracefully in his own house in the hills of New Hampshire, reminiscing about his days at sea and perhaps of the glorious days in England, and undoubtedly still thinking about he beloved Merryn. Mary Wallace spent much of her free time painting and decorating the house.

One day, about five years after Mary had moved into the house with Don Pedro, the peaceful atmosphere was rudely disturbed. It was a cool evening and the sun was just about to set. Don Pedro was out in the large garden to the rear of the house, sitting quietly underneath a tree. Mary was in the house, when she heard a commotion followed by a great shout of pain. She rushed out into the garden to find Don Pedro beneath a tree with a short, curved sword in his chest, dying quickly. Mary recognized it as a seaman's cutlass, and attempted to pull it out of the wound; but it was too late. A pale, shaken Don Pedro waved her away, perhaps not wanting to be saved. He asked that she bury him underneath the hearth stone of the house, to bless his last resting place. He told her that she and her descendants would own the house forever. He assured her that he had included the bequest in his will and made arrangements at the local registry office so that she would have no difficulty in obtaining her inheritance. Once again he blessed her and thanked her for the service she had rendered him. With one last sigh and Merryn's name on his lips, Don Pedro passed into the great beyond.

For several days Mary Wallace was too shaken to do anything about the murder. When she made enquiries no one would help. The Wilsons, very aged and frail themselves, could only suggest that perhaps one of the men from the *Aurora*, dissatisfied with the arrangements Don Pedro had made with them, might have come and taken revenge on his former captain. But that was conjecture. No one knew for sure who had killed Don Pedro in his declining years.

Mary inherited the house without difficulty and lived in it until her death in 1814. Her descendants obtained it after her. After that, the house changed hands many times. But it still stands, proud and very beautiful, in an isolated area of Henniker, New Hampshire, known to one and all as the "Ocean-Born Mary House."

Chapter Eight

Chief Rolling Thunder knew nothing about the demise of his blood brother. Ever since their one and only meeting, the Indian and Don Pedro had not been in touch again. Whether by accident or by fate, the Indian knew that their meeting had been important; he believed that, if it were meant for them to meet again, the powers that had brought them together in such an unusual way would again arrange it.

Rolling Thunder had much to keep him occupied as the years passed by. He was the chief of a medium-sized tribe of Long Island Indians, trying very hard to live side-by-side with the white man, not coming into conflict with him. He tried to keep his Shinnecock tribe as peaceful as possible, avoiding clashes with other Indians in the general area. He did his best to save what he could of the tribal lands from the encroachment of white settlers. At the same time, he traded with them in order to enhance his tribe's cultural level and wealth.

Gradually, the memory of Don Pedro and his pirates faded into the background and almost left his memory. Over half a century had passed and Rolling Thunder was well on in years; he spent much of his time thinking about the succession, for he knew his death was near. His own son, Thunder Cloud, was able and strong, and he knew that the tribe would be in good hands if Thunder Cloud took charge.

One night, he could not sleep and tossed restlessly, hour after hour. When he finally drifted off into deep slumber, he had a strange dream. Don Pedro appeared to him as alive as he had ever been, perhaps even more so, for his countenance was rosy and fresh; he looked younger than the Chief remembered him.

"Will you take care of my treasure chest?" the spirit in the dream asked. It was at that moment that the Indian, dreaming, realized that his friend and blood brother, Don Pedro, was no longer in the flesh. Don Pedro then informed him that he had been murdered by some of his own men, and that his body lay buried far away in New Hampshire. When Rolling Thunder offered to go up to his grave-site and bring the body back to wherever Don

Pedro wished, the spirit of the pirate thanked him, but said it was of no concern any longer since he was alive and well in the spirit world. What troubled him, however, was that his murderers might get the treasure chest, and this he wanted to prevent.

"What do you want me to do?" Rolling Thunder asked, still in the dream state.

"Go back to where we put the chest," the spirit of Don Pedro demanded. "Dig it up and move it elsewhere. If you wish, you may take the contents for yourself, but do not touch the accursed opal, for it has destroyed me. Do not touch it, I beseech you, for the love of God."

Rolling Thunder thanked the spirit, assuring him that he wanted no part of the treasure. He promised to go back to where it lay, and to move it elsewhere.

"Let no one see you do it," Don Pedro warned him, "or you may suffer death at the hand of a greedy murderer."

"Have no fear," Rolling Thunder replied. "At my age life has lost much of its attraction. I will go alone."

"I don't really care who finds it, someday in years to come," Don Pedro continued, "so long as those who have killed me will not benefit from it."

Again Rolling Thunder promised upon their oath as blood brothers that he would go and fetch the treasure chest from its hiding place and move it elsewhere. When he had done so, he saw Don Pedro's spirit smile with a face bathed in contentment, and slowly fade from his dream. Immediately thereafter Rolling Thunder woke up with a jolt. He realized that this had not been an ordinary dream. As an Indian he knew that there was another world beyond this one and psychic phenomena were no novelty to him. He took them very seriously. As soon as the sun rose, he readied himself to set out for the spot where he knew the treasure chest lay buried deep in the sand.

He went alone and he went on foot, despite his years. He knew very well that this was not going to be an easy task and he was well-prepared for it. Reaching out to his own god, Manitou, he fortified himself with prayer. When he reached the spot where he knew the prirate's treasure chest lay beneath the sand, he was ready.

The tree had grown in circumference, for fifty years is a long time, even for an old tree. Nevertheless, he had no trouble locating the spot, for it was the only tree which stood by itself. As soon as he could, he started to dig, making sure that no one could see him. From time to time he would rest, taking a sip of water from a container he had brought with him. The sun already stood high when his shovel struck something hard. He could hardly suppress a cry of satisfaction, for he knew he had found the treasure.

With almost superhuman strength, he managed to budge the heavy chest. It became clear to him that it would indeed take superhuman strength to get it out of its hole and across the sand to a new place. This, even with the power of his god behind him, he realized he could not do alone. He almost despaired at his task, feeling great anxiety over his inability to keep his promise.

But then an idea hit him: he remembered seeing the white men using certain small carts to carry their goods, and Rolling Thunder decided to use the same method. Hastily concealing the chest, he went back to his tribe.

The next day he returned, driving a small cart which he had bargained for with one of the white traders at a nearby post. The horse was old, gentle and willing and Rolling Thunder knew he would have no difficulty reaching the spot quickly and returning. As soon as he could, he dug up the chest again. This time, he managed to drag it up onto the cart. The job took several hours, and the effort exhausted him. But something stronger than himself made him get up and get on the cart and move. He already knew where he was headed for: not far away from the dunes was the tribe's sacred burial ground. No one would dare disturb the treasure chest there. The horse was slowed down by the weight of the heavy chest and it took longer than he had anticipated.

About an hour after he had left the dunes, he arrived at the burial ground, where he made sure that he was alone. He quickly found a spot that had been left vacant for a very important reason. This was the place reserved to receive his own body in time, but now he decided to use it for a different purpose. Digging as far down as he could, he placed the heavy chest into the grave, covered it up again and left. He knew that he had placed the chest deep enough for it to remain hidden, even when his own body was interred in the grave. Being a Chief, he knew that he would be buried in an upright position, but he had made allowance for that and there was still a thick layer of earth between the chest and the area in which his body would be placed at some future date.

Once again time went on and Rolling Thunder went about the business of being Chief, giving very little thought to Don Pedro's pirate chest. He was pleased that he had been able to carry out the wish of his friend, and having done so, dismissed the matter. Winter came round again and the cold wind from the sea made the Indian peoples' lives more difficult, as it always had. Only trading with the white man made it possible for them to continue their existence as they had for centuries past, for they no longer had the large land-holdings that had supported them before, and what hunting was left was not enough.

Here, on the edge of the white man's civilization, an Indian tribe had a difficult time surviving, and even so resourceful and wise a chief as Rolling Thunder realized that perhaps it was time for the tribe to move elsewhere. But he also knew that he would not make that move with them whenever it came. At the same time he noticed a certain restlessness among the young men of the tribe. In particular there was twenty-seven-year-old Standing Bull, a distant cousin of the chief's, and as arrogant a young man as had ever crossed his path. Standing Bull made no bones about his intentions: he felt he was better equipped to lead the tribe in these difficult times. Ultimately, word of his utterances came to the ears of Rolling Thunder and he could no longer ignore them. He decided to confront the young man and have it out. But he would do it peacefully, if at all possible.

"Look," Rolling Thunder said as he and Standing Bull faced each other in the Chief's tent, "look, I understand your needs, I understand your desire to improve our conditions. But we have been on this land for so long that it would be difficult to move elsewhere and start anew."

"Our land indeed!" the young man replied. "Why don't we take it back? What was once ours can be ours again."

Rolling Thunder shook his head. "You preach war, I preach peace," he said softly. "If they followed you we would all be wiped out."

Disdain crept across the young man's face. "You talk like an old man," he hissed, "and that is exactly what you are—too old to do anything."

Anger rose in Rolling Thunder's mind. He jumped to his feet and with a powerful blow he struck the young man across the face. But Standing Bull had a knife in his hand and with one strong movement put it in Rolling Thunder's heart.

At this moment, attracted by the noise of the discussion, the men of the tribe rushed into the tent where they found their beloved chief near death on the floor.

"Do not hurt him, I forgive him," Rolling Thunder said, his voice becoming feeble.

But the men of the tribe knew what their law prescribed as the fate of the murderer, and so did Standing Bull. Tomorrow at sunrise he would be tied to a post, and every man in the tribe would shoot an arrow into his body. He would then be buried outside the sacred burial ground, forever barred from entering the Happy Hunting Ground.

Blue Feather, the shaman of the tribe, knelt next to his Chief's fallen body. He looked up and shook his head. An hour later, Rolling Thunder had himself entered the Happy Hunting Ground.

After the official period of mourning, the tribe gave their Chief the kind of burial a Chief is entitled to. The grave site had been prepared soon after his death and thus Rolling Thunder's body, anointed and blessed, was put to rest above Don Pedro's treasure chest, just as he had thought it would be.

The shaman stared down at the gravesite

for a long time without speaking, as the men of the tribe watched in silence. Finally he spoke.

"May no man ever touch this grave, for I lay a curse upon those who may dare to. A curse so powerful that no one will survive it. Anyone who disturbs this grave shall be destroyed. I ask Manitou to be my witness to this, as I invoke the powers that have served me well and the powers that I have served all my life. May the powers protect the holy grave of my beloved brother and chief from outsiders who would dare disturb his peace. So be it."

"So be it," the men repeated. One by one, they went away, without a backward glance.

PART TWO

Chapter Nine

The years flew by swiftly. What was once Indian land became the white man's land, forcing the Indians to move farther and farther inland and eventually to congregate in small areas that became known as reservations. The people who moved into the area where the chief was buried did not know they were living close to the Indians' sacred burial ground. There was no way the Indians could take their honored dead with them, of course; and to tell the white settlers what it meant for them to have that particular piece of land was useless. But in their hearts the Indians knew only trouble could result from any attempt to touch the sacred soil, to build on it, to disturb the peace of those buried in this land. Nevertheless, none of the departing

Indians ever told the settlers who came after them what this particular piece of land had meant to them, and so it became more and more a memory shared only by those who had once lived there, but totally unknown to those who settled on the land in later years.

Among the white settlers was a group of people originally from France who had found their new world both hospitable and friendly. When they settled in the area they decided to call their village the town of friendship, or Amityville. At first there were just a few hundred of them, but as time went on, the little village grew until it became a sizeable township, right at the water's edge and extending quite far inland. The people who came after the original settlers made their living as fishermen and in agriculture. By and large, they lived peaceful lives, devoid of much excitement and change. No longer were there Indians in the immediate vicinity, and life became more and more similar to that of other towns and villages in the area of Long Island. The years rolled on, and the people of Amityville took part in the development of New York State along with others. Very few inquired into the history of that particular piece of land.

The year was 1902. Long gone was the open space of the fishing village. Instead there were tree-lined avenues, neat houses and an overall sense of orderliness. The track near the burial ground was now a street with numbered houses. On one corner stood a house made of wood which had been built long before the street itself was created. The people who lived in it knew that the house dated back to 1792. This was not particularly surprising in this part of Long Island, where old houses abounded. Naturally it had been renovated since then, and certain changes and embellishments had taken place, but the original house was still there, and the people who owned it treasured it very much.

The number outside read 112 Ocean Avenue, for the ocean was but a stone's throw away. Mr. and Mrs. John Peterson, who owned the house, loved every moment they spent in it. He had a little store in town where he sold fishing tackle, and she was a school teacher. They had one child, a boy, now twelve years old. But something about their boy had troubled them for years. There was a certain nervousness about him that did not quite match the tranquility of the little town where they lived. In school, Peter was a good student, but even there the teachers complained about his nervousness and restlessness; he had occasional bouts of what they could only describe in those days as a form of anxiety. For no reason at all, he would bolt from the classroom, run out into the hallway and not reappear until summoned sternly by one of the teachers. When the distraught parents took young Peter to a doctor he shook his head, finding absolutely nothing wrong with the boy. That of course was a time when Sigmund Freud had yet to be universally accepted. All the good doctor could do was to give the boy a cursory examination which indicated that there was nothing particularly wrong with him.

When Peter's thirteen birthday approached, his parents decided to throw him a party. They invited his best friends and some of the neighbors to come and celebrate the day, and they looked forward to a happy occasion. Lately the boy had been much calmer than before and they assumed that it was just a question of growing up that had troubled him.

Unfortunately, the week before the birthday was filled with heavy rains which did not seem to want to let up. For days on end the rains came down on Long Island, causing Amityville to be flooded and leaving the streets awash with sand and dirt. Nevertheless, Mr. and Mrs. Peterson decided to go ahead with the planned party, even if it should rain on the day. As luck would have it, the rain stopped the night before. As the waters gradually receded, a great deal of mud was left behind in the streets and houses of Amityville. Some basements were nearly filled with it.

The morning of the birthday party came. The sky was still overcast and gray but at least the rains had stopped, and young Peter rose early to play in the yard. His parents were still asleep, for they had a day of work and much activity in front of them. As Peter played in the yard behind the house, his shoes became covered with mud; but this did not stop him from continuing with his game of football. He was playing with a small ball which he had had in his possession since the age of six and which was to him a very precious object. Peter was used to playing alone, being an only child, and this ball had become, in a sense, his faithful companion.

It was difficult to control the ball on the soft, wet soil of the backyard. He miscalculated one kick completely: the ball bounced away towards the rear of the yard. Peter ran after it.

A few feet away from where the ball had come to rest, he noticed something white sticking out of the soft soil. His curiosity was aroused, and he approached it. Not sure what he had found, he used his right foot to push away some of the mud clinging to it. As he did so, he discovered to his horror that he was uncovering a skull, a human skull bleached white by age.

Peter gave a little cry of dismay, but then he gathered his courage. He had been reading books dealing with ghosts and skeletons and, like so many children, he loved stories about Hallowe'en and witches. What he had before him now was obviously a human skull, that much he knew. He raced back to the house and looked for his sand shovel, which he had had for years and which was commonly used for playing in the sand at the nearby beach. With the shovel in hand, he returned to the spot where the skull was still sticking out of the soil.

Hastily he started digging around it, hoping to unearth more of what he assumed was a skeleton. But the soil was soft at the top; as yet the rains had not fully penetrated below; perhaps the soil was too heavily packed. At any rate, he was unable to uncover much more than the skull and part of the neck.

Disgusted with his ability to do more than he had done, he hesitated. What was he to do about this? Suddenly he had an inspiration. Why not take the skull as a trophy? With all the power he could muster he kicked the skull with his foot. Brittle from the ravages of time and perhaps further weakened by the flood, the skull broke off. Peter shovelled the loose earth over the hole where it had been, covering up the rest of the skeleton. He then took the skull with him and decided he was going to put it in his room, to point out to his classmates. Perhaps he could put it to good use on Hallowe'en, which was then only a month away.

While he was walking back, he stumbled and the skull fell to the ground. As he bent down to pick it up, he realized that he had left his ball somewhere along the way. He went back to look for it but, try as he might, he could not find it.

Well then, he thought, if my ball is lost in the mud, let this be my new ball; it did not occur to him to be surprised at how little his loss affected him. He drew back his right leg and kicked the skull so hard that it flew across the yard as if it were another ball! As it did so, it seemed to him that he heard an angry shout coming from the direction he had just left. But he paid no attention to it, thinking that it was simply a neighbor yelling at his children. Peter picked up the skull, cleaned it with some water, and then returned to the house. He put the skull on the shelf in his bedroom.

The birthday party took place several hours later. There were altogether fifteen children in the house and everyone had a good time. One of Peter's classmates, Alfred by name, made his way into Peter's room and discovered the skull among the books on the shelf.

"What that?" he asked, pointing at the skull.

"Oh that," Peter replied as if it were the most natural thing in the world, "that is a skull I found."

"No kidding," said the other boy. "Where?"

But Peter wouldn't tell him. He thought that the whole incident was a bit peculiar to begin with, for what was a skeleton doing in the backyard? For a moment, he had had thoughts of communicating his find to his parents, but then changed his mind. They might disapprove of his action and he secretly felt ashamed of having broken off the skull and played football with it. The best thing was to say nothing and, if his parents were to see it, simply say that he had been given the skull by a friend or that he had bought it somewhere, or whatever came to mind. When you are thirteen years old, you don't think these things through.

But Alfred was not satisfied. Before Peter could say anything he had grabbed the skull and taken it from the shell.

"He's ugly, isn't he," he exclaimed, looking at the skull and sticking his tongue out at it.

"Put it back," Peter commanded, with perhaps more emphasis than necessary.

Alfred was frightened by the tone of Peter's voice and obeyed. He turned and started down the stairs to the main floor. As he did so, his foot got caught in the stair carpet. He stumbled and fell headlong down the stairs. His head smashed against the edge of a step and he lay still. Immediately everyone rushed to his aid; but it was of no use, the boy was dead.

Peter got only one quick look at his friend's face, but it was enough to send him from the room, howling with terror. For what Peter had seen was so horrible, so unearthly, he could not even describe it. His father stepped up immediately to gaze at the poor dead boy's face, but all Mr. Peterson could see was a face distorted in death, to be sure, but not particularly frightening. What had Peter seen that his elders could not?

When the commotion had died down and the party had been hastily disbanded, Peter's father wanted to know where the boy had got the skull. He had found it, Peter said, and since his father was preoccupied with the terrible accident that afternoon, nothing further was said about it. The question was not brought up again and Peter was allowed to keep his trophy. But he never touched it again.

The following week Peter's father went on a business trip. When he returned to the house a week later, he had contracted a strange fever and subsequently died, even though the family had summoned one of the best medical men from Manhattan.

In his last tortured moments, Peterson, burning with high fever, kept mumbling about The Great Evil One staring at him, a phrase the doctor was quick to dismiss as the ravings of a fever-wracked, dying man. Mrs. Peterson, on the other hand, wondered whether her poor husband was not perhaps being confronted by the devil himself, though she had no firm belief in such things and later dismissed that notion entirely.

Her husband's sudden passing left her in a state of shock, but it forced her to pull herself together in order to devote her energies to Peter's education. She was to be both father and mother to him henceforth. In her heart she could not quite divorce herself from the notion that the atmosphere in the house was somehow responsible for the tragedies that had of late come their way. But her rational outlook usually enabled her to overcome this notion, and she never talked about it to anyone, least of all Peter. The boy had enough to cope with in the unexpected loss of his father.

Thus Peter grew up in a fatherless home. By the time he reached fifteen, he had been forced to leave school because of his erratic behavior, and his mother, hard pressed to maintain the house, could no longer do so and sold it. The boy was then placed in what in those days was called a home for difficult children. His mother moved to Manhattan where she took a position with an export-import company that had done business with her late husband.

The house passed into the hands of one Franklin Doorman, who had heard the strange story about the skull and the accident but paid absolutely no attention to such matters. He was not a superstitious man and considered the incidents strictly coincidental. He and his wife, Dora, lived in the house for seven years. Whether they had any strange experiences in it or not we will never know, but at the end of seven years, when everyone thought that the Doormans were happy and content in their house, they suddenly moved out. They put the house up for sale for much less than they had paid for it and left town in a hurry.

A few months after the Doormans had left the house on Ocean Avenue, the Amityville town librarian, Miss Nancy Perkins, came across a tragic newspaper story. The story was from a Milwaukee newspaper, and it described the strange death of a couple named Franklin and Dora Doorman, who had of late come to Milwaukee from Long Island, New York. According to the article, the couple had been walking down one of the city's main business streets, and had stopped in front of a jewelry store to gaze at the display in the window. This was in the middle of the day when most people were at work, but the Doormans had not yet settled into jobs so they had decided to stroll down the street and look around. At that very moment a piece of heavy masonry had detached itself from one of the high floors of the building, and as it came crashing down upon the sidewalk it hit the couple, killing them both instantly.

Miss Perkins could not help wondering whether there was any connection between this unlikely tragedy and the Doormans' association with the accursed house in Amityville.

A young couple bought the house next and decided to spend their honeymoon in it. They came from nearby Patchogue but for business reasons had decided to move to Amityville. Robert and Gail Riccardi were only in their late twenties, and in the mood to strike out for greener pastures. He was a doctor and she was a nurse. One day her mother, Mrs. Tina Doremus, came to visit and stayed the weekend. Since the house had been bought and sold with all its contents intact, the skull was still there. The mother-in-law took a strange liking to this trophy and took it off the shelf in what used to be Peter's room, fondling it and handling it as if it were a relic of some sort. But then, accidentally, or by design, she dropped it to the floor, where it landed with a hollow thud. "Dammit," she said. "Why do they keep such junk around the house?" Hastily she picked it up and put it back in its place.

When Mrs. Doremus had touched the skull, something akin to an electric shock had gone through her body. It was almost as if she had come into contact with a force from another dimension, a force so powerful it left her momentarily speechless. As she gathered her wits, anxious not to let her daughter and son-in-law see her distress, she had the distinct impression that a pair of piercing eyes were looking down at her from somewhere near the ceiling of the room. But there was no one there. At the same time she felt a strong wave of anger, almost hatred, extended toward her, and it seemed to her that someone very irate was close to her, though of course there was nothing, or no one, visible to her eyes.

When the young couple and the wife's mother went to the beach the following day to take a swim in the ocean, the mother, known as an excellent swimmer, nevertheless drowned. All efforts to revive her failed. "Funny thing," the lifeguard remarked, "she looks like she had some kind of struggle out there in the water."

A struggle . . . with whom? The Riccardis

could not make sense of it. Somehow they felt responsible for Mrs. Doremus' death, since they had asked her to stay with them at the house on Ocean Avenue. This guilt weighed heavily on both of them and even a talk with their minister did not dispell it.

Heartbroken by the tragedy, the couple kept to themselves for over a year. When World War I broke out in Europe, the young doctor volunteered to go to England. He never returned. Only much later did Mrs. Riccardi learn what exactly had happened to her husband over there, when a former buddy of the doctor's, Gary Soletano, paid her a brief visit at another address she had by then moved to. It appeared that Dr. Riccardi had volunteered to go on a rescue mission to get some trapped American soldiers from behind enemy lines. All had gone well for the team of rescuers, and they were on their way back to their own lines when suddenly, so Soletano related, a heavy wind had arisen all around them, and when it had died down just as suddenly, Dr. Riccardi lay dead at Soletano's feet, killed by a bullet that must have come from their own lines!

On the death of her husband Mrs. Riccardi had sold the house in Amityville to the first person who wanted to buy it. The purchaser happened to be a local builder. He liked the house, but he didn't much like the location, so he moved it to what he considered a much better spot, at the corner of Carmen Street and South Island Place. There he rented it to a family of five who lived in it for twenty-five happy years. Nothing negative was ever heard about that house again and it still stands on the same corner.

The lot on which it had stood, however, became empty and, in a strangely menacing way, stared people in the face. An empty lot on a built-up street like Ocean Avenue made the tongues wag: why was the lot empty? why wasn't someone building? But no one came to build. For years, the land remained empty, overgrown with weeds and high grass; and before long people forgot the reason for the site's disuse.

Finally, in 1928, someone had either sufficient courage or suffecient ignorance of the circumstances to build a new house on the notorious lot at 112 Ocean Avenue, Amityville, Long Island. His name was Monahan, and he decided to build himself the nice wooden colonial Dutch house which still stands on that spot. Mr. Monahan was an elderly man with a family. When he died, he left the house to his daughter and her husband. The son-in-law's name was Fitzgerald. We do not know whether Mr. Monahan or Mr. and Mrs. Fitzgerald had any unusual experiences in what was then a new house; perhaps they did, perhaps they did not.

At any rate, some years later the house was sold to a Mr. and Mrs. Riley. Nothing out of the ordinary happened to the Rileys, at least according to their own testimony to the townspeople. But, nevertheless, they decided to sell out relatively soon after they had moved into the house. The reason was simple: they were getting a divorce. This was in the 1950s and the house was on the market for awhile. Then the house was purchased by the notorious DeFeo family.

What was once a happy, middle-class family of Italian background turned into something else again as soon as they had moved into the house. There was something about the atmosphere of that house on Ocean Avenue that changed peoples' characters and made them do things they would not normally do. The change, of course, was gradual. It didn't happen overnight. There were indications of trouble to come which were ignored. There were incidents that the DeFeos could live with and there were incidents that seemed threatening; all of this is well-known. A book has been written about it. A motion picture has been made of it.

On one occasion young Ronald DeFeo found himself stepping into the living room of their house just as his mother and father were having a heavy argument. Now arguments occur in the best of families and the DeFeos, being Latin, were perhaps more prone to be vociferous at times than calmer people. But this argument was different, or so it seemed to the boy. His father was about to lay hands on his mother, and young Ronald could not stand by idly and allow him to do it. He rushed upstairs to his room, grabbed his Marlon rifle, ran back downstairs and put the muzzle to his father's head. Everybody froze: would the boy pull the trigger? After what appeared to DeFeo an eternity, Ronald lowered the rifle and walked out of the room, without so much as a word being spoken by anyone.

Finally the strange influences from beyond the veil reached a climax. In the middle of a cold, foggy night, in November 1974, Ronald, then twenty-two years old, woke from a disturbed sleep. He got out of bed, not really fully awake, or so he says, took down his rifle and went methodically from room to room in his three-story house, killing off every member of his family—six people in all. He doesn't remember doing it. He denies that he knew what he was doing, but the facts were clear: Ronald DeFeo had killed his family. In the subsequent trial, his attorney, a brilliant lawyer named William Weber, tried to plead insanity for his client, but the Court ruled otherwise. Young Ronald DeFeo was sent up to Dannemora Prison, to serve a sentence of life for the murder of his family.

But did he commit the crimes? Was there something in him that made him do it, something stronger than his will power? Young DeFeo thinks so. Unfortunately, possession has no standing in a court of law. There was no question about it: Ronald DeFeo confessed to the shooting. The evidence was clear: it was his rifle with his fingerprints on it, and there was no one else in the house who could have done it—no one, that is, of flesh and blood.

But there were some questions which continued to baffle the police. How was it that six members of the family, each sleeping in a different room, on three floors of one house, would allow themselves to be murdered in cold blood without resisting, without warning each other, without running out to get help, not even crying out? For there were no witnesses who heard an outcry; there was no one who heard the shooting, and yet, the shooting took place. It is a puzzle the the police have never solved. A private investigator retained by the family of the murdered DeFeos thought that the young man must have had an accomplice, for he could not have carried out the murders alone. But this was merely an assumption on the part of the investigator who had absolutely no belief in such things as possession. He was unable to give any evidence to the effect that there was in fact an accomplice, nor was there any. So the DeFeo case, as it was called, became one of the famous unresolved mass murders, even though the young man who pulled the trigger had been convicted and put away in the maximum security prison at Dannemora in upstate New York.

Even in a maximum security prison like Dannemora, however, Ronald DeFeo was not truly alone. The angry spirit of the wronged Indian Chief whose skeleton had been desecrated kept a close watch on his unwilling instrument. Many a time young DeFeo knew the Indian was there with him, but how was he to communicate such a thing to the guards? All he would gain would be another examination by a psychiatrist already committed to the notion the DeFeo was in fact faking his insanity.

As he sat in his cell at Dannemora, Ronald recalled some of the terrible moments of the past, long before he knew what was wrong with their house on Ocean Avenue. Such as the time when his father . . . whom he had killed . . . had accepted that the house had a curse on it and had summoned a priest to bless it. Whatever was in the house was more powerful than the priest, who ran from it, terror in his eyes, trying to escape the clutches of an angry spirit. He remembered the time his father had planted lilies around the house because he had read somewhere that they kept evil spirits away. The morning after, all the flowers had been dead . . .

While young Ronald DeFeo began to serve six consecutive terms of twenty-five years for each of his victims, a total of 125 years in prison, knowing that he was unlikely to see freedom again in this incarnation, the house passed into other hands. Once the terrible news of the tragedy had disappeared from the headlines, a local real estate man offered it for sale again. This time a family of nondescript middle class people were the buyers. They were attracted by the unusually low price being asked for the property and they knew quite well why it was being sold so cheaply. But as they did not believe in the supernatural, it did not seem to bother them at all. They moved into the house and tried to enjoy it as much as possible, for it was truly a nice house, nicely located, with the water right at the back of it, where one could keep a motor boat, as the DeFeos did.

At first, the curious came and stood in front of house, very much to the annoyance of the family who had purchased it. There was very little they could do about it. So long as the tourists and other curious visitors were not trespassing on the property, they could not very well forbid them to be there. They tried to discourage would-be visitors by altering the number on the house but that didn't throw anyone off for very long. Visitors came, especially on weekends, and endless streams of cars would slowly pass by the house at 112 Ocean Avenue, trying to look at it as they passed, trying to figure out what it was in this strange house that made young DeFeo commit the six murders. Eventually, the attraction became less and less novel; as the film dealing with the house in Amityville went off the screen, so did the interest of the public at large.

As the years went by, an occasional visitor would come and stare at the house, but the owners no longer had a problem of dealing with mass invasions of their privacy. The weekends became gradually more and more tranquil, as they had always been, long before the DeFeos had occupied the house on Ocean Avenue.

The years went by, and Amityville prospered; it grew and grew, until it was one of the most attractive towns in central Long Island, the goal of many vacationers and those who wanted to buy homes near the water. Some of them remembered that there was something strange about the name Amityville in the past; but as the years went on, fewer and fewer of them knew exactly what it was that reminded them of the name Amityville, and even fewer cared. In time, Amityville had lost its horror, and became just another town on Long Island.

Chapter Ten

In New York City there lived a young man by the name of Paul Dickens. Paul was thirty-two and worked for an advertising agency named Smith, Collins, and Rosoff. He was, in fact, one of the top executives at the agency, making an excellent salary and considered one of the bright minds of the agency business. But despite his commercial success, Paul's heart really wasn't with the agency. I must hasten to add that the did not tell that to his bosses, the owners of the agency, nor to the clients whose accounts he handled, but confided such matters only to his inner thoughts and to his fiancee, whose name was Sybil Connor. Sybil, aged, twenty-seven, was an understanding woman, who would never betray her future husband in such matters as his true vocation.

What then was this true vocation that Paul so jealously guarded from outsiders? Ever since, at the age of twelve or thirteen, he had got hold of some fascinating books dealing with the subject, Paul had been a confirmed treasure hunter. To be sure, he had yet to find his first treasure trove, but he always visited places where treasure *might* be found, such as the spot on Long Island where Captain Kidd allegedly buried his, or the area off the shore of Miami Beach where sunken treasure lay unclaimed, waiting to be discovered. Unfortunately, Paul was not a deep sea diver, so the treasure of Florida was in no danger of being discovered by him. Nor was pirate treasure still to be found in the waters of Bermuda, where Paul liked to vacation with Sybil. In fact, Paul's desire to find treasure was confined strictly to land, where he seemed to be on steadier footing and where he could possibly be successful in the long run.

To Paul Dickens, pirates were not simply wrongdoers who should be punished for their terrible deeds. Pirates were his heroes and, since he had never met one in the flesh, he had no first-hand experience of how it felt to be a passenger on a boat about to be sunk or just having been boarded by the pirate's crew. Oh, Paul knew about all the terrible things that the pirates used to do in the old days, and he did not condone them. On the other hand he did admire the swashbuckling heroism of some of these men, apart from their wrongdoings and the resultant bloodshed. All things considered, he saw certain parallels between modern businessmen and some of the doings of eighteenth century pirates. Of course in the advertising game people weren't exactly put to the sword or made to walk the plank, but they were put out of business just as ruthlessly as they were put out of life by the ancient pirates.

Since Paul had no qualms about pursuing his work at the advertising agency and doing what was best for his company, even if it meant putting someone else out of business, he didn't have any qualms about cheering for the pirates of old for doing their thing in their way. Sybil, on the other hand, being a sensitive woman, felt that some aspects of the piracy business were certainly not to be condoned and she frequently discussed this with her fiancé. The discussions never led anywhere, because in the end they simply kissed and made love. But there was one thing to be said about all this: the excitement of finding buried treasure would in no way be hindered by the fact that it had been acquired illegally or through bloodshed. After all, so many years had passed and nothing could resuscitate the victims, the former owners of such treasures. Consequently, Sybil heartily agreed with Paul that looking for buried treasure was an innocent pursuit and did not necessitate her condoning the cruelty of pirates and those who had assembled the treasure in the first place.

As he grew more affluent, Paul acquired a summer home. It was really a weekend house primarily, but one could live there all year round if one wanted to. At first he had looked for such a house in nearby Connecticut, but, finding nothing to his liking, he had then spent weekend after weekend driving farther and farther afield with Sybil, looking for a house that would suit his fancy. That fancy was in the direction of something very romantic, perhaps an old house, a colonial house, something at least 150 or 200 years old. But it also had to be convenient and, of course, the price had to be right.

Eventually their search for a summer home took them to the state of New Hampshire. There, not far from Nashua, they found what they had been looking for: a pleasant late eighteenth century house in excellent condition with all the trimmings, two acres of land and easily accesible from either Boston or New York.

After they had settled into their new summer home they took an additional interest in the state of New Hampshire, where they were now part-time residents. Paul went to the local library in Nashua, which was one of the best libraries in that part of the country. He started to rummage through books about New Hampshire and, of course, its history. One day his eyes fell upon a volume that attracted his interest immediately. It was a book called *Yankee Ghosts*, written many years before about New England's hauntings and legends. Something within himself, perhaps a kind of hunch or psychic intuition, made him take the book down from the shelf and ask permission to borrow it. Hastily returning to their home in the hills he started to read. Picture his surprise when he discovered that one of the stories in this book dealt with his favorite subject, a pirate and buried treasure!

It would appear that at Henniker, New Hampshire, farther upstate, there was a house known as the Ocean-Born Mary House which had been built by a retired pirate. The author had visited it because of ongoing reports of hauntings and had extensively delineated the events in his book. Excitedly Paul brought the book to Sybil and asked her to share his enthusiasm for its contents.

"What is it?" Sybil asked and looked at the timeworn cover.

"It's about that house at Henniker, the pirate house," Paul replied excitedly. "Do you want to hear about it?"

Now Sybil knew that when the subject of pirates and pirate treasure came up there was nothing to be done but listen. The evening was still young, there wasn't much on television that night, so she decided they might as well go into the matter at length. Having made themselves comfortable by the fireplace, with a fire burning in it, setting the mood for what was to follow, she turned to her fiancé and asked him to read to her from the book.

"Ocean-Born Mary died in eighteen four-teen," Paul said, "but the house has changed hands many times since her death. This is what the book says:

"During the nineteen thirties, it belonged to one Louis Roy, now totally disabled and until recently a permanent guest in what used to be his home. The house was sold by him to the Russells not long ago.

"During the great hurricane of nineteen thirty-eight, Roy claims that Mary Wallace's ghost saved his life nineteen times. Trapped outside the house by falling trees, he somehow was able to get back into the house. His mother, Mrs. Roy, informed him that, being very psychic, she had actually seen the tall, stately figure of Ocean-Born Mary moving behind him, as if to help him get through. About ten years ago, *Life* told this story in an illustrated article on famous haunted houses in America. Mrs. Roy claimed she had seen the ghost of Mary time and again, but since she herself passed on in nineteen forty-eight, I could not get any details from *her*.

"Then there were two state troopers who saw the ghost, but again I could not interview them, as they, too, are now on the other side of the Veil.

"A number of visitors claim to have felt 'special vibrations' when touching the hearthstone, where Don Pedro allegedly is buried. There is, for instance, Mrs. James

Nisula, of Londonderry, who has visited the house several times. She and her group of ghost buffs have 'felt the vibrations' around the kitchen, she says. Mrs. David Russell, the present owner, felt nothing.

"I promised to look into the Ocean-Born Mary haunting the first chance I'd get. Hallowe'en or about that time would be all right with me, and I wouldn't wait around for any ghost coach, either.

" 'There is a lady medium I think you should know,' Mrs. Russell said when I spoke of bringing a psychic with me. 'She saw Mary the very first time she came here.'

"My curiosity aroused, I communicated with the lady. She asked that I not use her married name, although she was not so shy several months after our visit to the house, when she gave a two-part interview to a Boston newspaper columnist. Needless to say, the interview was not authorized by me, as I never allow mediums I work with to talk about their cases for publication. Thus, Lorrie shall remain without a family name and anyone wishing to reach this medium will have to do so without my help.

"Lorrie wrote me she would be happy to serve the cause of truth, and I could count on her. There was nothing she wanted in return.

"Somehow, we did not get up to New Hampshire that Hallowe'en weekend. Mr. Russell had to have an operation, and the house was unheated in the winter except for Mr. Roy's room, and New England winters are cold enough to freeze a ghost.

"Although there was a caretaker at the time to look after the house and Mr. Roy upstairs, the Russells did not stay in the house in the winter, but made their home in nearby Chelmsford, Massachusetts.

"I wrote Mrs. Russell postponing the investigation until spring. Mrs. Russell accepted my decision with some disappointment, but she was willing to wait. After all, the ghost at Ocean-Born Mary's house is not a malicious type. Mary Wallace just lives there, ever since she died in eighteen fourteen, and you can't call a lady who likes to hold on to what is hers an intruder.

" 'We don't want to drive her out,' Mrs. Russell had repeatedly said to me. 'After all, it *is* her house!'

"Not many haunted-house owners will make a statement like that.

"Something had happened at the house since our last conversation.

" 'Our caretaker dropped a space heater all the way down the stairs at the Ocean-Born Mary house and, when it reached the bottom, the kerosene and the flames started to burn the stairs and climb the wall,' Mrs. Russell said. 'There was no water in the house, so my husband went out after snow. While I stood there looking at the fire and powerless to do anything about it, the fire went out all by itself right in front of my eyes, when my husband got back with the snow it was out. It was just as if someone *had smothered it with a blanket.*'

"This was in December nineteen sixty-three. I tried to set a new date, as soon as possible, and February twenty-second seemed all right. This time I would bring Bob Kennedy of WBZ, Boston, and the 'Contact' producer Squire Rushnell with me, to record my investigation.

"Lorrie was willing, asking only that her name not be mentioned.

" 'I don't want anyone to know about my being different from them,' she explained. 'When I was young my family used to accuse me of spying because I knew things from the pictures I saw when I touched objects.'

"Psychometry, I explained, is very common among psychics, and nothing to be ashamed of.

"I thought it was time to find out more about Lorrie's experiences at the haunted house.

" 'I first saw the house in September nineteen sixty-one,' she began. 'It was on a misty, humid day, and there was a haze over the fields.'

"Strange, I thought, I always get my best psychic results when the atmosphere is moist.

"Lorrie, who is in her early forties, is Vermont-born and raised; she is married and has one daughter, Pauline. She is a tall red-head with sparkling eyes and, come to think of it, not unlike the accepted picture of the ghostly Mary Wallace. Coincidence?

"A friend of Lorrie's had seen the eerie

house and suggested she go and see it also. That was all Lorrie knew about it, and she did not really expect anything uncanny to occur. Mr. Roy showed Lorrie and her daughter through the house and nothing startling happened. They left and started to walk down the entrance steps, crossing the garden that lies in front of the house, and had reached the gate when Pauline clutched at her mother's arm and said, 'Mama, what is that?'

"Lorrie turned to look back at the house. In the upstairs window, a woman stood and looked out at them. Lorrie's husband was busy with the family car. She called out to him, but as he turned to look, the apparition was gone.

"She did not think of it again, and the weeks went by. But the house kept intruding itself into her thoughts more and more. Finally she could not restrain herself any longer, and returned to the house, even though it is a hundred and twenty miles from her home in Weymouth, Massachusetts.

"She confessed her extraordinary experience to the owner, and together they examined the house from top to bottom. She finally returned home.

"She promised Roy she would return on All Hallow's Eve to see if the legend of Mary Wallace had any basis of fact. Unfortunately, word of her intentions got out, and when she arrived at the house, she had to sneak in at the back to avoid the sensation-hungry press outside. During the days between her second visit and Hallowe'en, the urge to go to Henniker kept getting stronger, as if someone were possessing her.

"By that time the Russells were negotiating to buy the house, and Lorrie came up with them. Nothing happened to her that Hallowe'en night. Perhaps she was torn between fear and a desire to fight the influence that had brought her out to Henniker to begin with.

"Mediums, to be successful, must learn to relax and not allow their own notions to rule them. All through the following winter and summer, Lorrie fought the desire to return to Ocean-Born Mary's house. To no avail. She returned time and again, sometimes alone and sometimes with a friend.

"Things got out of hand one summer night when she was home alone.

"Exhausted from her last visit—the visits always left her an emotional wreck—she went to bed around nine-thirty in the evening.

" 'What happened that night?' I interjected. She seemed shaken even now.

" 'At eleven p.m.,' Lorrie replied, 'I found myself driving on the Expressway, wearing my pajamas and robe, with no shoes or slippers, or money or even a handkerchief. I was ten miles from my home and heading for Henniker. Terrified, I turned around and returned home, only to find my house ablaze with light, the doors open as I had left them, and the garage lights on. I must have left in an awful hurry.'

" 'Have you found out why you are being pulled back to that house?'

"She shook her head.

" 'No idea. But I've been back twice, even after that. I just can't seem to stay away from that house.'

"I persuaded her that perhaps there was a job to be done in that house, and the ghost wanted her to do it.

"We did not go out to Henniker in February, because of the bad weather. We tried to set a date in May, but the people from WBZ found it too far away from Boston and dropped out of the planning.

"Summer came around, and I went to Europe instead of Henniker. However, the prospect of a visit in the fall was very much on my mind.

"But it seemed as if someone were keeping me *away* from the house much in the same way someone was pulling Lorrie toward it!

"Come October, and we were really on our way, at last. Owen Lake, a public relations man who dabbles in psychic matters, introduced himself as a friend of mine and told Lorrie he'd come along, too. I had never met the gentleman, but in the end he could not make it. So just four of us—my wife, Catherine, and I, Lorrie and her nice, even-tempered husband, who had volunteered to drive us up to New Hampshire—started out from Boston. It was close to Hallowe'en all right, only two days earlier; if Mary Wallace was out haunting the countryside in her coach we might very well run into her. (The coach is out of old Irish folktales; it appears in numerous ghost stories of the Ould Sod; I'm sure that in the telling and retelling of the tale of Mary and her pirate, the coach got added.)

"The countryside is beautiful in a New England fall. As we rolled toward the New Hampshire state line, I asked Lorrie some more questions.

" 'When you first saw the ghost of Ocean-Born Mary at the window of the house, Lorrie,' I said, 'what did she look like?'

" 'A lovely lady in her thirties, with auburn-colored hair, smiling rather intensely and thoughtfully. She stayed there for maybe three minutes, and then suddenly, *she just wasn't there.*'

" 'What about her dress?'

" 'It was a white dress.'

"Lorrie never saw an apparition of Mary again, but whenever she touched anything in the Henniker house, she received an impression of what the house was like when Mary had it, and she had felt her near the big fireplace several times.

" 'Did you ever get an impression of what it was Mary wanted?'

" 'She was a strong-willed woman, I sensed that very strongly,' Lorrie replied. 'I have been to the house maybe twenty times altogether, and still don't know why. She just keeps pulling me there.'

"Lorrie has always felt the ghost's presence on these visits.

" 'One day I was walking among the bushes in the back of the house,' Lorrie said. 'I was wearing shorts, but I never got a scratch on my legs, because I kept feeling heavy skirts covering my legs. I could feel the brambles pulling at this invisible skirt I had on. I felt enveloped by something, or some-one.'

" 'Mrs. Roy, the former owner's mother, had told of seeing the apparition many times,' Lorrie stated.

"As a matter of fact, I have sensed a ghost in the house, too, but it is not a friendly wraith like Mary.'

"Had she ever encountered this other ghost?

" 'Yes, my arm was grabbed one time by a malevolent entity,' Lorrie said emphatically. 'It was two years ago, and I was standing in what is now the living room, and my arm was taken by the elbow and pulled. I snatched my arm back, because I felt the spirit was not friendly.'

" 'What were you doing at the time that it might have objected to?'

" 'I really don't know.'

"Did she know of anyone else who had had any uncanny experience at the house?

" 'A strange thing happened to Mrs. Roy,' Lorrie said. 'A woman came to the house and said to her, "I've come back to see the rest of the house." Mrs. Roy was puzzled—"What do you mean, the *rest* of the house?" The woman replied, "Well, I was here yesterday, and a tall woman let me in and only showed me half the house." But, of course, there was nobody at the house that day.'

"What about the two state troopers? Could she elaborate on their experience?

" 'They met her walking down the road that leads to the house. She was wearing a Colonial-type costume, and they found that odd. Later they realized they had seen a ghost, especially as no one of her description lived in the house at the time.'

"Rudi D., Lorrie's husband, is a hospital technician. He was with her on two or three occasions when she visited the house. Did he ever feel anything special?

" 'The only thing unusual I ever felt at the house was that I wanted to get out of there fast,' he said.

" 'The very first time we went up,' Lorrie added, 'something kept pulling me toward it, but my husband insisted we go back. There was an argument about our continuing the trip, when suddenly the door of the car flew open of its own volition. Somehow we decided to continue on to the house.'

"An hour later, we drove up a thickly overgrown hill and along a winding road at the end of which the Ocean-Born Mary house stood in solitary stateliness, a rectangular building of gray stone and brown trim, very well preserved.

"We parked the car and walked across the garden that sets the house well back from the road. There was peace and autumn in the air. We were made welcome by Corinne Russell, her husband, David, and two relatives who happened to be with them that day. Entering the main door beneath a magnificent early American eagle, we admired the fine wooden staircase leading to the upstairs—the staircase on which the mysterious fire had taken place—and then entered the room to the left of it, where the family had assembled around an old New England stove.

"During the three years the Russells had lived at the house, nothing uncanny had happened to Mrs. Russell, except for the incident with the fire. David Russell, a man typical of the shrewd New England Yankee who weighs every word, was willing to tell me about *his* experiences, however.

" 'The first night I ever slept in what we call the Lafayette room, upstairs, there was quite a thundershower on, and my dog and I were upstairs. I always keep my dog with me, on account of the boys coming around to do damage to the property.

" 'Just as I lay down in bed, I heard very heavy footsteps. They sounded to me to be in the two rooms which we had just restored, on the same floor. I was quite annoyed, almost frightened, and I went into the rooms, but there was nobody there or anywhere else in the house.'

" 'Interesting,' I said. 'Was there more?'

174

" 'Now this happened only last summer. A few weeks later, when I was in that same room, I was getting undressed when I suddenly heard somebody pound on my door. I said to myself, oh, it's only the house settling, and I got into bed. A few minutes later, the door knob turned back and forth. I jumped out of bed, opened the door, and there was absolutely nobody there. The only other people in the house at the time were the invalid Mr. Roy, locked in his room, and my wife downstairs.'

"What about visual experiences?

" 'No, but I went to the cellar not long ago with my dog, about four in the afternoon, or rather tried to—this dog never leaves me, but on this particular occasion, something kept her from going with me into the cellar. Her hair stood up and she would not budge.'

"The Lafayette room, by the way, is the very room in which the pirate, Don Pedro, is supposed to have lived. The Russells did nothing to change the house structurally, only restored it as it was and generally cleaned it up.

"I now turned to Florence Harmon, an elderly lady, a neighbor of the Russells, who had some recollection about the house. Mrs. Harmon recalls the house when she herself was very young, long before the Russells came to live in it.

" 'Years later, I returned to the house and Mrs. Roy asked me whether I could help her locate 'the treasure' since I was reputed to be psychic.'

"Was there really a treasure?

" 'If there was, I think it was found,' Mrs. Harmon said. 'At the time Mrs. Roy talked to me, she also pointed out that there were two elm trees on the grounds—the only two elm trees around. They looked like some sort of markers to her. But before the Roys had the house, a Mrs. Morrow lived here. I know this from my uncle, who was a stone mason, and who built a vault for her.'

"I did not think Mrs. Harmon had added anything material to the knowledge of the treasure, so I thanked her and turned my attention to the other large room, on the right hand side of the staircase. Nicely furnished with period pieces, it boasted a fireplace flanked by sofas, and had a rectangular piano in the corner. The high windows were curtained on the sides, and one could see the New England landscape through them.

"We seated ourselves around the fireplace and hoped that Mary would honor us with a visit. Earlier I had inspected the entire house, including the hearthstone under which, allegedly, Don Pedro lies buried, and the small bedrooms upstairs where David Russell had heard the footsteps. Then, too, each of us had stood at the window in the corridor upstairs and stared out of it, very much the way the ghost must have done when she was observed by Lorrie and her daughter.

"And now it was Mary's turn.

" 'This was her room,' Lorrie explained, 'and I do feel her presence.' But she refused to go into trance, afraid to 'let go.' Communication would have to be via clairvoyance, with Lorrie being the interpreter. This was not what I had hoped for. Nevertheless, we would try to evaluate whatever material we could obtain.

" 'Sheet and quill,' Lorrie said now, and a piece of paper was handed her along with a pencil. Holding it on her lap, Lorrie was poised to write, if Mary wanted to use her hand, so to speak. The pencil suddenly jumped from Lorrie's hand with considerable force.

" 'Proper quill,' the ghost demanded.

"I explained about the shape of quills these days, and handed Lorrie my own pencil.

" 'Look lady,' Lorrie explained to the ghost, 'I'll show you it writes. I'll write my name.'

"And she wrote in her own, smallish, rounded hand, 'Lorrie'.

"There was a moment of silence. Evidently, the ghost was thinking it over. Then Lorrie's hand, seemingly not under her own control, wrote with a great deal of flourish 'Mary Wallace'. The 'M' and 'W' had curves and ornamentation typical of eighteenth-century calligraphy. It was not at all like Lorrie's own handwriting.

" 'Tell her to write some more. The quill is working,' I commanded.

"Lorrie seemed to be upset by something the ghost told her.

" 'No,' she said. 'I can't do that. No.'

" 'What does she want?' I asked.

" 'She wants me to sleep, but I won't do it.'

"Trance, I thought; even the ghost demands it. It would have been so interesting to have Mary speak directly to us through Lorrie's entranced lips. You can lead a medium to the ghost, but you can't make her go under if she's scared.

"Lorrie instead told the ghost to tell *her*, or to write through her. But no trance, thank you. Evidently, the ghost did not like to be told how to communicate. We waited. Then I suggested that Lorrie be very relaxed and it would be 'like sleep' so the ghost could talk to us directly.

" 'She's very much like me, but not so well trimmed,' the ghost said to Lorrie. Had Mary picked her to carry her message because of physical resemblance, I wondered?

" 'She's waiting for Young John,' Lorrie now said. Not young John; the stress was on Young, perhaps it was one name—Youngjohn.

" 'Who is Youngjohn?' I asked.

" 'It happened in the north pasture,' Mary said through Lorrie now. 'He killed Warren Langerford. The Frazier boys found the last bone.'

"I asked why it concerned her. Was she involved? But there was no reply.

"Then the ghost of Mary introduced someone else standing next to her.

" 'Mrs. Roy is with her, because she killed

her daughter,' Lorrie said, hesitatingly, and added, on her own, 'but I don't believe she did.' Later we found out that the ghost was perhaps not lying, but of course nobody had any proof of such a crime, if it was indeed a crime.

" 'Why do you stay on in this house?' I asked.

" 'This house is *my* house!' Ocean-Born Mary reminded me.

" 'Do you realize you are what is commonly called dead?' I demanded. As so often with ghosts, the question brought on resistance to the need of facing reality. Mary seemed insulted and withdrew.

"I addressed the ghost openly, offering to help her, and at the same time explaining her present position to her. This was her chance to speak up.

" 'She's very capricious,' Lorrie said. 'When you said you'd bring her peace, she started to laugh.'

"But Mary was gone, for the present anyway.

"We waited, and tried again a little later. This time Lorrie said she heard a voice telling her to come back tonight.

" 'We can't,' I decided. 'If she wants to be helped, it will have to be now.'

"Philip Babb (another name the pirate used, later) allegedly had a secret passage built under the house. To this day, the Russells are looking for it. There are indeed discrepancies in the thickness of some of the walls, and there are a number of secret holes that do not lead anywhere. But no passage, as yet. Had the pirate taken his secrets to his grave?

"I found our experience at Henniker singularly unsatisfactory since no real evidence had been forthcoming from the ghost herself. No doubt another visit would have to be made, but I did not mind that at all. Ocean-Born Mary's place is a place one can easily visit time and again. The rural charm of the place and the timeless atmosphere of the house make it a first-rate tourist attraction. Thousands of people come to the house every year.

"We returned to New York and I thought no more about it until I received a letter from James Caron, who had heard me discuss the house on the Contact program in Boston. He had been to the house in quest of pirate lore and found it very much haunted.

"James Caron is in the garage business at Bridgewater, Massachusetts. He has a high school and trade school education and is married, with two children. Searching for stories of buried treasure and pirates is a hobby of his, and he sometimes lectures on it. He had met Gus Roy about six years before. Roy complained that his deceased mother was trying to contact him for some reason. Her picture kept falling off the wall where it was hung, and he constantly felt 'a presence.' Would Mr. Caron know of a good medium?

"In August nineteen fifty-nine, James Caron brought a spiritualist named Paul

Amsdent to the Ocean-Born Mary house. Present at the ensuing seance were Harold Peters, a furniture salesman, Hugh Blanchard, a lawyer, Ernest Walbourne, a fireman and brother-in-law of Caron, Gus Roy and Mr. Caron himself. Tape recording the seance, Caron had trouble with his equipment. Strange sounds kept intruding. Unfortunately, there was among those present someone with hostility toward psychic work, and Gus Roy's mother did not manifest. However, something else did happen.

" 'There appear to be people buried somewhere around or in the house,' the medium Amsdent said, 'enclosed by a stone wall of some sort.'

"I thought of the hearthstone and of Mrs. Harmon's vault. Coincidence?

"Mr. Caron used metal detectors all over the place to satisfy Gus Roy that there was no 'pirate treasure' buried in or near the house.

"A little later, James Caron visited the house again. This time he was accompanied by Mrs. Caron, and by Mr. and Mrs. Ernest Walbourne. Both ladies were frightened by the sound of a heavy door opening and closing with no one around and no air current in the house.

"Mrs. Caron had a strong urge to go to the attic, but Mr. Caron stopped her. Ernest Walbourne, a skeptic, was alone in the so-called Death room upstairs, looking at some pictures stacked in a corner. Suddenly, he clearly heard a female voice telling him to get out of the house. He looked around, but there was nobody upstairs. Frightened, he left the house at once and later required medication for a nervous condition!

"Again, things quieted down as far as Ocean-Born Mary was concerned, until I was shown a lengthy story—two parts, in fact—in the *Boston Record-American*, in which my erstwhile medium Lorrie let her hair down to columnist Harold Banks.

"It seems that Lorrie could not forget Henniker, after all. With publicist Owen Lake she returned to the house in November, nineteen sixty-four, bringing with her some oil of wintergreen, which, she claims, Mary Wallace asked her to bring along.

"Two weeks later, the report went on, Lorrie felt Mary Wallace in her home in Weymouth near Boston. Lorrie was afraid that Mary Wallace might 'get into my body and use it for whatever purpose she wants to. I might wake up some day and *be* Mary Wallace.'

"That's the danger of being a medium without proper safeguards. Such mediums tend to identify with personalities that come through them. Especially when they read all there is in print about them.

"I decided to take someone to the house who knew nothing about it, someone who was not likely to succumb to the wiles of amateur 'ESP experts,' inquisitive columnists and such, someone who would do exactly what I required of her: Sybil Leek, the famed British psychic.

"It was a glorious day late in spring when we arrived at Ocean-Born Mary's house in a Volkswagen staton wagon driven by two alert young students from Goddard College, Vermont, Jerry Weener and Jay Lawrence. They had come to Boston to fetch us and take us all the way up to their campus, where I was to address the students and faculty. I proposed that they drive us by way of Henniker, and the two young men, students of parapsychology, agreed enthusiastically. It was their first experience with an actual seance and they brought with them a lively dose of curiosity.

"Sybil Leek brought with her something else: 'Mr. Sasha,' a healthy four-foot snake of the boa constrictor family someone had given her for a pet. At first I thought she was kidding when she spoke with tender care of her snake, coiled peacefully in his little basket. But practical Sybil, author of some nine books, saw another possibility for a book in 'Life with Sasha' and for that reason kept the snake with her. On the way to Henniker, the car had a flat tire and we took this opportunity to get acquainted with Sasha, as Sybil gave him a run around the New Hampshire countryside.

"Although I have always had a deep-seated dislike for anything reptilian, snakes, serpents, and other slitherers, terrestrial or maritime, I must confess that I found this critter less repulsive than I had thought he would be. At any rate, 'Mr. Sasha' was collected once more and carefully replaced in his basket and the journey continued to Henniker, where the Russells were expecting us with great anticipation.

"After a delightful buffet luncheon—'Mr. Sasha' had his the week before, as snakes are slow eaters—we proceeded to the large room to the right of the entrance door, and Sybil took the chair near the fireplace, while the rest of us—the Russells, a minister who was a friend of theirs, two neighbors, my wife, Catherine, and I gathered around her in a circle. Our two student friends joined the circle too.

"It was early afternoon. The sun was bright and clear. It didn't seem a good day for ghosts. Still, we had come to have a talk with the elusive Mary Wallace in her own domain, and if I knew Sybil, she would not disappoint us. Sybil is a very powerful medium, and something *always* happens.

"Sybil knew nothing about the house as I had told our hosts not to discuss it with her before the trance session. I asked her if she had any clairvoyant impressions about the house.

"'My main impressions were outside,' Sybil replied, 'near where the irises are. I was drawn to that spot and felt very strange. There is something outside the house which means more than things inside!'

" 'What about inside the house? What do you feel here?'

" 'The most impressive room I think is the loom room,' Sybil said, and I thought, that's where Ernest Walbourne heard the voice telling him to get out, in the area that's also called the Death room.

" 'They don't want us here . . . there is a conflict between two people . . . somebody wants something he can't have . . .'

"Presently, Sybil went into a trance. There was a moment of silence as I waited anxiously for the ghost of Mary Wallace to manifest itself through Sybil. The first words coming from the lips of the entranced medium were almost unintelligible.

"Gradually, the voice became clearer and I had her repeat the words until I could be sure of them.

" 'Say-mon go to the lion's head,' she said now. 'To the lion's head. Be careful.'

" 'Why should I be careful?'

" 'In case he catches you.'

" 'Who are you?'

" 'Mary Degan.'

" 'What are you doing here?'

" 'Waiting. Someone fetch me.'

"She said 'Witing' with a strong cockney accent, and suddenly I realized that the 'say-mon' was probably a seaman.

" 'Whose house is this?' I enquired.

" 'Daniel Burn's.' (Perhaps it was 'Birch.')

" 'What year is this?'

" 'Seventeen ninety-eight.'

185

" 'Who built this house?'

" 'Burn . . .'

" 'How did you get here?'

" 'All the time, come and go . . . to hide . . . I have to wait. He wants the money. Burn. Daniel Burn.'

"I began to wonder what had happened to Mary Wallace. Who was this new member of the ghostly cast? Sybil knew nothing whatever of a pirate or a pirate treasure connected by legend to this house. Yet her very first trance words concerned *a seaman and money.*

"Did Mary Degan have someone else with her? I hinted. Maybe this was only the First Act and the Lady of the House was being coy in time for a Second Act appearance.

"But the ghost insisted that she was Mary Degan and that she lived here, 'with the old idiot.' Who was the old idiot? I demanded.

" 'Mary,' the Degan girl replied.

" 'What is Mary's family name?'

" 'Birch,' she replied without hesitation.

"I looked at Mrs. Russell, who shook her head. Nobody knew of Mary Wallace by any other name. Had she had another husband we did not know about?

"Was there anyone else with her, I asked?

" 'Mary Birch, Daniel, and Jonathan,' she replied.

" 'Who is Jonathan?'

" 'Jonathan Harrison Flood,' the ghostly voice said.

"A week or so later, I checked with my

good friend Robert Nesmith, expert in pirate lore. Was there a pirate by that name? There had been, but his date is giving as sixteen ten, far too early for our man. But then Flood is a very common name. Also, this Flood might have used another name as his *nom de pirate* and Flood might have been his real, civilian name.

" 'What are they doing in this house?' I demanded.

" 'They come to look for their money,' Sybil in trance replied. 'The old idiot took it.'

" 'What sort of money was it?'

" 'Dutch money,' came the reply, 'very long ago.'

" 'Who brought the money to this house?'

" 'Mary. Not me.'

" 'Whose money was it?'

" 'Johnny's.'

" 'How did he get it?'

" 'Very funny . . . he helped himself . . . so we did.'

" 'What profession did he have?'

" 'Went down to the sea. Had a lot of funny business. Then he got caught, you know. So they did him in.'

" 'Who did him in?'

" 'The runners. In the bay.'

" 'What year was that?'

" 'Ninety-nine.'

" 'What happened to the money after that?'

" 'She hid it. Outside, near the lion's head.'

" 'Where is the lion's head?'

" 'You go down past the little rocks, in the

middle of the rocks, a little bit like a lion's head.'

" 'If I left this house by the front entrance, which way would I turn?'

" 'To the right, down past the little rock on the right. Through the trees, down the little . . . '

" 'How far from the house?'

" 'Three minutes.'

" 'Is it under the rock?'

" 'Lion's head.'

" 'How far below?''

" 'As big as a boy.'

" 'What will I find there?'

" 'The gold. Dutch gold.'

" 'Anything else?'

" 'No, unless she put it there.'

" 'Why did she put it there?'

" 'Because he came back for it.'

" 'What did she do?'

" 'She said it was hers. Then he went away. Then they caught him, and good thing, too. He never came back and she went off, too.'

" 'When did she leave here?'

" 'Eighteen three.'

" 'What was she like? Describe her.'

" 'Round, not as big as me, dumpy thing, she thought she owned everything.'

" 'How was Jonathan related to Daniel?'

" 'Daniel stayed here when Johnny went away and then they would divide the money, but they didn't because of Mary. She took it.'

" 'Did you see the money?'

" 'I got some money. Gold. It says seventeen forty-seven.'

" 'Is anyone buried in this ground?'

" 'Sometimes they brought them back here when they got killed down by the river.'

" 'Who is buried in this house?'

" 'I think Johnny.'

"I now told Mary Degan to fetch me the other Mary, the Lady of the House. But the girl demurred. The other Mary did not like to talk to strangers.

" 'What do *you* look like?' I asked. I still was not sure if Mary Wallace was not masquerading as her own servant girl to fool us.

" 'Skinny and tall.'

" 'What do you wear?'

" 'A gray dress.'

" 'What is your favorite spot in this house?'

" 'The little loom room. Peaceful.'

" 'Do you always stay there?'

" 'No.' The voice was proud now. 'I go where I want.'

" 'Whose house is this?' Perhaps I could trap her if she was indeed Mary Wallace.

" 'Mary Birch.'

" 'Has she got a husband?'

" 'They come and go. There's always company here—that's why I go to the loom room.'

"I tried to send her away, but she wouldn't go.

" 'Nobody speaks to me,' she complained.

'Johnny . . . she won't let him speak to me. Nobody is going to send me away.'

" 'Is there a sea captain in this house?' I asked.

"She almost shouted the reply.

" '*Johnny!*'

" 'Where is he from?'

" 'Johnny is from the island.'

"She then explained that the trouble with Johnny and Mary was about the sea. Especially about the money the captain had.

" 'Will the money be found?' I asked.

" 'Not until I let it.'

"I asked Mary Degan to find me Mary Wallace. No dice. The lady wanted to be coaxed. Did she want some presents? I asked. That hit a happier note.

" 'Brandy . . . some clothes,' she said. 'She needs some hair . . . hasn't got much hair.'

" 'Ask her if she could do with some oil of wintergreen,' I said, sending up a trial balloon.

" 'She's got a bad back,' the ghost said, and I could tell from the surprised expression on Mrs. Russell's face that Mary Wallace had indeed had a bad back.

" 'She makes it . . . people bring her things . . . rub her back . . . back's bad . . . she won't let you get the money . . . not yet . . . may want to build another house, in the garden . . . in case she needs it . . . sell it . . . she knows she is not what she used to be because her back's bad . . . she'll never go. Not now.'

"I assured her that the Russells wanted her

to stay as long as she liked to. After all, it was her house, too.

" 'Where is Johnny's body buried?' I now asked.

" 'Johnny's body,' she murmured, 'is under the fireplace.'

"Nobody had told Sybil about the persistent rumors that the old pirate lay under the hearthstone.

" 'Don't tell anyone,' she whispered.

" 'How deep?'

" 'Had to be deep.'

" 'Who put him there?'

" 'I shan't tell you.'

" 'Did you bury anything with him?'

" 'I shan't tell. He is no trouble now. Poor Johnny.'

" 'How did Johnny meet Mary?'

" 'I think they met on a ship.'

"Ocean-Born Mary, I thought. Sybil did not even know the name of the house, much less the story of how it got that name.

" 'All right,' I said. 'Did Mary have any children?'

" 'Four . . . in the garden.'

" 'Did anyone kill anyone in this house at any time?'

" 'Johnny was killed, you know. Near the money. The runners chased him and he was very sick, we thought he was dead, and then he came here, I think she pushed him when he hurt his leg. We both brought him back here and put him under the fireplace. I didn't think he was dead.'

" 'But you buried him anyway?' I said.

" 'She did,' the ghostly servant replied. 'Better gone, she said. He'd only come back for the money.'

" 'Then Mary and Johnny weren't exactly friendly?'

" 'They were once.'

" 'What changed things?'

" 'The money. She took his money. The money he fought for. Fighting money.'

"Suddenly, the tone of voice of the servant girl changed.

" 'I want to go outside,' she begged. 'She watches me. I go out because her back is bad today. Can't get up, you see. So I can go out.'

"I promised to help her. Suspiciously, she asked, 'What do you want?'

" 'Go outside, you are free to go,' I intoned.

" 'Sit on the rocks,' the voice said. 'If she calls out? She can get very angry.'

" 'I will protect you,' I promised.

" 'She says there are other places under the floor . . .' the girl ghost added, suddenly.

" 'Any secret passages?' I asked.

" 'Yes, near the old nursery. First floor. Up the stairs, the loom room, the right hand wall. You can get out in the smoke room!'

"Mr. Russell had told me of his suspicions that on structural evidence alone there was a hidden passage behind the smoke room. How would Sybil know this? Nobody had discussed it with her or showed her the spot.

"I waited for more. But she did not know of

any other passages, except one leading to the rear of the house.

" 'What about the well?'

" 'She did not like that either, because she thought *he* put his money there.'

" 'Did he?'

" 'Perhaps he did. She used to put money in one place, he into another, and I think he put some money into the smoke room. He was always around there. Always watching each other. Watch me, too. Back of the house used to be where he could hide. People always looking for Johnny. Runners.'

" 'Who was Mr. Birch?'

" 'Johnny had a lot to do with his house, but he was away a lot and so there was always some man here while he was away.'

" 'Who paid for the house originally?'

" 'I think Johnny.'

" 'Why did he want this house?'

" 'When he got enough money, he would come here and stay forever. He could not stay long ever, went back to the sea, and she came.'

"I tried another tack.

" 'Who was Don Pedro?' That was the name given the pirate in the popular tale.

"She had heard the name, but could not place it.

" 'What about Mary Wallace?'

" 'Mary Wallace was Mary *Birch*,' the ghost said, as if correcting me. 'She had several names.'

" 'Why?'

" 'Because she had several husbands.'

"Logical enough if true.

" 'Wallace lived here a little while, I think,' she added.

" 'Who was first, Wallace or Birch?'

" 'Birch. Mary Wallace, Mary Birch, is good enough.'

"Did the name Philip Babb mean anything to her?'

" 'She had a little boy named Philip,' the ghost said, and I thought, why not? After all, they had named Mary for the pirate's mother, why not reciprocate and name *her* son for the old man? Especially with all that loot around.

" 'If I don't go now, she'll wake up,' the girl said. 'Philip Babb, Philip Babb, he was somewhere in the back room. That was his room. I remember him.'

" 'How did Philip get on with Johnny?' I wanted to know if they were one and the same person or not.

" 'Not so good,' the ghost said. 'Johnny did not like men here, you know.'

"I promised to watch out for Mary, and sent the girl on her way.

"I then brought Sybil out of trance.

"A few moments later, we decided to start our treasure hunt in the garden, following the instructions given us by Mary Degan, girl ghost.

"Sybil was told nothing more than to go outside and let her intuition lead her toward any spot she thought important. The rest of us followed her like spectators at the National Open Golf Tournament.

"We did not have to walk far. About twenty yards from the house, near some beautiful iris in bloom, we located the three stones. The one in the middle looked indeed somewhat like a lion's head, when viewed at a distance. I asked the others in the group to look at it. There was no doubt about it. If there was a lion's head on the grounds, this was it. What lay underneath? What was underneath the hearthstone in the house itself?

"The Russells promised to get a mine detector to examine the area involved. If there was metal in the ground, it would show up on the instrument. Meanwhile, the lore about Ocean-Born Mary had been enriched by the presence in the nether world of Mary Degan, servant girl, and the intriguing picture of two pirates—Johnny and Philip Babb. Much of this is very difficult to trace. But the fact is that Sybil Leek, who came to Henniker a total stranger, was able, in trance, to tell about a man at sea, a Mary, a pirate treasure, hidden passages, a child named Philip, four children of Mary and the presence of a spook in the loom room upstairs. All of this has been checked as entirely correct.

"Why should not the rest be true also? Including, perhaps, the elusive treasure?

"Time will tell."

For several minutes Paul and Sybil were

silent, thinking over what they had just heard. Then Paul spoke first.

"Well, it's obvious to me that the treasure is still there, somewhere, waiting to be found."

Sybil shook her head. "What, after all those years? Don't you think someone has been up there since the book was published and found it?"

"That remains to be seen," Paul replied. "My gut feeling tells me that it is still there, waiting to be discovered."

"And what do you propose to do about it?" Sybil demanded to know. She already knew the answer in her heart.

"We're going to go up there, day after tomorrow."

And so they did.

Chapter Eleven

At first Paul and Sybil had a difficult time convincing the inhabitants of the Ocean-Born Mary house in Henniker to let them visit. Of course they didn't tell them who they were or why they came; Paul thought it best to inform them that they were history buffs who had heard a great deal about the old house and were interested in New England architecture of past centuries. He also offered to pay twenty dollars for a specially arranged guided tour. All of this got them into the house.

But what about the treasure? Paul wondered. How was he going to have a chance to look for what? He felt that it was not an easy thing to discover without proper instruments, such as a metal detector. But on the other hand, if he could only get into the house for a few hours alone without the owners being present, perhaps his instinct might tell them where to look.

But all attempts to lure the owners, an elderly couple named Smythe, away from the house for even an hour, failed. They were suspicious of all strangers, especially those who came from New York City, and it was clear that Paul and Sybil were not exactly welcome once the tour had ended. Even his mentioning that they, too, were New Hampshire people now didn't help. Dejected, Paul and Sybil returned to their New England weekend house and not much was said about the matter for several days. Then, just as suddenly, the sober mood vanished and an air of expectancy returned to Paul's demeanor.

"I've got it," he said. "I know exactly what we must do."

Sybil shook her head. "Are you still trying to dig in that house in Henniker?"

"Yes," he replied, "and so will you."

As soon as he returned to New York City at the beginning of the week, he spent several hours on the telephone, without telling Sybil what he was doing. He was arranging an elaborate scheme for a special lottery, the winners of which would be the couple who owned the house. It might cost him as much as five or six thousand dollars but he was willing to risk that. The prize was much greater. Two weeks later the lottery tickets had been printed and he managed to get them into the hands of the Smythes. His hunch paid off. He had suspected them to be greedy enough to fall for the scheme, and so they did. They did not realize that this was a sting operation and that they were, in fact, the only ones who held tickets.

Another week passed. Then the lottery-organizer informed the Smythes that they had won first prize. The prize consisted of $500 and a free weekend in New York City. While this was going on, Paul visibly nervous, told Sybil what he had done. She thought it was very clever and hoped it would succeed. Sure enough, the Smythes accepted the challenge and the following week they packed up and left the house and went to New York for their lottery weekend, giving Paul two and a half full days to look for the treasure up in New Hampshire.

It was a lucky thing that Paul and Sybil's car did not encounter the Smythes' ancient jalopy on the road, so closely had he timed their arrival and the Smythes' departure for New York City. But he didn't want to wait a single minute. He knew, of course, that the Smythes had probably tipped off the local police department about watching the house in their absence. But that didn't bother him. If the author of *Yankee Ghosts* was right, there was no treasure inside the house, only the body of the pirate underneath the fireplace. The treasure was outside the house, underneath or near those big white stones, now almost invisible among the bushes. Paul had the latest electronic equipment with him, enabling him to discover anything metallic in the soil.

When they arrived at the house, it was mid afternoon and the light was still good. Should there be an encounter with a police officer, Paul was prepared to present himself as a visiting member of an historical society who had heard about the house and regretfully found the owners absent. To make sure his visit was not a total loss he and his wife wanted to look around the outside to get a feeling for the place. He was sure that no policeman could object to that. But he hoped that the surveillance of the house, if any, would only start at night and concern itself primarily with anyone trying to break into the house, which was not his intention.

Fortunately, he remembered where to look from his first visit. Quickly unpacking his equipment he went to work, with Sybil assisting him to the best of her ability. There was nothing, absolutely nothing. Not the slightest sign of anything metallic. Getting more and more upset, Paul took the equipment to other areas all around the house. The result was negative.

In desperation, because it was getting darker and darker, he took out two shovels and, together with Sybil, began to dig near the grave stones where Sybil Leek had indicated the treasure might be. This time there was something. His shovel hit on something hard. Feverishly, following through with his bare hands, he managed to pull out a little box, which almost fell apart in his hands.

The box was made of metal, but the metal had rusted. Inside there was something white or yellowish. He brushed aside the earth which had penetrated the box and cautiously, slowly, unfolded the piece of parchment inside.

"Not here," Sybil said, somehow fearing that they might be discovered. "Let's take this away from the house first."

"You're right," Paul agreed. He put the piece of parchment into his pocket, quickly covered the hole in the ground and, almost as if they were being pursued, the couple went back to their car and departed.

As soon as they had reached a quiet spot where they could pull off the road, he stopped the car and together they looked at his find. What they had in their hands was a yellowish piece of parchment, not very large, but in relatively good condition. The ink on it, brownish and spotted, had long faded but enough could be made out for them to read what had been written on it.

"Fool! You who disturb my rest shall find nothing. I killed him for nothing and you shall have nothing. John Howell has the last laugh after all, you fool. Yet I am glad I killed him for he wasn't one of us truly. Let there be no memory of Don Pedro and let there be warning to those who would assume his name: John Howell abused the honorable profession of the high seas and he lost his life over it. So be it. I have nothing to regret when I meet my maker. John Howell deserved what he received. Thomas Masterson, written in the year of our Lord 1769."

With an exclamation of disappointment, Paul dropped the piece of parchment. He looked at Sybil and smiled a wry smile. "We've come here for nothing," he said and started the engine.

"No," she replied. "We've come here to discover the truth."

"What do you mean?" Paul said as he slowly drove toward New York City.

"The truth," Sybil replied. "The truth is that the treasure is not at Henniker, but perhaps it *is* somewhere else."

"Of course!" Paul exclaimed. "It has been moved. It must have been moved!"

They almost flew back to New York City. Paul's enthusiasm was ten-fold now. He realized he had been barking up the wrong tree, so to speak, and had gone to the wrong house. But where to look? Where would he find the next lead? By now he was determined to unravel the secret of the treasure assembled by the late pirate Don Pedro. Nothing would stop him until he was successful.

As soon as he had some free time Paul went to the New York Public Library and asked to be shown the material they had on pirates of the late eighteenth century. There was quite a bit of it and the librarian warned him that it would take several weeks to work his way through it all, but Paul didn't mind. He was determined to succeed with his search. Aided and abetted by his fiancee he spent evenings and weekends at the library, going through every scrap of information about the pirates who roamed the seas off the American coast between 1700 and 1800.

In the end his search was crowned by success. After four weeks of gruelling research, he came across a mention of a book entitled *Pirate Lore* by one W.H. Carson, printed in London in 1964. This long forgotten work was said to contain the life histories of several famous pirates, among them Don Pedro, supposedly an English nobleman in disguise.

That was all Paul needed. The book, fortunately, was in the library, rare though it was, and within two or three hours after his discovery he held it in his trembling hands. His disappointment was profound when he found that the part dealing with Don Pedro was no more than a page and a half. But his eyes widened when he started to read. There were two paragraphs that caught his eye immediately.

"Don Pedro, alias Philip Babb, alias John Howell, was murdered by one of his own mates and presumably lies buried in New Hampshire at the Ocean-Born Mary house. As for his fabulous treasure, if it exists, legend has it that it lies buried in the sands of Long Island in the midst of an Indian burial ground near the little village of Amityville. Whether this is true or not we cannot say.

"One source mentions the rumor that the treasure includes a fabulous precious stone, known as Queen Anne's Opal. It is said that the opal was stolen from a Tibetan monastery and brings a curse on those who possess it. Perhaps, at the moment of his violent death, Don Pedro found time to regret that the ill-fated opal formed part of his treasure."

Paul looked up from the book and, almost as if he were in a trance, returned it to the librarian. He signed out of the library and went home. At last he knew what to do next.

Chapter Twelve

For a while Paul practically lived at the New
York Public Library, in the special section
reserved for local geneological research.
With the help of Sybil, and using every free
moment at his disposal, including weekends,
he tried to discover additional evidence
linking Don Pedro of Henniker, New Hampshire, with the short mention of the pirate
treasure on Long Island.

However much he read, he could discover
nothing further. All he had to go on was the
small amount of information he already had.
He could not spend more time on his search
without endangering his position with the advertising agency. Already his boss was
wondering why he was coming in late and
looking so haggard in the morning. Giving

him a knowing smile and suggesting it was his lovemaking that had caused this, got Paul off the hook for a while. But he realized that he could not go on much longer without risking his job.

"Enough is enough," he said one Saturday afternoon and took Sybil by the arm and walked out of the library, vowing not to return for a long, long time. Sybil was glad to hear it because she had become pretty bored with all this. If she had not loved Paul as much as she did, she would have walked out on the situation long before this. But, on the other hand, she had been swept up in the adventure of searching for the treasure, elusive though it might be. When Paul decided to stop looking for additional documents and get down to the search itself, she sighed with relief. Direct action was more her style.

"What do you intend to do about it?" she asked.

"Well," he replied, "this Amityville area isn't all that large. I think we should start by going out there tomorrow."

No sooner said than done. The couple arrived in Amityville, Long Island, where they visited the library and discovered that there had indeed been an Indian burial ground in the area. Paul and Sybil were intrigued to hear that it was believed to be on or near the site of 112 Ocean Avenue, the place where all those murders had happened, back in 1974.

Next, the couple tried to gather information from the "friendly townspeople." They were amazed to find that their questions produced nothing but closed mouths at the very mention of anything strange or supernatural connected with that house. It appeared that the townspeople simply did not wish to acknowledge the existence of anything unusual in their midst. Finally, with some prodding and a five dollar bill, he managed to elicit some information from the local bartender.

" 'Tis like this," the man said with a heavy Irish brogue. "They all know about it but no one wants to own up to it. The house, you know, was the scene of all that mayhem, and the townspeople don't like it. No, they don't like it one bit."

"I know that," Paul replied calmly, "but I would like to research it. I am writing a thesis," he added, when the bartender looked at him suspiciously. Was he perhaps one of those nosy journalists trying to write another sensational story for the Sunday sections, bringing a lot of unwanted tourists? the barkeep wondered. But this man did not look like a journalist.

"No," he replied, "I suppose there is no harm in that. But you are on your own sir. I cannot help you." And with that, five dollar bill or not, the barkeep turned and tended to other customers, leaving Paul and Sybil no alternative but to leave.

It wasn't difficult to find the house and they drove up to it, simply following a map.

There it was, 112 Ocean Avenue. They parked the car and got out. Paul rang the bell. He kept on trying for several minutes, but no one came to answer.

"I suppose they think we are curious tourists," Paul finally said with a shrug. "I can't say I blame them."

Nothing stirred inside the house, so they got back into the car and drove to the nearest real estate office. The sigh read "James Riley, Properties."

"I have an idea," Paul said. "Perhaps we could rent the place."

Mr. Riley, a ruddy-faced, rather jolly man in his fifties, was noncommital. Oh, yes, he knew about the house in question. Yes, it was occupied and so far as he knew, the owners did not have any intention of either selling or renting the house to anyone.

"What would it take to convince them, say for a month of so?" Paul asked. He looked at the real estate man with the air of a multi-millionaire from Texas. But the man was not impressed.

"Oh, I don't know. They may not want to at any price. What figure do you have in mind?"

The question caught Paul by surprise. He swiftly calculated what he could venture in this situation. "Well, suppose you offer them a thousand dollars a month for two months on our behalf."

"But why?" Mr. Riley said. "Why would you want to rent that particular house, unless it is because of . . . well, you know what I am talking about."

"Precisely," Paul replied, brazenly, "precisely that. We have read about it and we would like to experience the thrill of spending some time in that house. We are not afraid. We are crime buffs, and this is part of our research. We happen to have a month of vacation coming up," he lied, "and it would be the perfect place to spend it. Would fifteen hundred dollars a month do it?"

Mr. Riley shook his head. "I really don't know, but I will take your offer to them. Why don't you give me a call tomorrow morning?" The matter was closed so far as he was concerned.

"Wait a moment," Paul said. "Why don't you ask them what they want for a one month rental? Of course, we will guarantee that we will leave the place in the same condition we find it."

"That's understood," Mr. Riley said, glancing at his watch. "Leave it to me. Like I said, call me tomorrow morning."

There was nothing more to be said. It was clear to Paul that if he were to enter the house it would have to be done with the owners' approval. He was prepared to pay any amount, but that was not, as yet, necessary. So far he had done quite well, he thought. The bait was out. He could not imagine that the owner of this house, who was, as far as he knew, a middle class man of modest means, would refuse fifteen hundred dollars for a month's rent. But then again, he couldn't be sure.

That night Paul could hardly fall asleep. Tossing restlessly in his bed, he finally drifted off to a fitful doze, during which he spoke of Amityville, several times awakening his fiancee.

Early the next day he called Mr. Riley, fearing that the answer would be no. But to his surprise the man sounded a lot more friendly this time.

"Well now," the voice on the other end of the telephone said, "it appears that the owners of the house feel not entirely unfavorably toward your request."

"Great," Paul said. "What do they want?"

But Mr. Riley was in no hurry to tell him. "Why don't you come on out and we will talk about it? These things are best discussed in person."

"Well, of course, I will be glad to do that," Paul replied. "But have they given you any indication of their demands?"

"Yes, they have," Mr. Riley said, without the slightest change of voice. "Come on out and we will discuss it."

There was a click on the telephone and Paul realized that the conversation was over. These Long Islanders! he thought. They are worse than the New Englanders. But he realized there was nothing he could do but obey. As soon as he could that afternoon, he excused himself at the office and drove out to

Amityville by himself. Sybil refused to come along this time. She had things to do in the city. When he arrived at the real estate office it was already seven p.m., but the man had offered to wait for him.

After a handshake and the other polite preliminaries, Paul looked at the man expectantly, waiting for the news. And the news was not long in coming.

"To begin with . . ." Mr. Riley said, then paused infuriatingly to light his pipe, "they want an insurance policy for five hundred thousand dollars to make sure that nothing in the house is disturbed."

"Five hundred thousand dollars!" Paul exclaimed. "Why, the house isn't worth anything like that!"

"To them it is," Mr. Riley replied. "Want to hear the rest?"

Paul nodded.

"In addition," the real estate man continued, "in addition you will not publicize your visit here for any reason whatsoever; furthermore, you will guarantee that any journalists or other curious people will not be encouraged to come here while you are in residence."

"I have no intention of publicizing our visit, not at all."

"Good," said the real estate man. "Then that is not a problem. Now we come to the final condition—money."

"Yes," Paul said. "What do they want? For one month, remember."

"Yes, I remember. Five thousand dollars—take it or leave it."

Paul was shocked. "Five thousand dollars for one month's rent! *That* house?"

"That house," Mr. Riley nodded. "Precisely. Are you interested?"

Paul gasped. He had not been prepared for that. But he had come this far and there was no turning back now. "Draw up the contract," he said, swallowing hard. "When can we move in?"

"In two weeks' time, the first of the month," the real estate agent said. "They will take a little vacation. The money will go toward it."

With that Mr. Riley got up and went to another desk at the far end of the room. He opened the drawer, took out some papers, returned to Paul and put the papers in front of him.

"What's that?" Paul asked.

"That's the agreement," the other man said. "All you have to do is sign it and give me a check."

"You mean you already prepared the agreement?" Paul said with amazement. "Suppose I hadn't agreed to it?"

"Oh, but you would have. I can tell when a customer is ready. You were coming for a closing, not an inquiry."

Paul silently cursed himself for having been so eager, but he signed the document without even reading it. He then drew out a check and made it out to Mr. Riley. Five thousand dollars for one month's rent. Well, it wasn't going to ruin him, he thought; still, it was a lot of money.

The two men shook hands and Paul left to go back to the city. All of a sudden he felt very hungry and tired. It was time for dinner, he thought, but there was more to it than that. His energy had been sapped. He was glad to get away.

"Be back on the first," Mr. Riley said, as he followed Paul out of the office, closing up for the night.

Chapter Thirteen

Sybil thought the idea of moving into an accursed house just marvelous, for deep in her heart she always had had her doubts about the validity of such curses and about occult phenomena in general. The idea of a vacation in such off surroundings somehow stimulated her romantic interest in Paul. She was glad he had decided to pursue the matter further.

One of these days, she thought, Paul would decide to marry her. That was what she had wanted all along, but in this modern age where people live together sometimes for a lifetime without taking formal vows, she hadn't thought of pressing the point. She was quite content to let matters stay as they were, because Paul took very good care of her and there was always the remote possibility that she would not want to go further than their present, rather liberal arrangement. She had a well-paying job of her own, all the security she wanted, and she wasn't really dependent on Paul economically. On the other hand, living with him prevented her from having any other entanglements with other men and, while it provided her with emotional security, it also kept her from a whole world of otherwise enticing males. Paul represented to her all that she wanted in a man, even though occasionally he would drive her up the wall with his peculiar insistence on things that didn't really matter all that much. But then nobody was perfect, Sybil argued with herself, and there was a deep bond between them which, while not perhaps passionate love, was the next best thing to it.

All in all, she looked forward to having a vacation with him in such a thrilling place as that house in Amityville, Long Island. Her enthusiasm mounted as they packed the belongings they would take with them.

When they arrived at the house with a van attached to their car, excitement ran high in both of them. True to the agreement, the owners had left everything intact, for after all they were covered for any possible damage.

There was no one there to receive them. The real estate agent had provided them with the keys and apparently word of their temporary residence in the house had not spread, for there was no one standing around, waiting for their arrival or wondering what they were doing there. That was just as well, for Paul was not prepared to answer any questions at this point. Among his luggage was a certain kind of equipment generally used to determine metal in the ground or radiation levels in the area. He had rented it to determine whether, in fact, there were any unexpected energies or influences in that house. No, Paul had insisted all along, this wasn't going to be a fishing expedition but rather a scientific experiment, hopefully crowned by ultimate success.

On this Sunday morning Paul and Sybil unloaded the truck, put their belongings piecemeal into the house, parked the car and the van, and went inside. The whole operation took less than an hour and again it was fortunate that there weren't any passersby. But at eleven in the morning, people were either at home sleeping off "the night before" or in church. The house seemed oddly cold when they entered it. The furniture was, of course, all in place and Paul couldn't help wondering at the bad taste of the present owner, who had furnished it rather garishly in a contemporary style. But that was the owners' business and he knew that they would have to live with it for a month.

They decided to set up their headquarters in the largest of the bedrooms on the second floor, to the left of the stairwell. This was actually the master bedroom where the present owners slept. Within the hour, Sybil had rearranged things slightly so that the room took on some of their own individuality, putting the knick-knacks left behind by the owners into a corner or under the bed.

The house was clean and yet there was an ominous feeling of a *presence* everywhere they went. Both Sybil and Paul sensed it. Was this because of what they knew about the house and their expectancy of strange phenomena, or because there was, in fact, something in the house that the eye could not see? Whatever the reason, it didn't bother them: that is one of the advantages of being well-trained in the pursuit of strange adventure; you grow used to the unfamiliar. But they acknowledged to each other that there was indeed something peculiar about the house.

By now it was one o'clock in the afternoon and both felt pangs of hunger. Fortunately, they had brought with them enough food for the day, for they had decided to avoid going shopping that Sunday, giving them a chance to get acquainted with the house first. Sybil had put the food in the refrigerator downstairs while Paul roamed around the house inspecting the rest of the rooms. There was nothing particularly sensational about them, yet the same cold, clammy feeling pervaded every one of them. Undoubtedly, Paul thought, the residue of those terrible DeFeo murders clings to the atmosphere, a phenomenon well-known in parapsychology.

When he heard what he thought was Sybil's voice calling him to come downstairs for lunch, he replied, "Coming, darling," and started to descend the stairs. At this moment a strong gust of wind hit him in the rear. Had he not quickly grabbed the wooden stair railing, he would have fallen helter-skelter down the stairs. He descended in the normal way and walked into the kitchen, a little shaken by the experience. He expected Sybil to have lunch ready on the table, but she was nowhere to be seen in the kitchen. That's odd, Paul thought. Why did she call if she isn't ready? He sat down to wait. After two or three minutes, when nothing happened, and Sybil did not return, he began to call out for her. Her voice answered him but it sounded muffled, as if she were far away. After a moment of reflection, he realized that Sybil was in the downstairs bathroom.

"Come on out," he shouted.

The muffled voice of his fiancee replied. "I can't, I can't! Come and get me."

Paul jumped to his feet and raced to the bathroom. He easily opened the door from the outside. "What's the matter with you? Is your imagination running wild?" he said as a somewhat pale Sybil emerged.

"Imagination, nothing!" she replied in a tone of anger mixed with fear. "I went to the bathroom and then I couldn't open the door from the inside. Something or someone held it."

"Oh, come on," Paul said incredulously.

But he knew that his reassurance was hollow.

So the house was still haunted. Nothing much was said between them as they walked into the kitchen. Sybil began to prepare lunch. After a moment of thoughtful silence, she began, "If this sort of thing is going to continue I am going to leave here. I didn't come here to fight ghosts."

"Don't worry about it. This is just their— well, reception committee, telling us they are still here. They are probably harmless."

"*Probably!*" she almost shouted. "How do we know?"

Paul did not know what to say. He decided not to tell her about his little adventure on the staircase.

It was a good lunch, though Sybil had prepared it in a hurry. It helped calm their nerves. Suddenly Paul felt rather tired, more so than he expected to be. But then it had been a hectic morning; loading and unloading all the luggage took its toll, he thought. "I think I am going to lie down for half an hour or so," he announced and arose.

"I'm tired too," she said. "I guess all the excitement and all the things we had to do this morning caused it."

"Of course." He took her by the hand and together they went upstairs to the bedroom. There they loosened their clothing, took off their shoes and lay down on the bed. So tired had they become that within seconds they were both fast asleep.

The following morning they arose, having slept for eighteen hours. They felt refreshed and yet strangely remote from all that was going on around them. It seemed as if an invisible curtain had descended between their minds and the outside world; and yet they were functioning normally, as they went about the business of making breakfast. They thought that it was simply the aftermath of all the strain they had gone through during the previous day.

They spent the rest of the morning acquainting themselves with the surrounding area, taking a walk up and down Ocean Avenue and looking at some of the other houses nearby. Somehow they felt alien in this environment, not at all as they had hoped they would feel. Two houses down the street someone peered out of a window at them; as soon as they looked up, the person withdrew rapidly. It seemed almost as if people were afraid to encounter them. Paul immediately dismissed this notion because, after all, who knew about them? Who knew what they were up to? As if she had read his thoughts, Sybil said, "I don't think the townspeople like us very much."

"What makes you think so?" Paul countered, although he knew in his heart she was right.

"It seemed awfully empty," Sybil said.

"What do you expect?" Paul replied. "Maybe everyone's having lunch."

"Are they?" Sybil said. "Or are they simply

keeping to themselves and don't want anything to do with us?"

"Well now," Paul replied soothingly, "it may well be that they don't take kindly to people from the city, but that generally is the attitude out here, I should think."

"Maybe," Sybil replied, not convinced.

Nothing more was spoken and they returned to the house. The rest of the day went quickly; they spent most of the time unpacking. Later, they went out once again to shop for additional supplies.

Over dinner Paul told Sybil that he had arranged to take the entire period off from work in order to do what they had set out to do properly. Sybil was somewhat surprised, for she knew that the amount of money that he would lose in this matter was more than he could afford. She, too, had taken time off.

"Don't worry about it," Paul said. "I had two weeks coming anyway, and I am taking two extra weeks off without pay."

The following morning their search began in earnest. Paul connected his electrical equipment in order to cover every inch of ground inside and outside the house, to see if anything metallic was hidden in the ground. Sybil helped him set up the equipment and then divided her time between looking after domestic chores and anxiously peering out the window to see if he had discovered anything yet.

Paul found nothing on the first day and nothing on the second. He finished his inch-by-inch coverage of the house and grounds in the afternoon of the third day, trailed dispiritedly into the sitting-room, slumped into an easy chair and shook his head.

"I don't understand it. Nothing. Absolutely nothing."

"Is the equipment working properly?" Sybil enquired.

Paul nodded. He knew everything was in order. How could there be no results? There had to be some metallic objects in the grounds; maybe not a treasure but some nails or some broken piece of metal. But nothing, absolutely nothing had been discovered. He simply could not understand.

At the end of the fourth day of their residence Sybil convinced him that perhaps there was something wrong with the equipment or, if not the equipment, with the way he handled it. Paul reluctantly agreed and telephoned a friend who knew someone in the Army Corps of Engineers who might be able to help. The following day a man by the name of Charles Rogers arrived and unpacked some equipment very similar to Paul's. Mr. Rogers, or rather Captain Rogers, was an expert with the metal detector. There was no question as to the knowledge he possessed nor about the excellent condition of his equipment. Yet he did not turn up any metallic objects either. He departed the following day, shaking his head and regretting that he had not been of some use.

But news of the arrival of Captain Rogers

had gotten around the village. People kept appearing in the street, staring at the house. At first only villagers became aware of the change in occupancy, but somehow word got around outside Amityville as well. Strangers came to gape at the house; cars drove slowly past it. All this attention did not go down well with Paul, not to mention Sybil, because it happened at all hours of the day and night.

Around this time, Sybil noticed a strange change in Paul's behavior, which could not be entirely blamed on the curious bystanders outside or on his failure to discover the treasure. Where once he had been gentle and charming, he was now curt and nervous. More than once he cut her off in the middle of a sentence, something he had never done before.

They were now in the middle of their second week of residence in the house. While it was in some ways a vacation, in other ways the strain and expectancy of their quest was far from restful. Even Sybil began to become a bit neurotic about the whole thing, although she enjoyed the hunt. What worried her more and more every day was the increasing strangeness of Paul's manner. His face seemed oddly tense, and his eyes had taken on a nervous flicker which she had not noticed previously.

It was toward the end of the second week that there was a knock on the door. When Paul went to open it, he found a young man standing outside, who identified himself as a reporter from the *Long Island Journal*. He wanted a story.

"A story about what?" Paul exploded. "There is no story in this house!"

"Yes there is," the young man said. "May I come in?"

"Certainly not," Paul replied and slammed the door. The anger was still plainly visible on his face as he returned to Sybil. "The nerve of this guy, coming here trying to get a story from me! Some story he could get. Failure—nothing works. I don't understand it."

"Look," Sybil said, trying to calm him, "why don't we just call it quits and go home? We had a good try."

"What!" Paul exploded again and hit the table with his fist. "After all that I have put into this? I've got to have that treasure. I'm not going to leave here without it."

Sybil had never seen him like this. There was a look of greed on his face, as if getting the treasure was now a matter of life and death. And so it was, for Paul, at least. It had become a quest he refused to abandon. No matter how long it would take, no matter what he had to do, he had come here to find Don Pedro's treasure and he was not going to give up.

Sybil thought for a moment. "Perhaps we ought to try bringing in a psychic, to see what she can pick up?" she suggested, fearful that he might explode again. But to her surprise Paul only stared at her, thinking it over.

"An excellent idea," he finally said. "Yes, that is exactly what we ought to do. We need a good medium to help us find the treasure."

"I am sure this will help and maybe we will get some leads that we can follow up on," Sybil said. "Do you know anyone who might be able to help?"

"Well now," Paul replied, scratching his head, "I am not terribly well-informed about mediums and clairvoyants, but I do recall having read about a very famous one who used to be a vocal coach and then became a medium for many years. I wonder if she is still around."

"What was her name?" Sybil asked.

"Edith Mason—no, *Ena* Mason . . . Ena Mason, that's it! I remember now. There was a big piece about her in one of the newspapers at the time when she solved the Rubenstein murder case, remember?"

"No, as a matter of fact, I don't," Sybil replied. "If you think she will do, why not call her?"

"I will. I will," Paul said. For a moment the old Paul seemed to be back again, but only for an instant. The glint in his eyes was back a second later; his hands trembled as he looked through the telephone directory for the medium's number. But Ena Mason was not listed in the Manhattan telephone directory.

"How do you know she lives in Manhattan," Sybil asked, quite logically. Paul agreed that she had a point.

The following morning he called the American Society for Psychical Research and enquired about the whereabouts of Ena Mason. He was told she lived in Connecticut and he was given her phone number and address. That evening Paul seemed almost his old self again.

Chapter Fourteen

When Paul had reached her, Ena Mason agreed to come to the house, but not until the following weekend. Her clients kept her busy and there were bookings for months ahead. But Paul insisted and offered to double her usual fee.

"It isn't the money," Mrs. Mason said. "I have obligations to these people. They have been waiting a long time to see me, but I promise I will come on the first available day. You will have to be satisfied with that."

Finally the weekend came and Ena Mason arrived promptly at eight p.m. as she had promised. Mrs. Mason was in her sixties, and she was of stately appearance, very poised and obviously in full control of her abilities. She arrived driven by her husband who left and promised to return promptly two hours later.

"Two hours!" Paul exclaimed. "Do you think you can finish this in two hours?"

"Yes, I can," Mrs. Mason replied. "I have done this sort of thing before." With that she entered the house and began to walk around slowly, as if to take in the atmosphere first. "Terrible, terrible," she mumbled, more to herself than to her hosts. "This house has very bad vibrations—killings, death all over the place."

"Yes, we know that," Paul said, somewhat impatiently. "This is the DeFeo murder house, you know. It's pretty famous."

"Oh?" Mrs. Mason said. It was obvious she had not given it a thought or perhaps she didn't even know about it. Paul would not accept the latter explanation. As far as he was concerned, everyone must know about the house, including Mrs. Mason. He was so obsessed with 112 Ocean Avenue and the treasure it might contain that he felt everyone must feel as he did. He didn't realize that a busy medium such as Mrs. Mason couldn't care less about one more haunted house. To her they were all part of her job.

Slowly she went up to the third floor, looking into every room, followed closely by Paul and Sybil. "The vibrations in the house, as I said, are very bad. Their presence is here, all over the place; people who have been killed and cannot find rest. We must release them."

"Well, now," Paul said and there was an

edge to his voice, "that's all well and good, but the real reason . . ."

"Shush," Sybil said before he could go any further.

"Of course, we understand," Sybil said to Mrs. Mason. "If there are any unhappy souls hanging on in this atmosphere, by all means, let us release them."

More and more Paul's insistence on finding the treasure did not sit well with her. Sybil was no longer skeptical about the occult. She felt sorry for the spirits who had remained behind in the atmosphere of their passing; she felt the suffering and the terrible feeling of being lost between two worlds which they brought with them, and it troubled her a great deal.

"Well, now," Mrs. Mason said, "let us sit down somewhere and begin."

They went back to the ground floor, and in the living room Mrs. Mason took a comfortable easy chair near the fireplace, sat back in it, removed her shoes and closed her eyes. Paul and Sybil sat opposite her, waiting for what would happen next. They had never been to a seance. They had never been in the presence of a medium of the stature of Mrs. Mason and all this was quite new to them. But somehow they felt they were getting nearer to the solution of their quest and that there would be some movement at last towards the finding of the treasure. Perhaps they would also learn about other things they had not counted on, but which were part and parcel of the atmosphere in the house.

For the first time Sybil felt afraid. Paul, however, was so engrossed in the treasure hunt and what it meant to him, that nothing else mattered.

After several moments during which Mrs. Mason seemed to fall asleep, followed by heavy breathing, her body shook violently and she sat bolt upright. Her face was seemingly possessed by another personality, although her eyes remained closed. When she spoke, at first in a faint, trembling voice but gradually gaining in strength, it was in a man's voice.

"This is my land. You are intruders. Go or I will kill you."

"My God!" Sybil exclaimed, her hands reaching for her throat. "What is this?"

But of course Mrs. Mason could not answer them. She had left her body and allowed it to be taken over temporarily by an entity from the past. From the facial expression that now confronted Paul and Sybil it was clear that it was an Indian who was using the medium to communicate. Sybil remembered the research they had done about the area. Again the strange voice came from the lips of the entranced medium:

"Go while you can. This is my land. No one will stay here and live. No white man shall be on this land. This is my land."

Paul could not contain himself any longer. Not having been prepared for this nor having had any training in how to act in such circumstances, he jumped up and said, "I must find the treasure. I must find it. That's why I came here!"

The voice coming from the lips of the entranced medium was even more tremulous now, and there was a tinge of anger in it. "Treasure not yours. Whoever touches treasure shall die. Beware! You have been warned!"

But this only enraged Paul further. "Nonsense," he shouted. "I have a right to find it. I have worked hard for it. That treasure is mine!"

Once again the Indian spoke through the medium. "Beware, white man, or you shall die."

Suddenly Mrs. Mason fell back into the chair, almost collapsing. Paul jumped to his feet. "Don't touch her," Sybil said, remembering having read somewhere that you should not touch a medium while she is in trance. The two of them stood there waiting for Mrs. Mason to recover. After a moment of heavy breathing, she opened her eyes, seemingly unaware of what had transpired.

"Are you all right?" Sybil enquired, a little worried, because she had never witnessed anything like this.

"Of course I am all right," the medium said tartly. She rose from the chair, stretching and yawning, as if she had just slept for many hours. Paul and Sybil were not aware that this was how a trance medium usually felt after a heavy session.

"This was really terrifying," Sybil said. "I mean, the Indian and all that."

"Indian?" the medium enquired. "What Indian?"

"You mean you don't remember anything?" Paul asked incredulously.

"As a rule I don't," the medium replied, "because I am not really *there*. You see, when I go into a deep trance state, my true self, my personality, is absent from my body. It sort of lingers on in the immediate vicinity connected with the body by a thin rod of energy made of something parapsychologists call ectoplasm. You can't see it, but it's there just the same. If it were severed, I would die instantly."

"I see," Paul said. "While you are away, what happens to your body?"

"The whole point in deep trance mediumship," Mrs. Mason explained patiently, realizing that she had a neophyte on her hands, "the whole point is that you lend your body, as it were, to an entity, to a spirit, who wishes to communicate through it with those in the flesh, such as you and your lady. There are very few of us deep trance mediums around because it is a very exacting, very tiring kind of work. Also, you really have to know your business and you have to learn to relax completely so that there is no interference with the entity wishing to come through. Of course there are times when it is undesirable because the entity is dangerous, disturbed, or otherwise not in a position to operate the body of the medium properly. There are always dangers involved, you understand. But since I have done this for some thirty odd years, I have learned to cope with any potential dangers or problems."

"Then when you are outside your body, so to speak," said Sybil, more and more engrossed in what she had heard, "how does the stranger, I mean the spirit, enter your body and speak through you?"

"That is pretty simple, really, if you look at it from their point of view," the medium replied and sat down again. "It is as if they were putting on a shirt or a suit, slipping into the top of my head, where one of the principle solar plexus is located. The other one is in the stomach region. Once they are in the body, they will then operate it very much the same way a driver operates an automobile. Naturally it seems strange to them at first, and sometimes they have difficulties adjusting to my particular vibrations. But by and large spirits learn to adapt to the new surrounding, the new body, pretty well. Usually there is a guide present—a superior spirit who is in charge of the communication, and who helps if there are problems."

"Pretty well arranged, isn't it?" Paul said and smiled. "I really didn't know any of this. I've read a little about parapsychology, but the way you present it, it sounds all so simple."

"It's far from that, young man," Mrs. Mason said sternly. "It is much more complicated than I make it sound. It's just that I am so used to it that to me it seems natural, which it is, and uncomplicated. But I wouldn't suggest that anyone not properly trained should attempt to do what I do."

"Not a chance," Paul said and shook his head. "I wouldn't recommend it to anyone. It looked pretty scary, what went on. Of course, you don't remember any of it, do you?"

Mrs. Mason shook her head.

"Do you want me to tell you about it?" Paul said.

Again Mrs. Mason shook her head. "That won't be necessary. As long as you remember everything that came through and draw your own conclusions from it."

"I have," Paul replied, becoming more businesslike about the whole thing now. "What do we do next?"

"Well, now," Mrs. Mason said, "you are, I believe, looking for something in this house."

"That is entirely correct. In fact it is an understatement," Paul said.

"Has the entity who spoke through me been helpful at all?" Mrs. Mason enquired.

"Helpful? Far from it!" Paul shouted. "In fact, he threatened us if we didn't leave this place."

"That's too bad," Mrs. Mason replied, matter of factly, "but it sometimes happens, especially when Indians are involved . . ."

"Now what do we do to find what I am looking for? Is there any way that you could use ESP?" Paul asked.

"Indeed there is," Mrs. Mason replied with a nod. "Apart from being a deep trance medium, I am also a very accurate clairvoyant."

"How does that differ from what we just saw?" Sybil inquired.

"Well, when I do deep trance work, I am not really there, you understand. An entity uses my physical body to manifest itself: it speaks through me; it answers questions as if it were still in the physical world, although it's no longer a part of it. When I awaken from such a state I usually do not remember anything that has come through me during the trance. In this situation the entity speaks for himself, or sometimes a guide personality, that is to say, someone who supervises the contact to make sure that the instrument-that-is-I is not hurt or misused, will explain things to the sitter-that-is-you. In clairvoyance, on the other hand, I am fully awake, as myself, and use my extrasensory faculties to learn things, either from the past or sometimes in the future or things that are hidden."

"Hidden!" Paul exclaimed and jumped to his feet. "That is exactly it. Something is hidden in this place and I am trying to find it!"

Mrs. Mason seemed undisturbed. "Yes, I know," she replied very calmly, while Paul felt a bit foolish, having been so emotional about it.

"What do you think is my chance of finding what I am looking for?" Paul said, sitting on the edge of his chair.

"Well, I think your chances are excellent, but we will have to do some work, won't we?"

Both Paul and Sybil nodded.

"I am going to try to relax my body sufficiently to allow impressions to come through. This is not a trance, mind you, but simply a form of low level research. We call it traveling clairvoyance and it can be effective in locating missing persons or missing things, anything like that. Do you understand?"

While Paul and Sybil watched breathlessly, Mrs. Mason leaned back in her chair, closed her eyes and seemed to go into a light sleep. But her eyelashes indicated that her eyes were moving under the lids, and her breathing was regular, not as it had been prior to the onset of the trance before. Mrs. Mason was not asleep but was in a state somewhat deeper than normal wakefulness. After a few moments, which seemed painfully long to the couple, her lips began to move and she spoke in her own voice. At first she was hardly intelligible, but gradually her voice became stronger and inarticulate sounds were shaped into words.

"There is something hidden in the ground on this land," Mrs. Mason began, "something terribly important and valuable."

"Yes, yes," Paul said and leaned forward in the seat.

Mrs. Mason paid him no attention, as she continued. "It appears that a long time ago something was put into the ground, something that belonged to a man who has left this earth, also a long time ago. I get a name like Peter, Peter, maybe Pedro. Yes, it's the Spanish version of the name. He is connected with this. I feel there is a great deal of violence involved. Someone is being killed by another man. It's terrible. It's terrible! Of course this happened a long time ago. Somehow I feel there is a connection between this murder and what has been put into the ground. I can see it. It is a box—a rather large box, dark-colored. It is deep in the ground."

By now beads of sweat stood on Paul's forehead; the excitement had gotten to him. Sybil, on the other hand, seemed unusually calm. She was more fascinated by Mrs. Mason and the work she was doing than by the prospect of finding the treasure at last.

"Where is it? Where is it? Where should I look?" Paul finally said, unable to contain himself any longer.

"In the ground, deep in the ground," Mrs. Mason replied, her voice strong now, but her eyes still closed.

"But *where* in the ground? Where exactly should I look?" Paul said, trying to calm himself.

"Not far from the house," Mrs. Mason replied, "not far from the house, deep in the ground. You will be able to locate it."

"But why was I unable to find it? Why did my metal detector not work?" Paul asked; after all, he had searched everywhere with all the latest state-of-the-art equipment—he should have found anything which was there.

"You could not have found it," Mrs. Mason said, "because you were using an instrument that would not show it."

"What! There has to be metal there," Paul replied, taken aback by this.

"Yes, there is metal," the medium said. "There is a box of wood and inside there is lead—a leaden container of some sort. That is what I see, deep in the ground."

Of course, Paul thought. How stupid of me! If there had been a lead container, the instrument would not have found it. To discover lead and other very dense metals in the ground, he would have needed a different kind of detector. So there was hope after all.

"But why lead? Why would anyone want to put a leaden box into the ground?"

"To keep vampires away," Mrs. Mason replied without hesitation.

"*Vampires?*" Paul asked. "Are there such things as vampires?"

"No, there are not," Mrs. Mason replied. "There was an ancient belief that there were such things as vampires, and those who had buried whatever is in the ground thought that there might have been vampires coming after it so they took all the necessary precautions that they knew about in their time. This is a long time ago, my friend."

Vampires, indeed! Paul thought and smiled. Of course there were no such things, even though he had read in a local newspaper about a man who was going around holding himself out to be a "Vampirist," giving fancy lectures about creatures that only existed in man's imagination. But then a lot of people in this world follow their fancies and enjoy it, even though the creatures they talk about never existed.

"Will you lead me to this site?" Paul said eagerly, perhaps too eagerly.

"I will try," Mrs. Mason replied, "I will try."

But suddenly she opened her eyes and took a deep breath. "I am very tired," she announced, and yawned. "This has been a lot for me. Perhaps we should continue another day."

Paul, of course, was keenly disappointed, yet he knew that if the medium was too tired to carry on, the results might not be what he wanted them to be. He readily agreed to end the session for tonight and have Mrs. Mason come back the following night. He thanked her profusely for what she had done so far, and escorted her back to her car outside, where her husband had been waiting patiently for over an hour. He bade her good night and returned to the house.

Chapter Fifteen

Promptly at eight o'clock the following night Mr. Mason delivered Mrs. Mason to the house. After some preliminary discussion, Mrs. Mason took the same comfortable chair she had occupied the night before and Paul and Sybil seated themselves opposite her. The lights were lowered, yet there was enough to make out anything or anyone that might appear in the room.

"Shall I take the telephone off the hook?" Paul enquired.

"That won't be necessary," Mrs. Mason replied. "If it rings I won't hear it anyway, and one of you can answer it."

"Very well," Paul said. "What do we do now?"

"Nothing. Just sit quietly for a moment, empty your minds of *all* thoughts if you can to make yourselves more receptive to the energies, to the vibrations in this room. I need your assistance in this if I am to succeed. If you are tense or if your mind races from one thought to the other, we will not be successful. Do you understand?"

"Right," Paul replied, realizing how difficult it would be for him to empty his mind of his insistent desire to find the treasure. In fact, nothing else mattered to him anymore. For several days now he had not even called his office to find out how things were. Sybil had noticed that his tenseness had increased remarkably. More and more Paul seemed like a man possessed, driven by a strong ego that would not accept failure. Sybil felt uneasy in his presence now, but dared not tell him so. She hoped that, once the treasure was found (and she had no doubt that it would be found) Paul would revert to his usual sweet self. She did love him, and she had every hope that his strange behavior, caused by his extreme desire to find Don Pedro's treasure, might undergo a change for the better. She was willing to take the chance that it would.

Paul himself was looking forward to an exciting evening. He had no doubt that Mrs. Mason could perform what he expected her to do: namely, pinpoint the place where the treasure was buried. Although he had not been present at a session similar to the one they were now going to have, he felt no qualms about it nor did he expect anything particularly out of the ordinary. In fact, he felt it would be very much like a telephone conversation over a long distance in time and space. He had the tape recorder and pencil and paper as well and had set up a camera next to his chair, just in case there was something to record on film.

Once again Mrs. Mason closed her eyes, set back in the chair and allowed her body to become relaxed. After a while, the previous state of traveling clairvoyance overcame her and her voice, at first very low but gradually increasing in strength, was being picked up by Paul's tape recorder.

"I see the place," Mrs. Mason said, trembling with emotion, "I see a grave. Someone is digging a grave. They are Indians, many of them, and they seem to be very agitated. Now I see someone bringing a box and putting it into the ground. I hear voices, muffled voices, but I can't make out what they are saying."

Paul bent over to hear her more clearly. "Where is the place? Where is the grave?" he asked.

But Mrs. Mason did not reply directly. Instead she continued to speak, describing the scene from the past.

"Now they are bringing him—a man, a body—it is the body of a man. He is upright. They are placing him into this grave upright. They are burying him on top of the chest. The

Indians do not know the chest is there. Now they pass by and they throw something into the hole; I can't make it out. Now they are closing the grave. They are putting earth into it—more and more earth. I can hear the sound. Now I see the grave closed. The men turn away. They file past the spot. They are all gone now. The sky is gray and it is beginning to rain."

"Where is the spot? Can you show me where it is? Can you lead me to it?" Paul could hardly restrain himself now. He was ready to start digging this very instant. But again Mrs. Mason paid no attention to him. She was witnessing another scene now.

"I see another day. It is a gray day. I see a garden. It is this garden; yes, it is this land. The ground is waterlogged with much rain. I see a young boy playing in the garden. Now he is throwing a ball into the air. Now he runs after the ball."

Paul was unimpressed with this. He didn't want to hear about a boy playing ball in his yard. He wanted to know where the treasure was buried. But Mrs. Mason continued relentlessly.

"Now the boy is in the back facing the ball. His foot hits on something in the ground. He bends down. It is something white. I am looking at it. It is a skull; yes, it is a skull."

"Oh my God!" Sybil said, horrified.

"The boy touches it. He gets a shovel and digs around it. Now he picks up the skull. He is playing with it. He is using it as a football!"

Paul was ready to shake the medium to get more information, but Sybil restrained him. His excitement, however, had communicated itself to her as well. While Paul was trembling out of greed, she was trembling out of fear that Mrs. Mason might be hurt somehow by the spirit giving her this information.

"Where is it? Can you show us the place?" Paul said, trying to hold himself back as much as he could, but unable to disguise his eagerness.

"Terrible, terrible," Mrs. Mason replied, paying no attention to them. "This is a terrible thing that should not have been done! It should not have been done! This is sacred ground. The boy should not have done this. There will be terrible revenge upon all of them—all of them. The Indian says they must all die; everyone of them!"

Sybil drew back, her face white with fear.

Suddenly Mrs. Mason's eyes widened, as if forced open by an unseen hand. Her lips let out an unearthly scream, as she rose stiffly to her feet. She stared at Paul for a moment, as if she did not recognize him. Then, before he could stop her, she was running across the living room towards the door, with Paul and Sybil in hot pursuit.

"My God, I hope she won't fall," Sybil said.

But Paul was not concerned with such matters. Grabbing a flashlight as he passed the entrance door, he followed Mrs. Mason into the garden. When Sybil caught up with him, he was standing next to her as she pointed to a little mound at the extreme end of the garden. There was an expression on her face that Sybil had not seen before. It was a face paralyzed by sheer terror.

Somehow Paul and Sybil managed to get Mrs. Mason back to the house and revive her. A sip of brandy and some water helped, and a few minutes later she was herself again. This time she remembered nearly everything that had happened.

She warned Paul to be very careful; if he did not heed her advice, she added, he might suffer dire consequences. But Paul had no intention of giving up his quest. He thanked her, paid her the agreed-upon fee, and took her down to the waiting car. Her husband drove her away into the night. Sybil waved, but Mrs. Mason did not wave back.

Tomorrow they would start to dig. As Sybil returned to the house, a cold shudder ran down her spine. It wasn't because of what she had just witnessed, nor was it because of the terror that seemed to surround the business of finding Don Pedro's treasure. It was something more than that: an uncanny feeling of terrible things yet to come. But she felt powerless to stop any of it, unable to interfere with fate.

That night, Sybil could not fall asleep; she tossed restlessly for hours. When morning came, she was exhausted, and finally drifted off into a dreamless sleep. When she awoke, the sun was already high in the sky; Paul was already gone.

A look out the window showed her where he was: out in the garden by the little mound at the back, ready to begin his attack on the treasure of Don Pedro.

Chapter Sixteen

Paul's first attempt to find the treasure was far from successful. To begin with, the soil was hard, and he soon realized that he was not in as good shape as a treasure-digger—or a grave-digger—needed to be. He decided to get some better equipment, because the idea of getting a professional digger to help him was out of the question. It would not do for someone else to get his hands on what Paul considered to be his own treasure.

After an hour or two of trying to loosen the hard soil, he had to give up. Perhaps, he thought, if there were a heavy rain, that would soften the soil and digging would be a lot easier. But the sky was clear and no rain had been forecast. Nevertheless, stubborn as he was, Paul continued all morning to chip away at the area where he was sure the treasure lay buried. By noon he had managed to remove no more than a few inches of top-soil. If the treasure was buried as deep in the ground as the medium had indicated, he had an awfully long way to go. The sun stood high now and he began to feel warm.

Sybil came out to help him but, even though she was willing enough, she soon realized that this was beyond their abilities. She therefore returned to the house and waited. As she sat there a feeling of apprehension overcame her. Were they doing the right thing? Stronger and stronger was the feeling growing in her that they were dealing with something more than they could cope with; something threatening.

Far from superstitious, Sybil nevertheless had distinct fears of the unknown and she had always felt that there were things one should not meddle with. On the other hand, her curiosity was high: not so much out of greed, as was the case with Paul, but out of a desire to learn about the unknown. The idea of finding the treasure was indeed exciting to her.

As she was thinking of the pros and cons of their venture, now that success seemed to be within their grasp, the feeling of uneasiness became even more powerful. She got up and lit a cigarette, something she rarely did because she was trying to stop smoking. The cigarette did not calm her nerves. She returned to her chair by the window, watching Paul.

While she was sitting there, in a state of meditation or something akin of it, it appeared to her that there were voices all around her. A rush of air began to envelop her. At first, she barely noticed, but when the wind became stronger, she knew it must be real, because it moved the curtains at the window (which was closed) and chilled her skin as it passed by her.

As yet, she felt no panic, only curiosity. The voices were indistinct and garbled; she could not make out what they were saying. But they were human voices—of that she was sure.

She closed her eyes, leaned back in the chair, and tried to relax. She knew of her own ability to receive at times things that other people could not, and she hoped that this was a moment when such communication would occur.

The voices became stronger. She could make out a male voice shouting, "Get out! Get out!" Then she heard a plaintive female voice crying, "Help us!"

When she realized what the voices were saying she sat up in her chair, terror filling her soul. Who were the people who were crying out to her? Were they perhaps in mortal danger? She looked out the window at Paul who was still trying to dig and then back into the empty room. Was it all her imagination? Was she beginning to experience fantasies because of what she knew about the house? She decided to close her eyes again and lean back, to see if anything further would come through. The minutes ticked away. Then she heard the voices again, faintly at first, approaching rapidly; but they were not like the voices that had been there before. These were angry voices, shouting. She opened her eyes. There was nothing to be seen. By now the voices seemed close by— and then she realized that they were not spirit voices at all, but actual voices coming from outside the house.

Sybil rose quickly from the chair, opened the door and looked out. Sure enough, people were coming up the road toward the house, and they were indeed shouting.

My God, Sybil thought, they are coming to our house! By now the group had reached the front of the house. There were perhaps eight or ten of them, a motley lot, middle-aged people mainly. One man seemed to be their leader. While the others remained back in the street, arguing loudly among themselves, the leader, a man in his late forties or early fifties who was dressed in a business suit, marched up the steps to the house and ran the bell.

When he saw the door was already open, he asked, "May I come in, please? We would like to talk with you."

Sybil took a step backwards and the stranger came into the house. "Who are

you?" she demanded to know. "Who are
these people?"

The man in the business suit stood near the
door, apparently not wishing to come farther
into the house. He seemed ill at ease.

"We are residents of Amityville, ma'am,"
he said stiffly, "and we are here to tell you
that we don't like what is going on in this
house; not one bit."

"What do you mean?" Sybil wanted to
know. "This is our house, at least for a
month."

"Yes, we know you rented the house. We
know you are going to go back to the city
after that, and that's fine with us. But we
don't like what you are doing right now. We
don't like problems in this town. We have had
enough of it."

"Just a moment," Sybil said. She gently
pushed the stranger aside, stepped out into
the garden and called Paul.

"Paul, there is someone here who wants to
talk to us!"

Paul turned around, dropped the shovel
and slowly came back to the house. His hands
were dirty. His face was sweaty and his eyes
were glaring as if they were looking at a
treasure no one else could see.

"Yes?" he said, not exactly politely.

"Well," the stranger said, addressing Paul
now, "we represent the people of Amityville.
We know why you are here and we don't like
it. We would like you to leave this neighbor-

hood as it was before you came here. We don't want any more trouble."

"What's it go to do with you, what I am doing?" Paul demanded to know. "I'm not hurting anyone. I've paid for this house. I am going to be here a little bit longer and then I will go back to the city. We have a perfect right to do what we want while we are here. We are not disturbing anyone."

"Yes, you are, sir," the stranger replied stiffly. "You are stirring up old troubles."

"What troubles are you talking about?"

"You know perfectly well the story of this house. You know what happened here. There are stories of all kinds of strange things going on. Maybe they are true, maybe they are not, but they caused people to come here and disturb our way of life. We like our way of life. We don't want it changed. We don't want to be disturbed by outsiders. Do I make myself clear?"

Paul fell silent for a moment, thinking it over. When he replied, he was calmer but his voice had a cutting edge, which indicated to Sybil that inside, Paul was seething with anger.

"What I do in this house, which we have legally rented and paid for, is my business alone, so long as I don't endanger the safety of anyone else. There is nothing in the law that says I cannot dig in my own garden. So if you don't mind, just leave us alone. Goodbye."

With that, he turned and started to walk

back to the garden.

"Wait a moment," the stranger called after him. Paul stopped, turned around and faced him again.

"Look," said the stranger, "it isn't as simple as all that. You are digging for some pirate treasure that is supposed to be here. That sort of story gets around, see? People will come here from all over. This is a good town, a quiet town. We don't want any treasure hunts around here, understand?"

"Perfectly," Paul replied, much more politely than Sybil had thought he would. Again Paul thought it over before he continued. "Now then, here is my reply. I can understand your concern about undesirables coming to town. I don't want them either. I don't want anyone to come to this house, including you and your friends. What I do in my garden is my business. If you have heard some rumors or cock-and-bull stories, that is none of my business. I am doing some digging in the garden of a house that I have legally rented. That is all there is to it. If you have heard anything else, why don't you check another source? I have no comment whatsoever. If you don't mind, I would like to go back to my gardening. Good day, sir."

Paul turned and resolutely walked away, leaving the stranger standing there. Sybil thought the time had come to shut the front door. She went back into the house and closed the door. The stranger lingered outside for a moment, before going back to the other people in the street. There was some discussion and a moment later the group went away.

Sybil fixed a hasty lunch for Paul and herself. Paul gobbled it in five minutes and returned to the site to keep digging, regardless of the difficulties. To his amazement, the weather began to change just then. What had been a clear and sunny sky was now overcast. Despite the fact that the weatherman had predicted clear skies all day, in fact for several days, it appeared as if heavy rains were imminent.

Well, now, he thought, if it is going to rain, that is just dandy! That will soften up the soil and then I can really dig. He decided to take a short rest and wait for the rains to come. Going upstairs to one of the rooms, he left Sybil downstairs, seated by the window. She was doing what she had done before—going into a state of meditation, wondering whether what they were doing was right or wrong.

Whether it was the excitement of the unexpected visitor or the emotional tug of war going on within her, Sybil fell into an uneasy sleep. As she slept, it appeared that someone was trying to rouse her, for she heard an angry voice shouting in her ear, "Get out. Get out while you can!"

The voice became so insistent and so loud that it woke her. There was no one in the room. She rubbed her eyes, for sleeping in the middle of the day was not something she did very often and when she did, it always made her drowsy for an hour or so afterwards. As she tried to wake up completely, she noticed that she was not, after all, quite alone in the room. Looking across the large living room towards a window on the far side of the room, she saw a shadow directly in front of it. She rubbed her eyes again and thought that perhaps she had not fully awakened. When she opened her eyes again, the shadow was still there, only now it was darker.

To her amazement, she found herself neither afraid nor in a state of panic. Without so much as moving a muscle, she sat there looking toward the window on the opposite side of the room, watching as the shadow deepened. Gradually it took on the outlines of a human figure. What is it, she thought? In her heart she knew that she was having a visitation from a world with which she had, up until now, had no direct contact. By now she could make out the details as the figure solidified.

It was an Indian in full war regalia, who stood before the window staring at her in anger.

Oh my God, she thought, am I dreaming this? Her first instinct was to cry out to Paul —but then something stopped her. No, she thought, Paul would make it go away. I want to know what this is all about.

"Who are you?" she said to the apparition mentally, not daring to speak aloud. In the same manner the apparition replied to her. She did not hear his voice in the room, but she heard it in her mind as loud and as clear as if he had spoken.

"I am Rolling Thunder," the apparition said. "This is my land. This is sacred ground to my people. No white man may be here. You must leave."

"We will leave. We will leave," Sybil replied, getting more anxious now. "We will leave in a few days. But Paul wants to find the treasure first."

When her thoughts had expressed that idea, the Indian seemed even more angry. His eyes flashed as he sent back the message. "Do not touch the treasure! I am guarding it for my brother. You must not touch it or I will destroy you. Beware."

The figure began to fade and seconds later it had gone altogether. Sybil, fully awake now, rubbed her eyes. Had she dreamed it? Or had she been privy to a rare experience and, if so, why? Was the Indian spirit perhaps kindly disposed toward her for some reason, willing to warn her of impending disaster before it struck? It seemed the most comforting explanation. But how was she to tell Paul? At once she realized that whatever she might tell him, it would have no effect upon his plans. Sadly, she accepted that there was nothing to be done but to let fate take its course.

She settled once more in the chair and closed her eyes. This time her rest was peace-

ful. When she awoke an hour later she was
fully rested and relaxed. The experience was
clearly etched in her mind; she was determined not to tell Paul in so many words, but
perhaps to approach the matter indirectly. At
the same time she knew that her chance of
persuading Paul to give up the treasure hunt
and return home was next to nil.

An hour later the rains came. It was as if
the heavens had opened. Within the hour, the
garden was flooded. As Paul sat by the
window waiting for the waters to recede so
that he could start digging, it became clear to
him that nothing more could be done this
day. But tomorrow, he thought, I can get
down deeper to where the treasure is.

That evening, over dinner, Sybil tried to
intimate to Paul what had happened. She described it as a premonition of impending
disaster, but Paul waved her fears away.

"Please, no old wives' tales," he said.
"Don't confuse parapsychology with gypsy
fortune telling. We came here to find the
treasure. We know where it is now. We are
going to dig for it and we are going to find it,
and then we go home."

Sybil knew Paul well enough to realize that
any attempt to stop him was doomed to
failure. That night, when she had a moment
to herself, she prayed, asking God's help in
protecting them both from whatever might
come as a result of their interference with
ancient Indian sacred ground. Things had
gone too far for her to stop them and all she

could do now was to ask for protection.

The following morning the rains had stopped. The soil was muddy and soft. Early in the morning, Paul put on his boots, took the shovel, and walked out to where he had dug a hole the night before. The hole was now filled with water, but it didn't stop him. The soil was soft now and the digging went easier.

An hour later Sybil joined him. She had decided that she might as well be at his side, not so much because of the treasure, but in case anything untoward happened; if it did, she wanted to be there to help him.

The two of them feverishly shovelled away the muddy soil. Deeper and deeper they went: eventually they were up to their shoulders in what appeared to be an ever widening hole in the ground. But there was no treasure chest and no skeleton. Were they digging at the wrong spot after all? Paul decided to go to the west of their present hole and see whether perhaps he was missing the site by a yard or so. If that did not yield the results he wanted, he would do the same thing in the opposite direction.

"Be careful," Sybil begged, beginning to worry about what might happen, since they were pretty deep in the soil now. Again an uneasy feeling crept over her.

"I'll have to do this alone. There's not enough room for both of us." Paul dug sideways into the soil. Sybil stood back and waited. The moments went by, minutes feeling like hours.

Suddenly there was a cry from Paul. "I've got it. I've got it," he said. "I can see the skeleton!"

"Be careful, love," Sybil said, mindful of her premonition.

But Paul would not listen. He delved deeper, burrowing towards the whitish form he had glimpsed a yard or two away. For a moment he disappeared from Sybil's sight. His voice came back to her, muffled, but jubilant. "I'm getting there! I'm hitting pay dirt, so to speak," he said.

"Please be careful, though," Sybil called after him. But she was more or less speaking to herself.

As Paul disappeared into what appeared to be a large, odd-shaped hole in the wet ground, Sybil waited at the edge, unable to follow him. At this moment terror gripped and paralyzed her. She wanted to call out, "Don't! Don't!" But not a word came through her lips. Something stronger than herself kept her from communicating with him. While all this was going on she was keenly aware of the world around her; she heard the street noises and was even able to make out, in the distance, some angry shouts from people near the house. But none of this really penetrated her consciousness. Her eyes were fixed on the ground. By now, Paul had completely disappeared.

Suddenly she heard his muffled voice cry out; it held a note of achievement she had never heard him use before.

"It's here. It's here! I've got it!" His voice seemed fainter, perhaps because he had gone deeper into the ground than she had thought.

Paul had penetrated into what appeared to be a deep cave. It was not part of his excavations: this had existed before. The entrance had been re-opened, partly by the rain and partly by the pressure of some of the earth he had removed farther up. He did not realize, of course, that he had stumbled upon the ancient Indian burial grounds and that he was following subterranean passages which had been dug a long time ago.

The walls were crumbling but he paid no attention. So obsessed was he with his quest that even signs of imminent disaster would not have stopped him from proceeding farther. Wet earth dropped down on his head and matted his hair, but he paid no attention to that either.

It was dark in this deep recess but he had a strong flashlight with him and played it upon the walls. By now had had gone perhaps five or six yards away from the opening and his flashlight hit something different from the surrounding soil. When he saw that he had actually stumbled upon a large box of some sort, he realized that he had found the treasure at last.

It was at this point that he gave out the jubilant cry which Sybil heard. Totally oblivious to the dangers that might come with his position so far underground and without proper safeguards and getting as close as he could, he touched the box. No doubt about it. This was the treasure. But how was he to move it? Had Paul been less excited, he might now have returned to the surface and let matters rest for the moment, then come back the following day to reinforce the walls of the opening and remove the box with the help of Sybil.

But this he could not do: the fever of discovery was upon him, and with trembling hands he examined the box and the surrounding earth. As he bent down to see whether he could budge it with his bare hands, the heavy box began to move of its own volition. Perhaps loosened by the wet soil or by the force that had guarded it all this time, the box came crashing down on Paul and pushed him deep into the mud, burying his head completely.

Sybil was becoming anxious as the silence grew ominous. After several attempts to communicate with Paul by calling to him, she decided to go down to look for him. Paul had taken their only flashlight, but she had her lighter with her. Stepping carefully through the mud she managed to go down the short passage to where Paul's body was partially buried in the mud.

One look told her that she had come too late.

Chapter Seventeen

Once again the ancient curse had struck.

Stunned, Sybil stood transfixed for a moment. All kinds of thoughts passed through her mind. Her attempts to pull the body from underneath the heavy chest did not succeed. It was clear to her by now that there was nothing she could do for him anyway.

She realized that she would have to make some decisions. The natural thing would be to call a doctor or the police or both, but she immediately rejected this notion. If she could not save Paul's life, she could at least save his cherished goal from being taken by outsiders.

No thought of her own advantage crept into her thinking at this point, only what Paul would have wanted her to do had he survived. There was no doubt in her mind now. She had to do something about the body and about the heavy chest.

As she looked around the subterranean passage, she saw Paul's flashlight, which had dropped from his hands. Luckily it was still working. She searched the narrow chamber with its beam until she found the shovel. Wedging the flashlight in the soft mud of the wall, she began the grim task of digging around the chest. Eventually she was able to budge it sufficiently to pull Paul's body out from under it. Stopping every now and then because of exhaustion, she managed to pull his body back toward the opening and up to the surface.

She had used up so much energy by then that she collapsed on the ground, regardless of the mud, and slept for an hour before she woke up and realized that she had to move on.

More work had to be done. Hastily, she covered the opening in such a way that she could easily return to the passage underneath. This she accomplished by putting down a layer of branches, cut from some of the trees in the garden; then she added a layer of earth, camouflaging the opening to casual observers. She could explain the signs of digging as part of gardening procedure: they could have been planning to plant a tree, or simply trying to turn the soil for better growth or for flowers or fruit. She now began to drag Paul's limp body back towards the house.

With the help of the garden hose she managed to get the mud off his body, hands and face. She tried very hard not to faint at the sight of his dead body, telling herself that this inanimate mass of flesh had no connection with the man she had loved and lived with for so long. There was an expression of indescribable terror etched on Paul's face, as if he had seen something so horrendous and incredible that it had caused his heart to stop.

When she had cleaned him up, she pulled the body toward one of the old trees in the front part of the garden, laid him against it and put the shovel next to him. She was going to tell the examining physician that he had tried to do some digging and had suddenly collapsed. Since Paul had been a city man, who was not known for taking much exercise, and given his family history of heart disease, such an explanation might well be accepted, she thought. At any rate she could think of nothing better at the moment. After she had had a shower, she picked up the telephone with trembling hands and called for an ambulance. As she had expected, the doctor who arrived with the ambulance pronounced Paul dead and took the body to a morgue.

The following morning there was a routine examination and questioning.

The death was put down to heart failure,

due to overexertion. There were no complications. Sybil wondered whether this was due simply to good luck—or whether the local doctor wanted to get Paul's body out of Amityville with the minimum of delay, in the hope that his fiancée would go with him.

Two days later Paul was buried in a Brooklyn cemetery, where his family had buried their dead for the past fifty years. The only mourner was Sybil, who had not yet brought herself to notify anyone of Paul's passing. Paul was an only child and his parents had previously died; there were no close relatives.

She returned to Amityville immediately after the funeral. Their tenancy was due to expire in a couple of days, and Sybil was determined to do all she could to save the treasure. But, after a few strenuous hours of trying to move the chest, she realized that she would never be able to do it alone.

Naturally, the death of Paul had made all the local papers. In one account it was pointed out that the ancient curse had once again taken its toll and that it was inadvisable for outsiders to come to Amityville. There was nothing Sybil could have done to prevent such stories from appearing. But now that very adverse publicity helped solve her immediate problem. It was essential to have more time if she were going to remove the treasure. She called the owners and asked them to extend the lease for another month. Her heart was beating in her throat as she spoke with them, wondering if they actually thought that Paul had found the treasure. They could, of course, refuse to extend the lease, in which case the treasure would be lost. But the owners were more superstitous than she had counted on: Paul's death had convinced them that the house was, after all, not as safe as they had originally hoped. They were in no hurry to return, and when Sybil offered a sizeable sum to extend the lease for another month they readily agreed to remain on vacation in Florida and let Sybil stay on in the house. A sigh of relief passed Sybil's lips. She went to sleep that night totally exhausted, both physically and mentally.

She slept for twelve solid hours and when she awoke she could think clearly for the first time in several days. As soon as she did so, the terrible fact of the recent tragedy hit her fully. But this was no time to cry. Long before Paul's untimely demise, she had seen him in a totally different light: he had ceased to be the man she had once known. The bond between them had gradually loosened and she felt quite sure that, had he succeeded in acquiring the treasure, she would no longer have been part of his life. She had sensed, particularly during those past few weeks, that greed and total involvement with the material aspects of the treasure had so altered Paul's previously sweet and balanced disposition that there was no longer any room in his heart for her; he had lost the

capacity to have a relationship of the type
that she wanted. Still, he had been her fiance,
and she grieved for him. After all, he had not
deserved to die; but it seemed that anyone in
this house ran the risk of being affected by
the curse. Nevertheless, she decided to stay
on and complete what Paul had begun.

At first she thought she could get some
help to move the heavy chest from its hiding
place, and open it inside the house; but
eventually she rejected this notion. Whom
could she really trust? Paul surely would not
have wanted anyone else involved. On the
other hand, bringing the chest up herself
seemed out of the question.

So far no one had come to her door and
bothered her. The news of Paul's death had
not brought crowds of the curious, as she had
feared. If anything, the belief that the curse
had struck again kept people away from the
house. But she knew that she had to move
fast, before some nosey or greedy individual
got the idea that there was something
valuable hidden at 112 Ocean Avenue.

As if led by an inner voice, she descended
into the basement of the house, where she
rummaged among the rusty garden implements and other materials left by the owners.
Her surprise was great when she came across
a well-worn dolly which apparently had been
used to move heavy objects into the house. A
sudden thought struck her. She took the
dolly down to the rear of the garden,
uncovered the excavation and went down

into it. Then she returned to the house and found some rope. It took her five minutes to lash the ropes around the chest. Her next move was to position the dolly close by, and to build up a ramp of earth between it and the chest. She began pulling at the ropes in the hope that she might move the chest onto the dolly. To her relief she succeeded after only a few minutes.

By now the soil had dried up considerably and the walls were firmer. As soon as the chest was on the dolly she tied the ropes to the front of it and began to pull it towards the entrance to the excavation. This was no easy task because the floor was uneven, but she managed it: now the dolly with the chest on it sat underneath the opening. All that remained to be done was somehow to lift the chest out of the hole and get it up the garden and into the house. But how was she to do this without proper tools or proper equipment?

Once again her ingenuity came to her aid. She recalled having seen a winch in the cellar. The owners of the house had probably used it at one time to get their motor boat out of the water and onto dry land. She brought the winch to the hole and set it up securely over the opening. Then she tied ropes around the chest and began to wind the winch.

Twice the chest fell back onto the dolly, but, far from being discouraged, Sybil determined to find a way in which she could prevent this from happening again. every time the chest slipped back onto the dolly, she could hear metallic sounds from within.

Once more she had an idea which came to her out of the blue, perhaps inspired by someone on the other side of life, or perhaps from her own subconscious; wherever it came from, it was worth trying. Against the side of the house were some two or three dozen bricks, perhaps left over from some building work which the owners had abandoned. She managed to take the bricks to the opening of the hole. Then, gradually hoisting the chest a little bit at a time and putting a brick underneath, she raised the chest, inch by inch, until it was flush with the opening.

With one supreme effort, throwing her body backwards to support the winch, she pulled it toward the edge of the opening, then secured it with ropes so that it could not slip back again.

Exhaustion forced her to take a break. After she had rested for several minutes, she pulled the chest onto the ground, clambered into the hole, brought the dolly up and, with some effort, placed the chest on the dolly again. Now she felt she was halfway home. Pulling the dolly towards the house was child's play compared to what she had just been through.

The weather-stained, mud-smeared chest dominated the living room. Sybil stared at it for a moment, breathing deeply after her exertions. But she could not risk opening it yet, much as she wanted to. Passers-by might see her excavations. She ran to the opening and covered it again with layers of branches and earth. Once again, she returned to the house, ready to do the ultimate to complete Paul's quest: open the chest.

Half an hour later the chest was pried open. What Sybil saw was beyond belief. Before her was an array of gold bracelets, rings, a wide range of antique jewelry, gold doubloons and silver coins. It was an astonishing example of the booty which pirates would take from the passengers and crew of the ships they had captured. On top of it all, carefully wrapped in a separate box, was the glowing opal that had caused so much tragedy to those who had possessed it. The radiance of the precious stone fascinated her. She remembered that Paul had said the opal was reputed to bring bad luck to those who possessed it, but somehow she could not believe that anything so beautiful could be cursed. The story must be a myth; the evil in this house must be due to the desecration of the Indian burial grounds, not to the stone. She decided to dispose of the treasure as soon as possible, but to keep the opal for herself.

The next day Sybil spent most of the time filling in the hole and covering up all traces of her activities. It was not an easy task, for Paul had dug very deeply; and yet she managed it by the end of the day. In order to camouflage the site even further, she went into the village and bought some plants, which she then placed into the soft soil on top of the opening. As far as casual observers were concerned, this was simply an improvement in the garden.

Selling the hoard proved to be somewhat more difficult than she had anticipated. The first jeweler she approached with some of the bracelets wanted to know where she had obtained them. Since Sybil had no intention of disclosing anything about her find, she left the shop. Then she recalled that a friend had once advised her that, if she wanted to sell something without publicity, she should do so by auction. Quickly she contacted one of the top auction houses in Manhattan and placed the entire treasure trove into the skilled hands of the auctioneer. As far as the story she told him went, the valuables had been in her family for two centuries and an eccentric aunt had just left them to her. In view of Sybil's personal credentials as a reputable individual, the firm did not question this story; besides, auctioneers are less concerned with where something comes from than where it goes and how much it can be sold for.

The auctioneer had promised no undue publicity. The auction took place quickly, and Don Pedro's treasure was dispersed all over the world. It brought a goodly sum, nearly a million dollars. After the auctioneer had taken his percentage, some $700,000 was turned over to Sybil.

At first she thought that having that kind of

money was wonderful. But then she gave it further thought, for something about all this did not sit well with her. Within two or three days an idea had crystalized in her mind.

She went to the local library; there she asked the librarian where the nearest Indian settlement was in the area and when he pointed her to a small village no more than ten miles away, she drove there. The Indians she encountered were all up-to-date Long Islanders: were it not for their dark skins and the strange hair styles which some of them wore, one would have never suspected them to be of Indian origin. Sybil found the head man of the settlement. She wanted to do something to help Indian children have better lives, she explained to the puzzled head man; what could she possibly do to be of immediate value to them?

"It is simple," the head man replied. "We desperately need a new school."

That was it, Sybil thought. She donated half the money to the village to establish a school for Indian children. The rest, after taxes, would leave her with perhaps $150,000. It was a relatively modest amount, and she felt she had earned it by her work over the last few months, by restoring the grave to its previous condition, and by her donation to the Indian village. All in all, Sybil believed that she had done as well as could be expected under the circumstances and that the entire incident had reached its final chapter. Wherever Don Pedro was now, she thought, he should be satisfied—not to mention Rolling Thunder, whose grave was once again hidden. As for the people who owned the house, that was their problem and not hers; she knew very well that, no matter how much money she had realized from the treasure, she could not have persuaded them to move or to turn the land back into an ancient Indian burial ground!

With all that completed, Sybil felt almost at peace again. There was, of course, the opal which was still waiting to be mounted, so it could be worn in suitable fashion. As yet, she had no idea of the history and meaning of the gem in her possession.

Chapter Eighteen

Living alone in the house was a new experience for Sybil and one that she didn't dread as much as she had expected. Gradually the absence of Paul hurt less and less, although there were times when she felt his restless spirit was lingering around her. Of course she realized that this might be just her imagination and dismissed the notion.

In the next few days, however, she read enough about paranormal psychology not to dismiss the notion entirely. Paul had died in a way which was generally considered to provide a potential base for lingering in the earth's sphere; in other words, he might well have become what is commonly called a ghost.

Paul a ghost? What an idea! But there were

little things that made her wonder. To begin with, she never felt alone in the house. Even when she took a bath and closed the door tightly behind her (a silly thing to do since she knew there was no one else in the house), she had the uncanny feeling that she was being watched by someone or something that she could not see. Despite her growing psychic abilities, and she now knew she had them, she could not really make out what this someone or something was; she began to wonder whether her nerves were playing tricks on her.

But she discarded this explanation the first Thursday after the renewal of the lease. That day had been particularly warm. Coming out from the city after work, having a quick dinner and then spending another thirty or forty-five minutes working in the garden had made her tired; she had intended to take a quick bath and then go to bed. She was standing in front of the bathroom mirror, drying herself, when she suddenly felt a trembling sensation. At first the notion came to her that an earthquake was taking place, but she immediately dismissed such an idea because she had never heard of earthquakes in this part of the country. The mirror began to sway back and forth as if moved by unseen hands; a cold breeze swept through the bathroom and chilled her to the very bones. Then she noticed a flickering light near the ceiling. As she looked up, the light moved farther down until it came face to face with her, less than a foot away. Standing naked in front of the mirror and staring at this flickering light, she felt a strange lack of fear. Yet she was unable to move, almost as if she were paralyzed.

And then there was an enveloping sensation, as if someone were putting his arms around her body. There was no mistaking it. These were the arms of a man, and she let out a terrified scream. But the man's arms were not hurting her. They were fondling her. Could it be Paul, she thought? Could his spirit be trying to make love to her from the afterlife?

"Is it you, Paul? Is it you?" she said.

Immediately the sensation ceased. The spirit or whatever it was, had completely left.

Hastily she got dressed and went out of the bathroom. She returned to the living room, unable to go to sleep right away. If it hadn't been Paul's spirit, who then had tried to make love to her in the bathroom? Certainly not the vengeful Indian chief. Could it be one of the murder victims of the DeFeo family? But she dismissed this notion also because she realized that none of the victims had been young men; there were only an old couple and young children.

Who then, or what had put its strong arms around her? The puzzle remained and so did her nervousness. She decided to take some drops, something she had picked up in a health food shop that shouldn't cause her any side effects; hopefully, she thought, she would soon be fast asleep. In the morning things might look different.

Sybil's continued presence in the accursed house did not escape the notice of the local townspeople. Nothing more appeared in the local press, to be sure, and very few tourists came by, at any rate no more than used to in years gone by. Occasionally, a car would drive slowly past the house, and people would crane their necks, pointing the house out to each other; but no one rang her doorbell and she felt it unnecessary to ask for police protection from overly eager tourists or curious townsfolk.

The second week of her residence in the house passed relatively uneventfully. She hoped that perhaps the whole month would be peaceful. Then she would return to the city and resume her life, shattered though it was because of Paul's death. At least she would be free from any further misgivings or problems of a psychic nature. She longed to be among normal people again and to be in a world where things are pretty much understood and predetermined—a world where the unexpected and the unseen have little or no place.

Then one day somebody left a little book on her doorstep. In the morning, as she rushed out to leave for the city, she found it. The book was called *The Amityville Curse* and it dealt with the alleged curse put on the house and on any of those who dared live in it. While she thought the book was fiction, she nevertheless read it from cover to cover.

Reading it destroyed her precarious tranquillity. It made her realize that the curse had not been lifted by Paul's death, nor by the finding and proper dispersing of Don Pedro's treasure. What then did the spirits want? she asked herself with a certain amount of bitterness. What more could she do to pacify them? But she knew at the same time that the answers would not come to her easily.

When she returned from the city that evening and opened the front door, a heavy piece of plaster fell to the ground, narrowly missing her. She had not noticed it being loose, and yet there it came, crashing down from the ceiling. She shuddered, thinking that, had she been two or three inches further inside the house, she would soon be lying in the hospital or even in the morgue. Was someone trying to tell her something? she wondered.

When she had cleared away the debris, she proceeded to prepare dinner for herself. To her surprise she found that the cupboard was almost completely bare, for she had forgotten to shop the previous weekend. What was she to do? She did not feel like driving to a local restaurant. She was tired and wanted to go to sleep. Under the circumstances she decided to telephone a nearby grocery store, order a few simple things and prepare a makeshift dinner for herself. No sooner decided than done; the grocery promised delivery within the next twenty minutes.

She stretched out on the sofa in the living room, waiting for the boy from the grocery store to arrive. As she did so, she noticed a strange pattern of light playing on the ceiling. At first she thought it was due to passing cars, but when she got up and checked the windows she realized that there was no way that the lights could be the result of something outside. The origin had to be elsewhere. By now the lights were quite pronounced; they formed a flickering and ever-changing pattern—now round, now oval, now starlike. They were dancing on the ceiling as if to challenge her to make out what they might possibly be. As she observed the strange goings on Sybil became alarmed. Here was something that she could not readily account for in terms of normal physics. She rose from the couch and went directly beneath where the lights were doing their peculiar display on the ceiling. She could now make out something more than just lights: fainly etched inside the largest light was the outline of a human face!

"My God!" she exclaimed, realizing that she was witnessing another manifestation. At this moment the doorbell rang. Quickly she went to the door and opened it. It was the grocery boy.

"Come in. Come in," she said, perhaps more eagerly than necessary. The young man, a sandy-haired boy of perhaps eighteen or nineteen, stepped inside the house, carrying the supplies down the corridor, and then to the left into the kitchen. She paid the boy, gave him a generous tip and accompanied him to the front door. She watched him get into his little Volkswagen. For no reason she could have put into words, she stood at the door waiting for the car to drive off, down the tree-lined street and back to the village.

At first, the boy had trouble getting the engine started, but he finally did, and the car drove off. Sybil was ready to return to the house, when she saw the car swerve from the right side of the road, cross to the left side, and drive with full impact into a tree. She could not believe her eyes: there was the sickening sound of a crash, and then utter silence!

My God, she thought, he's killed himself! She ran out, leaving the door wide open, to see whether she could help. The accident had occurred perhaps a half block away from the house. When she reached the site of the crash, she realized that she had come too late. There, hanging out of the half-open door, was the delivery boy, his neck obviously broken.

Sybil somehow made it back to the house, somehow closed the door behind her, somehow summoned the police. After an ambulance had taken the body away, a police officer came to question her, since she was the only witness to the accident. There was very little to tell him except that the car had inexplicably crossed over to the other side of the road and then made directly for one of the trees.

"I can't understand it," she kept saying over and over again.

The officer nodded. "These things do happen sometimes," he said. "Perhaps the boy wasn't well or perhaps he didn't know how to drive."

"I don't know. He seemed a very responsible, healthy boy to me," Sybil said. "I can't understand how this could have happened."

The officer shrugged and left. Sybil was more shaken than ever. She sat down again in her living room and decided to meditate. As she did so, she had the feeling she was leaving her body and floating into the air. She had by now read enough about out-of-body experiences and astral projections to realize that this was nothing supernatural as such; it occurred to many people. She knew that sometimes people who are at the verge of sleep will actually travel outside their body and then return to it; often they would not even be aware of it, but put their experiences down to having had a very vivid dream.

Despite this knowledge which she possessed consciously, she was terrified when she suddenly found herself floating down the corridor and up the stairs to the second story of the house. Something or someone drew her into a room to the right of the stairs, the room in which young DeFeo had murdered his father! And there, big as life, she saw the dead/man with his bullet wound as fresh as the day he had been shot all those years ago.

Sybil let out a scream of horror and instantly was pulled back into her physical body, rushing through the air and feeling the walls between her and the living room. She landed inside her physical body with a thud, trembling with the horror of her most recent experience. Her eyes were wide open now and she realized that she had brought on this particular state through her meditation. Determined not to let this happen again, she made herself ready for bed.

But then the thought struck her. What if the phenomena in the house were to increase day by day? Should she just leave and let the people who had been living in the house prior to their arrival cope with it? Immediately she rejected the proposal as cowardly. She owed it to Paul's memory not to run away.

No, she promised herself, she was going to deal with the matter as rationally as possible. But the next step, she decided, was to call on the services of the medium again. Perhaps Mrs. Mason could figure out what had to be done to lift the curse and to bring peace to those on the other side of the curtain—and also to Sybil herself.

She ran to the telephone. To her immense relief, she heard Mrs. Mason's voice after the second ring. Sybil blurted out her story. The medium readily offered to come the following evening, once she had heard of the tragedy that had recently occurred.

That night, Sybil slept soundly. If she had any dreams, she did not recall them on awakening.

Chapter Nineteen

Once again, Mrs. Mason seated herself in the comfortable chair in the living room. An anxious Sybil sat opposite her, biting her fingernails while she waited for Mrs. Mason to go into her trance state.

After several moments, during which the medium coughed and spluttered, as was customary prior to the onset of trance, Mrs. Mason relaxed, her eyes closed, and her breathing became more regular. To all appearances she seemed asleep. After a while, which seemed like an eternity to Sybil, her eyes or rather her eye lashes fluttered, and the muscles around her lips began to move. Clearly, an entity was trying to manifest itself through her.

And then what had been a gentle, ladylike

face suddenly turned into a hard, masculine one; every line was etched sharply. The nose became acquiline; the medium, her eyes still closed, sat bolt upright in the chair. The entity operating her physical body now was someone other than Mrs. Mason. Sybil did not have to wait long before she found out who was confronting her.

"You see, white woman," the harsh voice said, "you see now the foolishness of trying to steal treasure from sacred burial ground? I kill your man and I kill you if you do not leave."

"I intend to leave," Sybil replied, totally prepared to defend herself. "But I want this anger, this hate to stop. What else do you want me to do? I have already done all I can."

"Not so." The Indian's voice was deep, totally unlike Mrs. Mason's normal speaking voice.

"What more do you want?" Sybil almost shouted. "Haven't I gone to the Indian village and given them money for a school?"

"Rolling Thunder says white woman must leave. White woman must go back to city. White woman must give back precious stone."

"You mean the opal?"

"Yes. Stone must go back where it came from."

"But I don't know where it came from. How can I do this?" Sybil said, almost in tears now. But her distress made no impression on Rolling Thunder.

"White woman must give back precious stone. White woman must leave sacred burial ground and never come back or I will kill her as I kill all others."

"But what about the curse? You've put a curse on this house!"

"You are right. No blade of grass shall grow in this soil until sacred burial ground is restored to Indian people. No house, no people."

"But that is impossible! I don't own the house. I am only here for a little while."

"You here long enough. You must tell them."

"But suppose they don't want to leave? What about the curse?"

"Curse go with you. You go. You return the opal. You must return land to Indian people. That is my command."

"But how can I do this?" Sybil cried out in desperation, for she noticed that the medium had sunk back in her chair, deeply asleep now. Clearly, the Indian had left her body. After a minute or two, Mrs. Mason sat up again, her face having regained its normal expression. Once again, Sybil realized that Mrs. Mason could not recall what had come through her lips. She had, of course, recorded every word that had been spoken and she now played the tape back for Mrs. Mason who listened intently.

"Well, that's quite an order, isn't it?" she finally commented.

"What should I do? How can I break this

curse?" Sybil asked.

"There's only one way you can deal with this," Mrs. Mason replied, and there was a grave timbre to her voice. "You are dealing with an ancient Indian ritual curse. Only an Indian ritual can dissolve it. I can't. You can't. It has to be dealt with the Indian way."

"But how? Whom do I call? What do I do next?" Sybil said. Tears rolled unheeded down her cheeks.

Again Mrs. Mason had an answer. "Well," she said very calmly, "I think I might have a solution for you. I have a friend who is a writer. He writes about strange phenomena, the occult, the paranormal, the world of spirits, and such. He is very knowledgeable and has learned a great deal. He is a little psychic himself and he might just be able to help you."

Sybil was clearly disappointed. What good would a writer be to her? All he could do was publish the story, which would merely bring more people to the house. She told the medium this, but Mrs. Mason shook her head. "No, that is not so. You see, this young man is not only knowledgeable where it counts— he's also Indian. Or at least part Indian, I am not sure how much."

"Why do you think he could help me?"

"Just a hunch," Mrs. Mason replied. "It came to me in a flash when you asked before. Perhaps the spirit guides are suggesting it. Perhaps it is my own intuition. Why don't you give it a chance? Talk to him. You don't have to go ahead with it, but give yourself a chance to explore this possibility. I feel very strongly about it. I feel that there might be a solution in this person, and that somehow you will be able to succeed where I cannot. You see, the Indian chief, while using me as his medium, will not listen to me if I speak to him as myself, the clairvoyant. I have no standing in his world. You understand me?"

Sybil nodded.

"Very well then," Mrs. Mason said and rose from the chair. "I shall call the young man tomorrow and I will ask him to get in touch with you at once."

"What is his name?" Sybil demanded to know.

"His name is Johnny Woodruff."

And with that Mrs. Mason let herself out the door, smiled at Sybil and went on her way.

Chapter Twenty

The following day, bright and early, the telephone rang in Sybil's bedroom. She had taken to sleeping in one of the rooms on the second floor, the one which to her held the least obnoxious vibrations. Naturally, she knew that the rooms had been tainted with murder during the DeFeo tragedy; but, having gone from room to room, she had finally decided to bed down for the rest of her stay in this particular room, which had belonged to one of the children. She had moved the telephone there.

She picked up the phone. A cheerful male voice announced that he was Johnny Woodruff, calling at the suggestion of Mrs. Mason.

"Oh, yes, I was expecting your call," Sybil

said, still a little sleepy. Last night's session had left a deep impression on her; it wasn't easy to shake off.

"Mrs. Mason told me you had a very special problem," the voice at the other end said. "She thought that perhaps I might be able to help you."

"Yes," Sybil replied with a tone of hopefulness in her voice. "Do you think you can?"

"I will try," Johnny Woodruff said. "When can I see you?"

"Anytime," Sybil replied. "Just come on out."

"All right. How about this evening?"

"Fine. What time would you like to make it?"

"I'll be there at eight. I have some business in the city but I will be there by eight o'clock. All right?"

"Absolutely, and thank you so much."

There was a click as Woodruff ended the conversation. For a little while longer Sybil went back to sleep. She had a weird dream. In this dream she saw herself walking through the house, slowly going from room to room. As she peered into each and every room of the house, she saw the victim of the DeFeo slayings on their beds, all of them dead, with the blood dripping from their wounds. But in the dream this did not bother her.

Then she came to the living room downstairs. She walked up to the fireplace and stood in front of it for a long time, or for what appeared to her in the dream as a long time. When one dreams one can never tell how much time is passing. There was no fire in the fireplace at that moment, but as she looked into it, suddenly there sprang up a flame and the fire seemed to light itself. She stood there, fascinated, unable to budge from the spot. Suddenly she felt a pair of arms around her, the arms of a man. She turned around to see who it was, but she could not see anyone; yet she felt the pressure of a pair of male arms embracing her, not in a threatening, but in a loving fashion.

"Who are you?" she demanded. At that moment she woke with a jolt. The dream was still very vivid in her mind. She was puzzled by what she had dreamt, wondering whether it had perhaps some significance in terms of what was yet to come—or more likely, she reasoned, the confused sum total of what she had experienced before. The matter of those unseen arms had never been settled in her mind, and this dream brought it freshly to her attention.

It struck her as odd that Mrs. Mason had not come up with evidence concerning some *other* spirit. But the fact that she hadn't, and knowing that a good trance medium would certainly pick up any such entity in the house, made her wonder what all this was: was it a projection into the future, or was it simply her own mind playing tricks? More puzzled than ever, she decided to get up and clean the house, and prepare herself for her meeting with Johnny Woodruff that evening.

Then a thought occurred to her. If she were to meet this young writer, should she not know a little more about him than the few words of introduction Mrs. Mason had given her? Getting dressed quickly, she drove down to the Public Library. There she approached the assistant librarian, who was busy going through index card files behind a glass partition.

"Do you by any chance happen to have any books by somebody named Johnny Woodruff?" Sybil began uncertainly.

The librarian said, "Johnny Woodruff. Isn't he a writer on the occult and stuff like that, the paranormal?"

Sybil nodded.

"Let me have a look." The librarian got up from behind her desk and went to a filing cabinet. There she went through a long row of index cards. After a few minutes she nodded.

"Yep, we have a couple of his books. Do you want to take them out or read them here?"

"Well, could I just have a look at one of them?"

"Well, which one? We've got *The World of Magic* and we've also got *Ghost Houses in America.*"

Sybil thought for a moment. "Let me have both of them, if you don't mind."

The librarian nodded and went about finding the books. A few minutes later she handed Sybil two small volumes, and told her to sit down in the library where there were comfortable chairs beside the long tables. She could stay there until five p.m. but if she cared to take the books out on a card she would have to fill out an application form. Sybil thanked her and said she would see; she thought she might be able to finish her reading at the library.

The librarian returned to her desk and Sybil was left alone with the two books.

She opened *The World of Magic* and started to read. After a page or two she realized that it was a history of magical incantations, having mainly to do with the past. This was not what she wanted, but she kept leafing through the book until a passage caught her eye. This was something, she felt, she ought to read and understand. The passage dealt with the meaning of incantations:

"The word *incantation* conjures up visions of witchcraft, but to incant merely means to implore in a rhythmical, orderly pattern. The superficial difference between prayer and incantation is that prayer may be uttered in any fashion, rhythmical or disorganized, since the meaning of the words and presumably the feeling behind them is paramount. The incantation, on the other hand, requires a specific way of speaking the words. Incantations are the prayers of pagans and magic. Always directed toward a superior power, they are requests for action on the part of a deity. They may or may not include 'counteroffers' on the part of the supplicant, such as promises, or sacrifices or animals or grain, as with some primitive religions. They consist of frequent repetition of words or phrases in monotonous tones or in sharply accented rhythms, coupled with definite physical movements. Some incantations are set to music and are sung. A typical Wicca (or Witchcraft) incantation addresses itself to the Mother Goddess or to Diana, describing her beauty and wisdom, and then asking her to help the supplicant in such and such a way.

It is possible to utter an incantation quietly in the privacy of one's room. Incantations are based on the *assumption* that the deity understands the significance of the words used. There already exists an agreement between man and deity that this particular formula will be acceptable to the deity in order to perform certain services for the supplicant. Man, to be sure, has no guarantee that this is so. He takes the word of his priest or of tradition perhaps only of his own heart for it. But his firm belief that the invocation used is the right one is a major factor in making it work. The supplicant has done something *positive* about the situation.

What exactly works in an incantation? I have personally witnessed incantations both by groups and by individuals and at the very least, a sense of elevation and purification of mind and body follows the ritual performance of the incantation. Doubt and negative thinking are replaced by confidence. Moreover, partial or even total identification with the deity may occur. In such a state of near-ecstasy, the supplicant imagines himself possessed by divine powers and goes about solving his problems accordingly. How can we say with certainty that some divine element does not *indeed* enter the body and mind of the supplicant at that point? If we accept the philosophy that God is within us at all times, it may well be that incantations awaken such dormant sparks of divinity within and make them work for us, together with our own human impetus. At any rate, properly performed and ritualistically staged incantations, when spoken or sung at the height of the emotional wave which accompanies such rituals, are frequently effective.

Do spells and curses really work? Scientifically speaking they are nothing more than highly concentrated *energy patterns* impressed with certain thoughts and directed towards another person or persons. Many curses have found their mark despite the fact that those affected did not believe in them. In a recent work dealing with the Habsburg family I discussed the effect of a family curse in great detail and showed that it had worked. I know of a noble Austrian family which was wiped out as a result of a seventeenth century curse which finally found its mark even though the original culprit was only remotely related to the later descendants.

Whenever energy passes from one place to another, it causes reactions. If we consider curses, blessings, and spells energy patterns, then these energy patterns may cause effects. Knowledge of an existing curse or blessing also influences those involved, whether or not they are willing to admit it. A person may accept the blessing or curse or wonder whether it will work; even if he doubts it, there is uncertainty involved, which is nearly the same as belief.

All rituals work to the degree they are able to penetrate to the emotional *center* of the worshiper."

Sybil put the book down and thought about what she had just read. It had taught her a good deal about rituals and incantations and curses and spells, but what about Indian rituals? Nothing in the passage in Mr. Woodruff's book dealt with Indians. Was he cognizant of the fact that this was an Indian matter, probably different from anything he had encountered before? Immediately Sybil rejected this notion: after all, Mrs. Mason would not have selected Johnny Woodruff if she had not felt he was capable of dealing with the matter at hand. Speculation at this point was idle: Sybil had seen and read enough. She felt there was no need to read the other book. She returned the books to the librarian, thanked her and left for the house.

By now it was nearly six o'clock and she prepared a simple meal for herself. This evening, to be sure, she might know a great deal more about how to deal with her problems, and she eagerly looked forward to meeting the mysterious Mr. Woodruff.

Promptly at eight p.m. the doorbell rang. She rushed, perhaps a little too eagerly, to open the door and found herself facing an attractive young man who seemed to be about her own age. He nodded politely to her and stepped in as she retreated. She noticed that his sharp blue eyes seemed to question everything he looked at and his movements were quick and deliberate as he walked down the corridor into the living room. He carried a small briefcase which he now put down on the couch next to himself.

"Can I get you something?" she asked.

"What do you have?" he replied.

She laughed. "How about a cup of coffee or a drink or some juice?"

"No drink, thank you, but a cup of coffee will do—milk and sugar. Thank you."

She went to the kitchen where she had earlier made some coffee for herself. There was just enough left in the pot. She took a cup from the pantry and poured his coffee. While she was doing this she thought to herself that her visitor really was rather good-looking. Immediately she dismissed such a notion. This was not a social call. This was grim business. She returned to the living room and offered him the coffee.

After a moment he looked straight at her and said, "Now then, I understand you have an Indian spirit here who would like to get rid of you."

"That's an understatement, Mr. Woodruff!" she replied. "He is trying to kill me, or anyone else who lives here. Furthermore, he would like to have this land for use as a sacred Indian burial ground, presumably with the house removed, and he doesn't want me to keep the opal."

"Ah yes, the opal. Mrs. Mason wasn't able to tell me much about it. May I see it?"

"Yes, of course," Sybil replied and rose. She had been meaning to put the opal in her deposit box but had not yet done so. Thus, it rested carefully wrapped in tissue paper in a little box safe in the back of the linen closet upstairs. A few moments later she came back with the box and handed it to the young man. He opened it and took out the opal. The light hit it in a peculiar way so that reflections from it touched the opposite wall. Both noticed something strange about the reflection: it seemed to be fluctuating and growing, as if the opal itself were moving when, in fact, it lay still in Mr. Woodruff's palm. As they watched in fascination the play of lights on the wall, Woodruff said, "It is very strange—I mean psychometrically speaking, I get some very strange vibrations from it. I almost feel holy. I feel religious, as if this were a religious object."

"That's entirely possible," Sybil replied. "I understand that it is of Tibetan origin. Paul, my late fiancé, found some reference to an opal having been stolen from a Tibetan statue in the eighteenth century and it is probably this one. It is supposed to be the 'Queen Anne opal,' and is supposed to be unlucky to all those who possess it."

"Really?" Woodruff said. Perhaps more hastily than necessary, he put the opal back in the box and handed it to Sybil.

"You're not afraid of it, are you?" Sybil said. She had not failed to notice the haste with which he had gotten rid of the opal.

He smiled. "In my business one is not afraid of anything, or one shouldn't be in it, don't you agree?"

"Yes, of course, but you seem to be in great

haste to get the opal off your hands."

Again Mr. Woodruff laughed. "That was sheer prudence. I did not want to be included among those whom the original owner or owners wanted eliminated for possessing the stone."

"What do we do now?" Sybil demanded.

The young man leaned back, closed his eyes for a moment thoughtfully and then replied, "As I see it, you have two problems to contend with. On the one hand, you have the Indian chief who wants his land back. On the other hand, you have the stone which he wants returned to its place of origin."

"How on earth am I going to do that?" Sybil asked. "If the story is true, and it comes from some Tibetan temple, does he expect me to go to Tibet and look for it?"

Again the young man smiled. "To an Indian chief in the spirit world such matters are of little concern. Only results count. And when it comes to promises and hopes, especially between blood brothers, as this appears to be, nothing can stand in the way of fulfillment. I am afraid your modern sense of practicality will have absolutely no influence on his feelings in the matter."

"But how—how am I going to satisfy this spirit?"

"That is why I am here, is it not?" the young man replied and looked straight at her. He held her gaze for perhaps a minute or two. At that moment something very strange happened: an energy of some sort passed between them and it seemed to Sybil that she was now hooked into his particular vibration. At the same time she found herself strangely attracted to this young man, A sense of relief and a positive feeling pervaded her being for a long, long moment. Yes, she thought, this man will help me.

"Then how do you propose to proceed, so far as the opal is concerned?" she asked tremulously.

"Here is what I suggest. In New Jersey there is a little known but very important monastery founded by Tibetan lamas. It has one of the great temples in the Western world. Would it not be appropriate to ask for the help of the priests of that lamasary and perhaps give the opal to them, either to enshrine it in their own temple or to get it back to Tibet by their own means?"

"A splendid idea," Sybil replied. She tried to forget the fact that the opal was probably worth a great deal of money, and that it was the most beautiful ring she had ever possessed.

As if he had read her thoughts, the young man shook his head. "No matter how much this stone is worth on the commercial market, and no matter how beautiful it is, you must get rid of it."

"I understand," Sybil accepted that she must make the sacrifice. "And I am ready to do what you ask. Your excellent advice shall be followed at once. How do we find this monastery in New Jersey?"

"It is a good thing that I happen to be very interested in Tibetan magick," Johnny said. He drew a piece of paper from his pocket, consulted it and then turned back to Sybil.

"The lamasary is called the Labsum Shedrub Ling Lamasary. It was founded a long time ago by Tibetan monks who were refugees from their homeland. It is perhaps two and a half to three hours away from the city."

"But we can't just drive up there and say, 'Hey, fellows, do you want our opal,' " Sybil objected.

"No, of course not," Johnny said. "I will call the abbot and start the ball rolling, so to speak. Of course it will take some explaining, but I think these people will understand. They are all trained in high magick and there should be no difficulty in getting them to accept and properly enshrine the opal in their temple. Whether or not they are willing to take it back to Tibet or have it sent there doesn't matter, especially since, as you know, Tibet is occupied by the Red Chinese. They may object, quite legitimately, to having this precious, sacred stone fall into the wrong hands. But it seems to me that if the stone were placed in a similar setting to the one it originally came from, our Indian chief might just be satisfied on behalf of his friend, who owned the opal. The stone would no longer be in the wrong hands, meaning yours and mine, but in a sacred environment. I might be able to persuade the angry Indian chief that this is in fact the best solution for the safety of the sacred jewel."

Sybil had listened to him with an expression of amazement. This young man was certainly capable of suggesting the most unusual plans, she thought. What a blessing that he had come into her life!

"When do you propose to undertake this journey?" she inquired.

Johnny thought this over for a moment. "I should think it will take me a day or two to make the necessary arrangements. Besides, I feel we must deal with the land first because your tenancy here is limited, I understand."

Sybil nodded. She had almost forgotten that another week and a half was left and no more. During that time the matter had to be settled.

By now it was past ten o'clock and she knew she had to get up early to go to work the following morning. Again Johnny seemed to read her thoughts, or sense them, for he rose and said, "I think it is time I went back to New York City now, but we must do what we have to do here as soon as possible. Now that I know where the problem lies, I think I can safely say that it will be taken care of. I will come back with all the necessary paraphernalia and we will have a go at the Indian chief's anger. Hopefully we can release you and anyone else who might live on this piece of land forever."

"How soon do you think you can do this?" Sybil asked as she led Johnny to the door.

"I realize that you only have a week and a half left here, but I have to check my astrological charts to make sure we do this on a propitious day. Everything counts when you are undertaking such a difficult operation as this."

"Operation? I don't understand," Sybil said, puzzled by the term.

He laughed. "A magickal operation, that is the term used. But don't worry about it. I will call you tomorrow morning and I will be out here within two or three days at the latest—perhaps tomorrow. I have to make sure we are doing it right. We don't want to fail, do we?"

"No, we don't," Sybil said.

For a moment he hesitated at the door, and looked at her again in the way he had done before, when she had felt "hooked" into his gaze. Once again a strong jolt of electricity, or whatever it was, passed between them. She didn't move.

"Well, thanks for everything," she said. On impulse, she leaned forward and kissed him. He looked amazed and pleasantly surprised, but didn't say anything. He merely smiled and walked out, leaving her standing there and wondering what had made her do it.

Long after the door had closed after Johnny, she realized why she had kissed him. The knowledge completely overshadowed who was left of her grief for Paul. In fact, it seemed to her now that Paul had just been someone who had paved the way for the main event: Johnny was the man she needed to fully realize herself. But how could she be so sure of this when she barely knew him? she wondered. An overriding desire to be with this man blotted out all rationality. For the first time since she had become involved in the strange world of Amityville and its compelling atmosphere, Sybil felt light and free again. This stranger was the bearer of good news, she felt, and if the tragedies of the recent past had paved the way for his coming, then they were something she could live with. This realization, coupled with the hopeful news and her expectancy of early action, made her feel really good for the first time in many weeks. That night she went to bed without the slightest worry or hesitation; she fell into a healthful, deep sleep and awoke just in time to get ready to go to the city. She didn't recall any dreams, upsetting or otherwise.

She had provided Johnny with her number at work and, sure enough, at eleven o'clock he rang her. His cheerful voice was just what she needed.

"I've figured it out," he said. "We are going to do it tomorrow night. Is that all right with you?"

"Is it all right!" she replied, perhaps a little louder than necessary, for her co-workers turned around. "Is it all right? What time, the day after tomorrow?"

"Not the day after tomorrow," Johnny

corrected. "Tomorrow, tomorrow at eight. I will be there."

Why had she thought it was to be the day after tomorrow, she immediately wondered? Was her unconscious mind playing tricks on her by postponing for still another day the confrontation with the forces in the house? But deep down Sybil was relieved at the thought that it would be tomorrow after all.

"Is there anything you will need? Anything I should get?"

"No, just get a lot of rest tonight and, oh, one thing. I hesitate to bring this up," he paused. She began to wonder what he wanted, what he meant.

"What is it? Is there anything wrong?"

"No, no, it's just rather a personal question to do with the ritual we are going to perform. You see, a lot of energy will be raised and both of us have to be in perfect shape."

"Of course I can understand that. I am fine, there is nothing wrong with me."

"You are not on any kind of medication?"

"No, nothing at all."

"One more thing, and please forgive the question. You don't have your period, do you? Because if you do, we must postpone it; otherwise you would be in danger."

She had not counted on that kind of question. "No, it isn't that time of the month. Anything else I should or should not be doing?" There was a tone of annoyance in her voice, for which she hated herself.

He sensed it. "Please forgive me for asking such a personal question, but if it were—that time of the month, your energies would be depleted and the additional strain could be a danger to your health. That is why I asked."

"Of course, you are forgiven. You are just doing your job."

"Yes," he replied, "I am doing my job and then some. I like my work. Have a good day."

Before she could say anything further, he hung up. Eight o'clock tomorrow night. What would happen, she had no idea. She knew, in any case, that she was in good hands.

Chapter Twenty-One

The following day dawned just like any other that she had spent in the house, and yet there was something very special about it. Sybil had a strange, undefinable feeling that a phase of her life had come to an end; naturally she ascribed this feeling to the forthcoming session with Johnny and the spirits, but at the same time, she realized that an inner change was also taking place. To be sure, she had not forgotten Paul's tragic demise: the wound was still there. But somehow it didn't hurt any longer. Somehow she was turning back to life and leaving what occurred in the past where it belonged, behind her.

Promptly at eight the doorbell rang and Johnny arrived. He carried with him a satchel. When he opened it, she noticed a rattle, a bell and what to her appeared to be a fly whisk.

"What are these?" she asked.

He shrugged. "Just implements for the ritual. Symbolic of course, but very necessary." He proceeded to place the objects on the cocktail table in front of the fireplace.

"We are going to do it right here," he said, "and hopefully all will be well after that."

"What exactly are we going to do, Johnny?" she enquired. Until now he had been quite secretive about the required ritual. All she knew was that it was something that he felt would satisfy the angry spirit of the Indian Chief Rolling Thunder, and thus free the house, its inhabitants, and the land from any further manifestations.

Johnny looked straight at her and his face was very serious. "I think you should understand that what we are trying to do is one of the most difficult magickal operations imaginable. We have, on the one hand, a justifiably angry spirit—justifiably because after all this is his gravesite, his tribe's sacred burial ground—and it's been desecrated. On the other hand, there are ourselves and others who might live on this land, in this house, who have a stake in remaining here peacefully. So there is merit on both sides. I do not intend to drive the spirit from this house or this land as if he were some intruder, which he isn't. I intend to give him something in return for making peace with us. That is the basic idea behind this particular ritual."

"How do you propose to do this? I am a novice at this sort of thing."

"I realize that. I will tell you exactly what you must do. But I will explain first." With that he took Sybil by the hand and gently sat her down on the couch next to him. She liked that, somehow; his taking her by hand added reassurance.

"Well now," he began, "I have done my homework well. I have refreshed my memory concerning ancient Indian tribal traditions and I am happy to report that what I have found will work, at least it will if we do it well."

"Won't we?" she said, a tiny bit worried.

He nodded. "Of course we will. That is to say, it depends on you, but I have no doubt that you will cooperate fully once you understand the purpose of what we are doing."

Sybil's curiosity was once more aroused. "Please tell me, I'm all ears."

"Very well," Johnny continued. "This particular ritual will open the gates to the other side, as it were. We request the presence of the spirit and hopefully he will oblige us."

"But if he doesn't what do we do then?"

"We will cross that bridge if we come to it, but given the previous events, I think he will oblige us and will want to make an appearance and to communicate. Once we have made contact, we will assure him that this is indeed his and his tribe's sacred burial ground, his land and not ours. But at the same time we will ask that he allow us to stay here and propose a kind of peace treaty between him and the white man. If he should agree, and I am hopeful that he will, then we must give him something in return. There has to be some sort of sacrifice to please him and to help him maintain face, for to an Indian, whether in flesh or in spirit, honor is very important. You see, he was assigned the task of watching over Don Pedro's treasure, and now that the treasure is gone he feels ashamed and believes that he has not done his duty by his blood brother. So in order to help him over this situation he has to replace what has been lost."

"What do you propose to give him instead?" Sybil couldn't think of anything that would be acceptable to the Indian, especially one in the spirit world.

"I am coming to that," Johnny continued. "There has to be a sacrifice, as I said, and you and I will be able to provide him with what he needs to maintain his honor. In one of the oldest tribal traditions, there is a ritual whereby a peaceful co-existence between the tribe and what is called the outsider, meaning of course the whites or the strangers, is possible, provided the whites, the strangers, will sacrifice one of their own. Since Indian society is essentially a male society, the sacrifice has to be female."

"What?" Sybil exclaimed. "We have to

sacrifice a woman to get peace in this house?"

"Yes and no," Johnny replied and smiled at her concern. "As it is written in the anxient text, a willing white maiden has to be sacrificed. The word 'willing' is very important. This is not a sacrifice where some poor victim is killed against her wishes, of course, but where she is sacrificed with her consent."

"But that is impossible!" Sybil replied, perturbed. "We are not going to commit murder here!"

"Nobody is speaking of murder," Johnny reprimanded her and looked straight into her eyes. "Remember, this is a ritual where everything is meant symbolically. A willing white maiden will be sacrificed but there will be no bloodshed. No one will get hurt. If we do this according to ancient traditions, the chief is bound to accept it and peace will result."

"Frankly, I don't understand what you are talking about," Sybil replied, more confused then ever, "but if you say that it can be done symbolically, I'm all for it."

"Then you are in full agreement with me on this?" he said unnecessarily, it appeared to her.

She nodded. "Of course I am."

"Very well. Then may I begin?" Without waiting for her reply, he rose and went to the cocktail table in front of the fireplace where he had earlier placed the implements he had brought from the city.

He pushed back a few chairs which stood nearby, creating an open area between the cocktail table and the fireplace. He then took a candle, placed it on the table and lit it. Then he turned back toward Sybil, and said, "I'll have to change now. Where is your bathroom?"

Puzzled, she directed him down the corridor to one of the bathrooms. What was he about to do, she wondered?

He emerged several moments later wearing a pair of long leather pants, a heavy belt, and Indian jewelry around his neck, and a headband with his hair flowing back from his head. Truly, she thought, he looks like an Indian now! Still trying to get used to this transformation, she stayed where she was while Johnny moved to stand in front of the cocktail table, which she realized now was serving as an altar. He raised his arms above his head, took a deep breath, and began.

"Manitou, Manitou, in the name of the Supreme Being Manitou, I open this gate so that those on the other side may come and speak to me. I am Tall Oak, son of the tribe of the Cherokee, ancient Shaman and hereditary priest. I, Tall Oak, request the presence in this circle of the great chief Rolling Thunder so that we may have a palaver."

Johnny then put his arms down and took the fly whisk, faced in the four directions of the compass, then ritually dusted the cocktail table-altar and placed the whisk back on it. Now Johnny took up a little drum which he began to beat.

The rhythm of the drum was hardly audible but in some way affected Sybil. She felt herself swaying with it, becoming one with the proceedings. At this very moment Johnny turned back toward her and waved her to come and join him. Feeling strange, Sybil stepped forward and stood beside him in front of the altar.

Once again Johnny spoke. Raising his right arm in a salute to the unseen spirit he said, "It is I, Tall Oak, who requests the honor of palaver with the great spirit Rolling Thunder so that ancient wrongs may be righted. Come forward, great spirit. Do me the honor of palavering with me. I am Tall Oak of the Cherokee, Shaman, and hereditary priest. I beg thee, great chief, to do me the honor."

Once again there was a moment of silence. Sybil felt herself totally engulfed by the atmosphere of the ritual. Johnny had put the drum down again and stood staring toward the fireplace, his body taut and intent. She could see every muscle on his chest and noticed that his face was curiously tight, as it gradually took on more and more the expression of an Indian. What was going on, she wondered? But she decided not to try to analyze what was happening now, but to go with it, no matter where it might lead.

Just as she was wondering whether anything would happen other than the strange feeling that was pervading her, she noticed a flickering light coming from the direction of the ceiling and dancing about the fireplace, as if in search of something or someone. A moment later the light moved directly toward where they were standing. Frightened, she raised her arm and covered her eyes in an instinctive motion to protect herself. But the light was not headed for her; it came directly to Johnny and then vanished into Johnny's head!

"My God," she thought, "I hope he is not hurt!" Suddenly a great concern for his welfare arose in her. She looked at Johnny now and realized that a transformation had taken place, so rapidly that she had not even noticed it. What stood before her was another person in Johnny's body! For a moment Johnny's lips moved silently as if the entity now dominating him was trying to get his bearings. And then a voice came from Johnny's lips, totally unlike his own.

"It is I, Rolling Thunder," the voice said, as Johnny's eyes flickered, giving him the appearance of someone being used by an exterior force. "What do you want of me?"

Suddenly Sybil realized that with Johnny in trance having become the spokesman for the Indian chief, there was no one else to conduct the ritual but herself. Panic pervaded her, but instantly she caught herself and forced it down.

"It is Tall Oak of the Cherokee, hereditary shaman of the tribe, and I, Sybil, who request the honor of palavering with thee," she began, remembering what Johnny had said. Apparently she had hit it right.

"I will palaver," the voice of the Chief said through Johnny.

"We are willing to recognize your rights to this land, the sacred burial ground, your gravesite, in return for giving us peace," Sybil said.

But the voice became angry. "No peace with white man! No one shall live on this ground. No blade of grass shall ever grow again. This is our land, our sacred burial ground."

"We are willing to give sacrifice."

"Sacrifice?"

"Sacrifice," Sybil continued. She heard herself saying, very much to her surprise, "We will sacrifice a willing white maiden, in the ancient ways, if you will conclude a peace treaty with us."

"You will bring back the honor of my grave?" the voice said. "You will give my bones eternal rest in the Happy Hunting Grounds?"

"I will, I will," Sybil replied, not knowing what to say next.

"It shall be so. In the name of Manitou there shall be peace between my people and your people. But if you do not give sacrifice, there shall be eternal war between us until no one survives on this sacred land; no white man shall live here, and all those who try shall perish by my anger, for I am Rolling

Thunder and this is my land. So must it be."

Suddenly Johnny's face returned to normal. His head went down to his chest, as if awakening from a deep sleep. Close to him stood Sybil very much excited, and not knowing what to do next.

"He has come through you. He had entranced you!" she cried.

But Johnny already knew. He nodded. "That was a possibility, since I am a deep trance medium as well. But now there is work to be done."

As if nothing had happened, he turned around and faced the fireplace once again, raised his arms and spoke.

"I call upon thee, Chief Rolling Thunder, to conclude forever a peace between you and your people and me and my people and my white friends, that this land may no longer bear your curse. To conclude this peace treaty between us we offer the sacrifice of a willing white maiden as it has been done in the old days. Give us the sign of your willingness to accept the sacrifice, and we shall proceed to do so."

Johnny stepped back, lowered his arms and stood rigidly facing the fireplace. Sybil, transfixed, watched in awe as a flame suddenly rose in the fireplace where no flame had been lit! Johnny, of course, realized what the flame was.

"I thank thee, Chief. I thank thee and may peace be between you and your people and my people and my white friends in this house on this land. In the name of Great Manitou I now will offer you the promised sacrifice, the willing white maiden selected for you and your tribe so that there may be peace between us."

While he was speaking Sybil felt strange all over: it was as if she too were entranced. At this moment Johnny turned toward her and extended his hand to her. Obediently she went over to where he was and stood facing him.

"What now?" she said hesitatingly.

"It is time to implement the bond between Rolling Thunder and us," he said solemnly. "You said you would help cement that bond and the time is now."

"Yes, I am willing to help you. But what am I to do?"

"You are the willing white maiden who will be sacrificed, you understand that?" he said and immediately held up his hand. "But don't worry, we are not about to kill you. What will happen now is far more pleasant, I hope. You see, my being part Indian—actually, two of my grandparents were full-blooded Indians—makes me eligible to perform this rite. Besides, I am hereditary shaman, an office that has come down to me through my grandparents. What I do is meaningful and more than symbolic; it is likely to be satisfactory to the other side. I therefore asked once again that Rolling Thunder accept your sacrifice as a willing white maiden, and that there be peace among us forever on this land."

Sybil felt a glow of excitement, and yet she could not move even a finger. It was as if she were enveloped by an unseen force that felt both electric and warming. The force made her tingle but, at the same time, it was frightening. Johnny stepped over to her and with quick deliberate movements stripped off her dress and undergarments while she stood motionless. With another quick movement, he removed his pants and stood there naked before her.

Then his strong arms went around her. As he embraced her, she suddenly remembered her psychic experience of before: the arms she felt now in the flesh were the arms she had felt clairvoyantly before, and she realized at that moment that what was happening now was indeed part of her destiny, part of her future.

Gently, Johnny lifted her up in his arms and placed her on the carpet between the makeshift altar and the fireplace. He then proceeded to make love to her. At first she responded hesitantly, but then with mounting passion as she realized that she was not only a willing victim for Rolling Thunder, but a woman falling in love with a man.

Chapter Twenty-Two

That night both Johnny and Sybil slept a peaceful, heavy sleep, devoid of dreams, or if they had any dreams, they did not remember them. When they arose the next morning, they looked at each other with new eyes and Sybil knew that she had received more than she had bargained for. The bitter memory of Paul had been purged from her, and her life looked a lot more promising than it had before. As for Johnny, he was clearly enchanted by his own discovery that he desired and longed for her.

"There is something else we must do, and do it quickly," he said as he got dressed.

Before breakfast, they went out to the gravesite at the rear of the property and together they arranged it in such a way that it

325

would be difficult for anyone to guess that there had been any digging on the spot. But before they covered up the opening Johnny descended into the excavation and took upon himself the responsibility of laying out the skeleton of the chief so that it could find eternal rest. There was nothing he could do about the missing skull. Instead, he placed an Indian talisman which he had brought with him in the place where the skull would have been. After they had covered the opening carefully, he put a small tablet into the ground, on which a protective seal, known to Indians as a symbol warding off all evil, had been placed.

"We are finished here, Sybil," he said and went back to the house with her. Immediately she called the owners and advised them that she was leaving two days earlier than planned. When she had done so, Johnny embraced her, and she knew then his feelings for her were not part of the ritual.

"I am going back to the city now, and I would like to see you later this evening." She nodded and went to the house to pack her things. She too would leave very shortly.

Later that evening Johnny came to her apartment and stayed with her throughout the night. But they were both distracted by the knowledge that they still had to take the opal to the Tibetan monastery.

The following Saturday they took off in Johnny's bright red sports car for the monastery in New Jersey. Very little was said, but thoughts of love ran back and forth between them. It was afternoon when they arrived. Johnny had telephoned ahead and they were expected. The abbot seemed excited at the prospect of receiving so precious a gem. Immediately he led them to his private study and offered them seats. Sybil produced the little box with the opal in it and handed it over to the abbot. Despite his calm manner, for he had been trained not to show emotions to easily or readily, the abbot let out a little cry of astonishment.

"It is as I suspected," he said and there was joy in his voice. "It is the sacred opal from Rva Sgreng! At last it is back with us. I cannot begin to tell you how thankful we are."

"What are you going to do with it?" Sybil asked.

"I made some inquiries after your friend called me. We have received dispensation from the Dalai Lama to place the opal in our temple."

"Will you not send it back to Tibet, where it came from?" Johnny enquired.

"Do you know what is happening in our homeland?" the abbot asked. "If we took the opal there, the Chinese would take it. The Dalai Lama feels we should be the custodians of the precious jewel for the time being, until our homeland is free. Then he will bring it back in a ceremonial procession and replace it where it came from."

"*Um many padmi hom,*" Johnny said.

"Um many padmi hom," the abbot replied.

Sybil looked at both men, wondering what they were saying. Johnny leaned over to her and said, "It's a statement of faith, having to do with Buddha being the heart of the lotus. We have just sealed the bargain, so to speak, and the opal is no longer in your possession."

"Does that mean that the—ah—special side effects of the opal will no longer affect me?"

"That is correct," Johnny replied. "You are free, for you have returned the opal. Now you can live your own life as you choose."

Sybil got up, ready to leave, but Johnny motioned her to stay seated for a moment longer.

"I believe you are celebrating the festival of Maitreya this afternoon," he said to their host.

The abbot nodded. "Yes; it is the festival of the coming Buddha, and you are welcome to stay. It will start in approximately two hours."

"I think that would be nice," Johnny replied, very much to Sybil's surprise, since she hadn't been asked. Something in Johnny's tone made her wonder what he was up to. Her mood was so festive and so relieved of all anxiety that she couldn't care less what he had in mind. She was in love with a man she had known for only a few days!"

The abbot rose as a sign that the audience was finished. "Is there anything else that I can do for you?" he asked politely.

Johnny rose and so did Sybil. "As a matter of fact, Your Eminence," he replied, "there is."

"Then please state it." The abbot smiled. "I would be happy to do anything in my power."

Johnny looked at Sybil with a compelling expression in his eyes.

"I believe it is traditional, since you are celebrating the festival of Maitreya, that any couple wishing to be married may do so at a moment's notice."

When he had spoken Sybil heard her heart beat faster. Had she heard right?

"Yes," the abbot replied. "Do you want to be married?"

"Yes, we do," Johnny said matter-of-factly. Again he looked at Sybil, waiting for her answer.

To her amazement and surprise Sybil heard herself say, "Yes, we do!"

"Well then," the abbot said cheerfully, moving toward the door of his study, "come with me so that we can register you properly. After all, we are in the United States and we must do things legally."

Two hours later Sybil and Johnny were joined in matrimony in the Buddhist manner, or rather in the Tibetan-Lamaist manner, which is somewhat more colorful than traditional Buddhism. Somehow Johnny had got hold of a ring which he placed on Sybil's finger during the ceremony. The abbot in turn gave them a signed photograph of His Holiness Tenzin Gyatso, the fourteenth Dalai

Lama. In the evening, they left the monastery, and returned to the city. The following week Sybil gave up her apartment and moved in with Johnny.

In the middle of her happiness, she found time to wonder about the house at 112 Ocean Avenue, Amityville, Long Island. By now the owners should have moved back in. Out of curiosity, Sybil telephoned them about a week later. Was everything all right? she asked. She pretended to be concerned only with the kitchenware and the other possessions which the owners had left in the house.

"Everything is perfectly fine," the voice of the owner resounded on the telephone. "You've been a very good tenant. I have only one question. You seemed to be planting something in the rear of the garden. What happened?"

"Well," Sybil replied after a moment's hesitation to gather her thoughts. "We tried but nothing would take there. I think the soil is not conducive to planting anything. If I were you I would just leave it alone—yes, indeed, I would just leave it alone."

"If you say so," the owner replied cheerfully, and hung up.

That night Sybil had an unusual and colorful dream. She seemed to awaken because a voice was trying to penetrate her conscious mind, yet she knew she was still alseep. Her eyes were closed but, with her inner eye, she discerned the tall figure of an Indian, dressed in full regalia of a chief. A voice, seemingly coming from far away and trailing off indistinctly in the end, penetrated her consciousness.

"I am Rolling Thunder, my child. I have come to say good-bye."

As Sybil watched, the Chief was joined by a white man in strange clothes. His outfit reminded her of some costume films she had seen. Clearly, he was some sort of seaman and yet his clothing seemed more elegant than that of an ordinary sailor. His face was peaceful and glowing, and he looked at the Indian with affection.

The white man looked down at her with a smile. When he spoke, it was with a clipped British accent. "I am Don Pedro and I came to tell you that you need not worry any longer. All is well. I am at peace. I have found my Merryn."

At this moment the picture faded and the figures of the two men gradually disappeared from her inner eye. She woke up with a jolt. Johnny was fast asleep next to her and she did not wish to wake him. What a strange dream, she thought—or was it a dream at all? With that, she went back to sleep.

The next morning Sybil woke early, filled with a restlessness for which she had no immediate explanation. Johnny was still fast asleep and she made sure he would not be awakened when she slipped from the room. It could not have been more than seven a.m., and all was very quiet. In the distance the muted noises of the city waking up to a working day barely intruded into her consciousness.

And then she realized what was so different about this morning: the atmosphere had changed; the restlessness was in herself, and she felt a need to get on with her life as soon as possible, and to get on with it *somewhere else*.

So the years went by, and Amityville, Long Island was just another growing community, filled with nice, average people going about their business. In the summer, the population would be enlarged by tourists or those who came from the city to spend a weekend. All in all, Amityville had long lost its sinister connotations, and people had ceased to connect the town's name with horror films.

It was now ten years after Sybil and Johnny had gotten married and in those ten years they hadn't been back to the house once. Was it because they felt that they had left the past behind, or was it because of some secret fear that in returning they might reawaken something not fully laid to rest?

In any event, neither expressed a desire to revisit the place where so many traumatic events had taken place. Johnny decided to publish in fictional form what he had been able to accomplish in the house; but he carefully avoided pinpointing the location, not so much because he wanted to protect the citizens of Amityville but because it might in some way affect the magical operation which he had so successfully concluded.

As for Sybil, she couldn't have been happier. Her life with Johnny was absolutely delightful and harmonious.

It was about that time that the house came on the market again. The current owners had lived there for eight years. They were no longer young and they wanted to move to the West Coast, partially because of the climate and partially because the husband, who was an air space technologist, thought he would find better employment there.

So the house was put up for sale once again. The real estate agent who handled it, Rooker and Purloin, one of the top firms in the area, quickly found another buyer in the person of Reginald Doar.

Mr. Doar was twenty-nine years old, unmarried, and the son of Richard Doar, county executive and a well-known politician in the area. Young Doar had always dreamed of owning the house where so much had transpired. For to him the Amityville horror and curse belonged to local history, and as a history buff the thrill of owning the actual house where all this had happened, was well worth the price he had to pay. Besides, as a successful attorney, he could well afford it.

But Mr. Doar was also a movie buff, specializing in horror films from past years. He decided to built a studio at the far end of the property where he could view the films he owned and enjoy them with his friends. The contractor promised him construction of such a studio within a matter of two months.

The following week work started on the studio. Using a medium-sized bulldozer, the construction crew began to clear the land at the rear of the property. As they did so, the shovel cut through the grave of the great Indian Chief, Rolling Thunder. When the shovel cut through the skeleton and broke it into smithereens, none of the men were surprised. In their line of work, they were always making similar discoveries. To them, the skeleton was merely a lot of old bones, of no particular significance. They threw them on a heap of refuse, to be carted away the next day.

None of this, of course, was known to Mr. Doar. The following night, after the bones had been disposed of, he was awakened in the middle of the night by an unnatural wind. At first he thought that Long Island was having an earthquake or a hurricane, but when he stuck his head out the window he saw that everything was quiet; in fact, deadly quiet. He went back to bed, trying to go to sleep.

But the wind became stronger, and everything in the house began to rattle. Frightened, young Doar sat up in bed and stared into the darkness of his room, where he saw a flickering light approach him. As he looked on in horror, the light turned into a luminous figure, outlined in two-dimensional fashion but still clearly discernible as a man. The man was an Indian, taller than most, and his eyes were burning fiercely. Then Doar heard a voice that seemed to come from far away.

"You have broken a bond," the voice said, "and now you must pay the price."

With that the wind and the howling became stronger. Unable to understand any of this, the young man quickly ran to the door and out into the garden, where there was no wind at all. While he was trying to figure out what to do next and to find a rational explanation for what he had seen, a huge flame burst out inside the house. Within moments the entire building was engulfed. As Doar stood by helplessly, unable to move, his home became a roaring inferno. By the time the fire department arrived, there was practically nothing left.

A month later the property was up for sale again, only this time there was no house on it. It was merely a piece of land with the burnt-out remnants of what was once a house and a few charred tree stumps. . . .

But nobody came forward to buy it. So, for all I know, it may still be available, in case you are interested.

People in Amityville have long since become accustomed to The Place, but they also tend to avoid it, especially at night. It isn't so much out of fear or preoccupation with events which, after all, lie so far in the past that few remember them personally; it is due to a keen sense of self-preservation. If you live in Amityville, you just mind your business and let that piece of land be.

There isn't a real estate man within miles

who would handle the sale of the ground. The town owns it, as of now, but all efforts to unload it have failed. To build on it is out of the question. A feeble attempt by one of the young town councilmen to "stop this nonsense and superstition" and make good use of a valuable piece of property got only one vote in council: his.

Lately, nobody has even bothered to consider the matter. The land remains there, and even those eager and nervous souls who proposed putting a high fence around it got nowhere with the town council. But the town did not want some enterprising journalist to dig up the old stories and have flocks of unwanted tourists swarming over the place, so they ordered a barbed wire fence to be put around it to keep people out. After all, it was town property now, and they had a right to do it.

The people who live on both sides and across from the land pretend it isn't even there. And there really isn't any need to walk onto the land: there is nothing to pick up, nothing to clean. Even the many dogs of Amityville, much as they love a place where they can run freely, never so much as come near the piece of ground. Little Joe Polinaro, the son of the barkeep at the Blue Onion, tried to take his mutt, Buddy by name, to do his business on that lot last February. The dog wouldn't go in and when Joe picked him up and carried him over the barbed wire fence, the animal shot out of there like a cannonball. It hasn't been seen since.